Accl
Go Go Gato

"From its hero to its milieu to its eccentric, three-dimensional characters, Max Everhart's *Go Go Gato* is a terrific read. The North Carolina minor-league baseball scene feels authentic and beloved, and I was always rooting for protagonist Eli Sharpe. The best news is that this excellent mystery is first in a series. Fans of Harlan Coben will want to check out Max Everhart, a major new talent!"

—Steve Ulfelder, Edgar Award-finalist

"*Go Go Gato* is the debut entry in a promising new series by Max Everhart, and it's a fast-paced, entertaining tale. Eli Sharpe is a very appealing character who combines just the right amounts of wit, humor, intelligence and courage, and it will be fun to watch him in action as the series continues to grow and develop."

—James L. Thane, author of *Until Death*

"Max Everhart scores a homerun with this first novel in his new Eli Sharpe mystery series. Eli finds much more than he bargained for in his search for a missing baseball player in this fast read, best enjoyed with a glass of George Dickel in hand since that's Eli's favorite 'poison.' Like a good curveball you won't see the twist ending coming at you."

—Paul D. Marks, Shamus Award-winning author

"This is an excellent read and the author's characters are very real; in particular, Eli Sharpe and his friend Ernest Carpenter. Readers will enjoy the plot, and root for Eli to discover the criminal before a more serious crime occurs."

—Suspense Magazine

GO GO GATO

ALSO BY MAX EVERHART

Eli Sharpe Mysteries
Split to Splinters (*)
Ed, Not Eddie (*)

The Rook Series
Alphabet Land (*)

Short Stories
All the Different Ways Love Can Feel

(*) – coming soon

MAX EVERHART

GO GO GATO

AN ELI SHARPE MYSTERY

Down & Out Books Edition: July 2018

Down & Out Books
3959 Van Dyke Rd, Ste. 265
Lutz, FL 33558
www.DownAndOutBooks.com

Cover design by Zach McCain

ISBN: 1-948235-09-9
ISBN-13: 978-1-948235-09-9

To my wife, Libby

CHAPTER 1

On a Wednesday morning in mid-June, Eli Sharpe was sitting at his desk treating jet lag with strong coffee when he heard a knock on his apartment door. After a second, more insistent knock, he added a dash of George Dickel to his Folgers and hid the pint in a desk drawer.

"It's open," he said loudly and stood up to receive his visitor.

In walked a tall blonde, her high heels stabbing the scuffed-up hardwoods, her perfume battling the smell of coffee and dust permeating Eli's six-hundred-square-foot studio apartment that doubled as a working office. Her perfume won the battle: Light Blue by Dolce & Gabbana. Same scent his third fiancée used to wear.

Eli introduced himself, but the tall blonde was more interested in appraising her surroundings than exchanging pleasantries. She frowned at a black futon he'd bought used at a flea market in Sarasota, Florida, nine years prior. She sighed at an ash coffee table he'd found at a consignment store in Austin, Texas. She peeled back an inch section of wallpaper that had been dangling for months.

Meanwhile, he examined her from head to toe. Athletically built, she was in her early- to mid-thirties, and judging by her erect posture and breezy confidence, she'd spent the last twenty years being The Pretty One. Maybe a swimmer or a tennis player—

cut biceps, no-nonsense but stylish short hair, parted on the left. Emerald green eyes. Fair skin pulled tight over attractive, even features and dotted with freckles. She wore a crisp white button-down with the sleeves rolled to the elbows, a gray pencil skirt, and ruby red high heels.

"So you live *and* work here?" she asked.

"I travel a lot for work. As for my living quarters, I prefer Spartan accommodations. Helps me think."

"Your living quarters don't exactly instill confidence. Not in clients, anyway."

"Which is why I usually meet them in a neutral location. Sorry, I didn't catch your name."

"How can you think with so many pictures of Nixon on the wall?" She touched a framed poster of Richard Nixon running for U.S. Senator. The caption read: THE MAN WHO BROKE THE HISS CASE!! Beside the campaign poster was a black and white picture of Nixon bowling in the White House basement. She moved on, running her painted fingertips over a collection of Nixon campaign buttons and bumper stickers.

"I don't get it," she said. "What's the obsession?"

"No obsession. Nixon was interesting."

"He was a criminal."

"An interesting criminal who did some good. He opened trade with China and Russia."

"And bombed Cambodia. Without permission from Congress or the people."

"Granted, he was quirky."

"I'd say you have a quirk or two also, Mr. Sharpe. You obviously spent more money on your presidential collection than the furnishings in this apartment."

Eli sipped spiked Folgers, unwilling to admit even to himself just how true her statement was. "I was on a redeye flight this morning, and if you say I'm quirky, so be it. But I'm also a simple kind of guy. All I ask is that people call me Eli and they introduce themselves on our first encounter."

"Are you this sarcastic with all your clients?"

"You're not a client. You're a stranger. A well-dressed one, but a stranger nonetheless."

"You're funny," she said without laughing and turned her attention to the bookcase. She picked up a well-worn John le Carré novel—*The Spy Who Came in from the Cold*, a present from Eli's uncle, a man he cared for far more than his own father. She flipped through the pages. She opened to the middle of the book, held it in Eli's direction. There were copious notes in the margins.

Eli said, "In my younger and more vulnerable days, I thought being a British spy was a viable career option."

She put the book back where she'd found it and examined a baseball sitting atop the bookshelf. It was signed by Pedro Martinez, the strikeout pitcher of Expo and Red Sox fame.

"Teammate of yours?" she asked.

"Not exactly. Pedro struck me out four times in one game. Afterward, I got his autograph. Silver linings and all that. If you won't tell me your name and why you're here, perhaps you could tell me how tall you are."

She put the baseball back, situated herself in a cushioned swivel chair, and aimed a no-nonsense look in Eli's direction. "My name is Veronica Craven. Ernest Carpenter at DMSI Investigations referred me to you."

"I never knew his first name was Ernest. That could come in handy someday."

"I like jokes. That was a joke, right?"

"An attempt at one, sure. So we have two things in common: we're both tall and we both enjoy jokes."

"We have something else in common. I'm a sports agent."

"You're too late. I'm retired." Eli turned and jerked a thumb at the only thing hanging on the wall behind his desk: a framed picture of Eli Sharpe in a Tampa Bay Devil Rays uniform with a Louisville Slugger resting on his right shoulder. The caption at the bottom of the picture read: "Eli Sharpe, 2B, 1999." Although the photo was fifteen years old, Eli didn't look drastically different. He was still tall and lanky. His hair was just as dark and just as thick, his face still boyishly handsome and almost entirely untouched by his years in the sun and his on-again off-again relationship with the bottle. "I was a third-rate infielder on a second-rate team," Eli said, turning back around. "I've begun a second career."

"I know," she said. "I spent the morning calling former and current clients of yours. For a man with such a..." she paused, crinkled her nose, "an interesting apartment, you have an impressive client list."

"I have an impressive bathroom, too. There's even a mini fridge in there." Eli smiled; she didn't reciprocate. So much for liking jokes. He made a cage of his hands. "Despite appearances, Miss Craven, I am a successful private investigator. As a former baseball player, I have working relationships with Major and Minor League team owners, general managers, scouts, broadcasters, sports writers, and players both current and retired." Eli opened his wallet, flashed his private investigator's license and his permit to carry a concealed weapon. "As you can see, I am licensed here in North Carolina as well as twelve other states. Locally, I have contacts in the Asheville PD, the local newspapers, and various government agencies around town. And, not to boast, but if you needed someone to show you the sights of this fair city nestled between the Blue Ridge Mountains, you could do a lot worse than yours truly."

"There's no need to give me your résumé," she said, smiling. "I did my due diligence. You get most of your cases through DMSI. Pro teams hire you to dig into the personal lives and financial records of ballplayers, hence, your most recent trip to Seattle. You make sure these players are worth the investment before big money contracts are signed. Is that correct?"

"More or less."

"Excellent. To why I'm here then. According to Mr. Carpenter, you excel at finding missing persons as well."

"I've found a few people. Computers, cellphones and a high-tolerance for asking the same questions over and over again helps. Who are you looking for?"

"A client of mine. Actually, he's more than a client to me." There was a hint of sadness and fondness in her voice, and something else Eli couldn't pinpoint. It was throaty—no, flinty—and the more she talked, the more Eli liked it. He liked the way she over-enunciated every syllable, liked how she maintained eye contact while talking, liked her runway model height and frank, emerald green gaze. He imagined she would be one tough cookie when it came time to negotiating a contract.

"What's your client's name?" Eli asked.

"Almario Gato."

"'Go Go' Gato? He's yours?"

"It's pronounced 'got-oh,' and yes, he is my client. I take it you've heard of him."

"I read the Bible. According to *Baseball America,* the Colorado Rockies gave Gato a one-point-two-million-dollar bonus when they signed him last June. He was seventeen. You brokered that deal?"

"Guilty."

"MBA or law degree?"

"Both, actually. UCLA, oh-one and oh-four. My father insisted."

"My old man insisted Jerry Garcia was one of Jesus' earthly representatives. But I managed a BS in Criminal Justice after my playing days were over. Three-point-seven GPA."

"Impressive."

Eli studied her face for traces of irony, but found none. He sipped his coffee, the whiskey singing his throat.

"So," Eli said. "Go Go is missing."

"For three days now, yes. Which is why I flew into North Carolina from Los Angeles."

"Have you notified the police? Filled out a missing person's report on Go Go?"

"FYI: Almario despises that nickname. And, no, I haven't informed the police. The police would inform the Rockies, and I would like to avoid doing that. For now."

"Fair enough. But if you're not here on the club's behalf, who is hiring me?"

"I am. What's your fee?"

"One thousand dollars a week, plus expenses. But I have questions first."

"I'll double your fee if you start right away."

"I'll work just as hard if you pay my standard rate. On a missing person case, I work pretty much around the clock. Tell me about the last time you spoke to Almario."

She bit her lip, readjusted her watch band. The watch—sterling silver with diamonds along the band—looked like an antique. There was something Eli couldn't make out engraved on the band.

"Saturday. Four days ago. He called me on my cellphone as he usually does after a game."

"What did you talk about?"

"His performance on the field. The Asheville Travelers had just finished a double-header. Almario struck out four times in the first game and was benched for the second. He was upset. Distraught, in fact."

"Even great players have off-nights. Was he upset about anything else?"

"A nagging knee injury, I think. Last July he tore his ACL. He had surgery and missed the rest of the season. Cut to the present and he still doesn't feel one hundred percent. Honestly, he was underperforming before the injury. Point-two-one-five batting average, seventeen RBI. Only twelve stolen bases. The team manager said his fielding was suspect as well."

"And aside from the rough game he called you about, how was Almario doing this season?"

"Poorly, I'm afraid." Her face hardened. Crow's feet appeared, which made her look older. And more alluring.

Eli reached into his desk, removed a pocket-size red leather notebook and jotted down the key points of what Veronica had just said. Missing three days. Knee injury. Low stats. Agent and player worried. Eli knew the Travelers' team manager from way back and made a note to talk to him about Almario.

Eli said, "That last phone call from Almario, did he say where he was calling from?"

"No, but I'm fairly certain he was calling from his apartment. Maria, Almario's fraternal twin, lives with him. She cooks, cleans and worries about him constantly. During my conversation with Almario, I heard banging pots and pans in the background. My guess, she was making one of his favorite dishes to cheer him up."

Eli asked for Almario's address and wrote it down: 23 Battery Park. The heart of downtown Asheville, among several hip ethnic restaurants, boutique art galleries, and vintage wine shops. Eli knew the building but had never entered it. He did, however, know you needed at least two commas in your bank account to call Battery Park home. He was also certain that Maria and Almario were the only Cuban-born, newly affluent teenagers to live in that building. Eli asked if there was anything else of importance Veronica could recall from the phone call.

"Music," she said after a brief pause. "Maria listens to Spanish popular music, and I heard some while I was speaking to Almario. Lots of horns. Acoustic guitars. Singing in Spanish."

Eli added the new details to his notebook. Pots and pans. Spanish music. He looked up from his writing, and then looked back down. He wrote something he didn't want Veronica to see and closed the notebook. He leaned back in his chair, asked Veronica to tell him about Almario. She straightened her shoulders. As she gave him the Boardroom Glare, he wondered how many men she'd cut down to size with her freckles and emerald eyes. Probably about as many women as she'd vanquished with her intelligence and ambition.

"I don't like being scrutinized."

"It's part of my job, Miss Craven."

"My name is Veronica, not Miss Craven." She crossed her legs, tilted her head to the side. She looked at Eli and then the picture of Eli in his baseball uniform and then back again. She nodded once as if she'd drawn an important conclusion about Eli Sharpe.

"I traded in the uniform and spikes for business casual." Eli opened the lapels of his favorite blue seersucker jacket, drawing attention to the frayed Rolling Stones T-shirt beneath. She didn't smile. He wasn't deterred. He put on his reading glasses—sycamore brown, ten bucks at the same thrift store he'd purchased the jacket. In imitation of a preening male model, he ran a hand through his shaggy brown hair. "Great Clips," he said. "Twelve bucks. With tip."

"I prefer men who wear contacts."

Eli shrugged, slipped his glasses into his jacket. "Tell me about your client."

"Almario is a five-tool player, the closest thing to a can't-miss prospect there is. He can run, field, catch, and hit for both power and average. His baseball IQ is off-the-charts, which makes his professional struggles that much more perplexing."

"My first year, I didn't hit my weight. And I've never weighed more than one-seventy."

"I appreciate the sentiment, but when Almario was a sophomore in high school, a scout for the White Sox assigned him an OFP of seventy-five out of eighty. So I say again: he's a can't-miss prospect."

Eli whistled to show his appreciation. He decided not to tell her that way back, his own Overall Future Potential was seventy-eight out of eighty. Even a savvy agent like Veronica needed to believe one of her best clients wasn't a bust.

She said, "I know what you're thinking. Potential doesn't matter. Results matter, and you're right. But Almario is special. A genuine phenom. When I first met him, he was playing shortstop for the Asheville Day School here in town." She stopped abruptly, stared down at the sunlight reflecting off the hardwoods. When she looked up, her face had softened, making her look like a pretty high-schooler wrapped up in a daydream, and Eli wondered how old Veronica Craven was. Thirty-three or four? Maybe younger? "It was a mesmerizing performance," she said, her professional demeanor returning.

"How mesmerizing?"

"Almario hit for the cycle with six RBI. He hadn't hit his growth spurt yet and was only five-foot-eight and weighed about one-thirty. He is as tall as me now. His arms are corded with muscle. He truly is a physical specimen."

Eli finished his coffee and thought about standing up, but changed his mind. Then he thought about the thirty-six games he played in the Big Leagues, and he tasted copper on his tongue. He checked the bottom of his coffee mug. Empty.

"Okay," he said a little louder than he'd intended, "if Almario is as gifted as you claim, and I have every reason to believe he is, then why is he still stuck here in Asheville with the Single-A club? It's been more than a year since he was drafted. Why hasn't he moved up the ladder? Why is he languishing in the bus leagues?"

Her eye twitched. A chink in the armor. But she quickly recovered and spoke calmly.

"I told you before, he has been injured. Full recovery takes time."

"But time is precisely what highly paid athletes don't have, Veronica. When I was coming up, the Tampa Bay Devil Rays, one of the worst sports franchises at the time, breathed down my neck because I wasn't producing fast enough. And all they had was a measly four hundred thirty thousand dollars a year invested in me."

No eye twitch this time. She re-crossed her legs, adjusted the band on her antique watch, and breathed evenly. "I'm well-acquainted with your playing career, Eli, and it is of no interest to me. Do us both a favor and don't project yourself into this situation."

Eli flashed a smile Dale Carnegie would have applauded. Second thing he'd learned on the job: find parallels between your own experience and the person being investigated. Makes it real. More personal. And the more personal the job, the more apt you are to achieve a favorable outcome. But Craven didn't strike Eli as the type to be interested in the psychology of investigation. Nor, he figured, would she be interested in hearing about the first thing he'd learned on the job: how to talk to potential clients.

Eli said, "My point is, I need to know more than just stats and OFP. I need to know as much about Almario, his background, and his state of mind as possible, if I'm going to find him quickly and safely."

"What do you need from me? Be specific."

Eli picked up a stress ball and tossed it into the air. Caught it. Sat the ball on top of his decade-old laptop, laid his hands flat on the desk. "You said he is more than a client to you, so you must know something that may be affecting his behavior."

"You mean something besides being a teenage orphan millionaire, just four years off a smuggler's boat from Cuba?"

Eli opened his mouth. Closed it. Waited a beat. "Yes, that would qualify. What about drugs? Alcohol?"

"I've advised him repeatedly on the perils of substance abuse."

"You didn't answer my question."

"It's possible he drinks. I couldn't say for sure."

"Girl trouble?"

"That seems a more likely possibility. Almario is impressionable and handsome. Extremely handsome. His beauty, if I may call it such, is a burden."

Eli nodded. He'd seen a picture of Almario Gato in *Baseball America* last year. The kid had a full, thick head of Bible-black curls, caramel-colored skin, blue-green eyes, and gleaming white teeth. Tall and lean with muscle, he was the kind of guy for whom the tuxedo was invented. Eli factored in Almario's naivety and healthy bank account, and the most likely candidate became girl trouble.

"Does Almario have a girlfriend?" Eli asked.

"I wouldn't know. What we have is more of a mentor-pupil dynamic. I encourage him to make wise decisions. We do not discuss his sex life. You really should talk to Maria."

"I intend to. Is there anything else I should know?"

"Maria received an email from Almario's Yahoo! account this morning."

Eli stood up, had a look out the window. In the distance, he spied the Blue Ridge Mountains. They were too hazy, too far away to be real. He turned around and sat on the edge of his desk, faced Veronica.

"I'll take the case. Under one condition."

"Which is?"

"You tell me how tall you are."

She stood up, smoothed out her skirt. "I'm exactly six feet tall."

They shook hands. She reached into the pocket of her skirt and pulled out a shiny black leather wallet. She handed Eli one thousand dollars in cash—all twenties—and a pre-paid Visa card for expenses. Eli wrote her a receipt, and then stuffed the cash and the card into his pants pocket.

"I'm six-one," Eli said. "But to be fair, you're a much snappier dresser."

"Yes, I am."

Eli walked Veronica Craven to the door, taking note of the heart tattoo on her left forearm. He opened the door for her, and she crossed the threshold and turned.

"What are you doing?"

"Bidding you good morning," Eli said. "I have a case to work."

"You need to come with me to see Maria Gato. I'll drive."

"Thanks, I have my own car. A truck, actually. It has four

wheels and everything."

Her iPhone buzzed, and she typed a text one-handed while the other hand pointed at Eli. "I'm sure you have a very manly truck, but I wasn't asking, I was insisting."

"Your rental car, it has air conditioning?"

"Yes. Why?"

"Because it's supposed to top out at ninety today." Eli opened his seersucker jacket. "And this is the last clean shirt in my wardrobe."

She laughed—snorted, actually—and quickly covered her mouth. She slipped her iPhone into her skirt pocket and began clicking her way down the hallway. "Just be outside in five."

"Make it ten. I need to make a few calls first."

As she disappeared down the first flight of stairs, Eli inhaled deeply. A familiar scent. Very familiar.

CHAPTER 2

After placing phone calls to the County Assessor and the County Recorder, Eli took a quick slug of George Dickel, rinsed his mouth with Listerine, and hustled outside, hoping like hell the humidity was at least tolerable. But hope didn't spring eternal. It was, after all, mid-June. In the South. The sun had risen above the Blue Ridge Mountains and was showing no mercy. The parking lot shimmered like a mirage, heat trails rising off the cars, most of which were in various stages of decrepitude. Donning a pair of cheap sunglasses, Eli blinked the sun spots off his retina and checked his Seiko: 10:47 a.m. He spotted Veronica Craven's black Mercedes SUV and moved toward it.

"You're double-parked," Eli said.

Veronica held up her pointer finger. She finished giving the person on the other end of her iPhone a stern talking to. When she finished, she blew her brains out with a finger pistol.

"Dare I ask?"

"Get in," she barked. "I've got the air on full tilt."

Eli climbed inside, his armpits already damp with sweat. The car smelled fresh-off-the-dealership-lot new with just a hint of Veronica's perfume. He leaned back in the leather seat and let the air conditioning chill the beads of sweat on his forehead.

Veronica pressed a series of buttons on the GPS. A computer-generated voice instructed her to turn right onto Patton Avenue.

Her iPhone buzzed, and she looked at the screen. She snapped on a pair of white Ray Bans and held the cellphone between thumb and forefinger as if holding a dead rat.

"Put that in the glove compartment. I need a respite from the twenty-first century."

Eli opened the glove compartment. A pack of Marlboro Ultra Lights fell out. A yellow Post-it was stuck to the side of the package: DON'T BE WEAK. Eli tucked the smokes and Veronica's iPhone inside the glove compartment.

The iPhone buzzed. Eli smiled.

Veronica checked her makeup in the mirror, gripped the steering wheel at ten and two, and steered into light traffic on Patton Avenue. As she headed east past the automotive dealerships, she commented on a string of night clubs, chain hotels and chain restaurants that dotted the four-lane highway.

"Sprawl," Veronica said. "This isn't the Asheville I've read about in travel magazines."

Anxious to defend his adopted city—especially *his* side of town, the less fashionable west end—Eli considered giving Veronica a condensed lecture on the history of Asheville, North Carolina. The Western North Carolina Railroad completed a line from Salisbury to Asheville in 1880, which later enabled George Washington Vanderbilt to construct the Biltmore Estate, the largest private residence in America. Over time, that one-hundred-seventy-nine-thousand-square-foot house transitioned into a multi-million-dollar company. Which lured in tourists. Who created thousands of jobs. Which caused the sprawl flashing by Eli's window at fifty-five miles per hour.

But Eli refrained from being the local know-it-all, remembering all the times he'd traveled to new cities and some cabbie wanted to play docent, wanted to tell him about the *real* Cleveland or the *hidden* Miami. Instead, he let the air conditioner chase away the remnants of his jet lag and thought about Almario "Go Go" Gato. He waited for Veronica to say something about the Blue Ridge Mountains, which stood alongside the highway, hovering over the valley below like stoic parents waiting for their kids to clean up their messy bedrooms. Eli gave her points for her silence. And for ditching the phone, even if she kept glancing anxiously toward the glove compartment every time it buzzed. The car rode smooth, hardly a bump. For a resident of Los Angeles, she drove cautiously, obeying all traffic laws. Eli had a perfect driving record. Well, almost perfect. There was that time he drove the Durham Bulls' chartered Greyhound into the right field fence during the seventh inning stretch. But that was history. Almost ancient.

With the city skyline steadily growing in the windshield, Veronica sped up. Crossing the bridge, she broke the silence.

"Is that river as dirty as it looks?"

"Nah, there was a storm last night. The banks flooded."

"Looks filthy to me."

"I assure you the French Broad is much cleaner than the L.A. River. But L.A. has other things going for it."

"Don't mention the smog," she said, "or the celebrities."

Her iPhone buzzed a twelfth time. Eli asked who she was talking to earlier.

"Are you sizing me up again?" she asked.

"Try being nosy."

"I assure you that call had nothing to do with Almario or his disappearance. I want you to find him." Something caught in her throat. She rubbed her eye beneath the sunglasses. "Truth be told, I *need* you to find him. I feel responsible. For him and Maria."

Eli pointed to an uneven line of dwarf skyscrapers ahead. He turned off the GPS. "I hate that robot voice. Go three blocks up Patton and turn left onto College. Two blocks down and make a left on Battery Park. Almario's apartment building is the five-story glass affair on the right. The one with all the outdoor terraces."

She drove three blocks and turned left. College Avenue was in full swing. Business men in Sharpe, hustling to their next deposition or investor's meeting. Skateboarders showing cops on bikes how to do a kickflip. Hippies walking mangy dogs. Street vendors peddling homemade jewelry and vegan sandwiches. Veronica stopped at a red light, pointed.

"Is that a doo-wop group?"

"In matching ice cream jackets, no less."

"I've been here a few times, but now I have to ask: how the hell did all *this* happen?"

Eli took that as an invitation and explained how Governor Samuel Ashe christened this town Asheville in 1797, how the Vanderbilt family inadvertently commoditized fresh air and stunning mountain views. After more than a century of tourism, the town had grown and now downtown was bustling with tall bank buildings, law offices, luxury apartments, ethnic restaurants, and art galleries. To use Veronica's word: sprawl.

"What about the artists?" Veronica asked. "The hippies?"

"They come to be inspired by the clean mountain air, too. And to chase the ghosts of artists past. Ever read *The Beautiful and the Damned?"*

"Not Fitzgerald's best work."

"No argument here. But he wrote most of it at the Grove Park Inn here in town. Nice hotel, if you can afford it. As for the hippies, Asheville has a good music scene and a tolerant vibe."

"Strange place."

"I love it," Eli said somewhat defensively. "Wouldn't live anywhere else." Eli rolled his window down. The doo-wop group was singing "Get a Job." He snapped his fingers.

Veronica rolled up his window, put the child safety lock on, steered the car forward. She changed the subject. "Actually, the apartment belongs to Maria. Almario bought it for her. The deed is in her name."

"I know. I called the county assessor. Almario doesn't own property anywhere in Buncombe County. I also learned that Almario purchased a marriage license two months ago."

A clenching of the jaw. Momentary and subtle, but there.

"Who is the bride?"

"Don't know yet. My contact at the county recorder's office was on her way to lunch. Said she'd fax me a copy of the license later."

"Did you explain to your contact that this was urgent? That Almario may be in danger?"

"Wouldn't do any good. The contact is my second ex-fiancée."

"Your ex does favors for you? I'm impressed."

"We're not friends. We're friendly. Our breakup was mutual."

Laughing, Veronica stopped the car in front of 23 Battery Park, checked her makeup a second time, and retrieved her iPhone. A good-looking black kid in a black suit and tie emerged from the building and opened Veronica's door.

"Welcome back, Miss Craven."

Veronica handed him a ten, and Eli followed her through the building's revolving door.

The lobby looked like the living quarters of a spaceship, circa 2210. White marble floors and walls. A large mural of a single pine tree backlit by ambient blue light. Three red velvet couches and two futuristic-looking chairs in about two-thousand square feet of lobby space. The concierge, a puffy-cheeked man in a black suit and mauve button-down, complimented Veronica on her Gucci high heels. Eli hustled into the elevator, disheartened to find still more white marble. Staring at his reflection in the marble's surface, Eli scratched the stubble on his face.

"What floor?" he asked.

Veronica pushed her sunglasses atop her head and produced a key. She unlocked a little red box above the other elevator buttons and pressed the only button inside. "The penthouse," she said. "Top floor."

"So you've already seen her today?"

"Yes, I drove from the airport to DMSI Investigations and then straight here."

"So you lied to me." Eli stood on his tiptoes and looked

down. "You're taller than six feet."

The elevator opened directly into the fifth floor penthouse.

"This way," Veronica said, and Eli followed.

The apartment was open concept with more white marble floors and walls. The main living area had twenty-foot ceilings and a large glass window overlooking the downtown cityscape and the Blue Ridge Mountains beyond. There was a fifty-inch plasma screen TV mounted on the wall, and a red velvet loveseat and matching armchair arranged around an ultra-modern coffee table made of dark wood with a white lacquered surface. Marquez's novel *Love in the Time of Cholera* lay dog-eared on the coffee table along with a statistics textbook. Eli shuddered at the memory of taking STATS 215—all those nights spent guzzling instant coffee and staring at a blank sheet of graphing paper. Something spicy was cooking somewhere, and his stomach groaned.

"Wait here," Veronica said and clicked her heels into the kitchen, which was separated from the rest of the space by a wall that only reached halfway to the ceiling.

Eli sat down in the velvet armchair and picked up Marquez's novel. He didn't read Spanish, but as he stared at the opening paragraph, he remembered the book's opening, something about death and the smell of almonds. He put the book back where he found it and walked to the large picture window. The traffic inched along Biltmore Avenue below. Sunlight gleamed off the hoods of cars and neighboring buildings. A small band of Phish fans milled around the fountain, strumming guitars for spare change and smoking cloves. Eli walked to a door leading out to the terrace. A selling feature for most, but he didn't care for heights. Or stainless steel furniture. He returned to the red velvet armchair and waited.

Several minutes later Veronica waved Eli toward the kitchen. She leaned in close, grabbed hold of his jacket lapels, and stared into his eyes. "No bullshit, Almario is all she has." She bit her lip and let go of his jacket, smoothed out the wrinkles she'd made. "At the moment, he's all I have."

Eli got his first look at Maria Gato in the kitchen, which was massive and cold like the rest of the apartment. Raven-haired with a dark brown face sprinkled with pimples, Maria stood over a steaming sauce pan, her marble-black eyes focused on what looked like chicken bubbling in a reddish sauce. Her skin tone was much darker than Almario's, and standing next to Veronica, Maria appeared dwarfish and plump, bordering on fat. Her clothes weren't flattering either: a baggy tie-dyed T-shirt splattered with flour and red sauce and Jordache blue jeans that hung loose off her wide hips.

Eli introduced himself, and Maria lowered her eyes as she shook his hand. Firm grip. Strong, callused hands.

Veronica opened a drawer, removed a clean white apron, and slipped it over her pencil skirt, tying it off in the back. She put a hand on Maria's shoulder. "Eli Sharpe, the quiet one here is Maria Gato, Almario's twin sister. Maria, Mr. Sharpe is the private investigator I hired to find Almario. He needs to ask you some questions. Don't worry, he's here to help."

Maria nodded a second time and continued stirring her pot with a wooden spoon.

Veronica nodded at Eli.

Eli said, "Veronica tells me you received an email from Almario yesterday. Is that right?"

"No, it isn't," Maria snapped. "The email was from Almario's address, but it wasn't him."

"Do you mean someone other than Almario wrote it?"

"Yes, someone else wrote it."

"How do you know?"

"The grammar. It was full of mistakes." Maria looked up from her pan for the first time and said something in rapid Spanish to Veronica, who answered in Spanish. "Sentence fragments, yes. A sentence must have a subject and a verb and express a complete thought. Whoever wrote the email broke this rule a lot. I mean, often."

"Break it a lot myself," Eli said. "Among many others."

"My brother speaks and writes perfect English. Our father was a language professor in Cuba." She crossed herself, kissed her fingers. "If we didn't make good grades, we were severely punished. Almario prides himself on his speaking abilities."

"His elocution," Veronica added helpfully and took the wooden spoon from Maria's hand. "You two talk, Maria. I will babysit the *achiote.*"

Maria reluctantly relinquished her post at the stove. She dug her hands into her pockets and then removed them, wiping them on her shirt. She glanced around the kitchen for something to do. Without a task to perform, her shoulders slouched, and she touched her hair, picked a pimple on her chin.

"You're worried about Almario," Eli said, "but I'm here to help."

Maria took her hands away from her face, ooze leaking from her chin pimple. Despite her bumpy complexion and somewhat greasy hair, she was still a pretty girl. It was her eyes. Dark but clear, they might have been the eyes of a Spanish princess from another century.

Eli said, "Maria, before you were born my father dragged my mother and me down to southern Florida, where I had my first taste of Cuban coffee. I must have been nine maybe ten at the time. I'd never tasted anything so delicious in my life. You wouldn't happen to have any on hand, would you?"

Maria snickered as her eyes sparkled with childish excitement. "In my country we don't call it Cuban coffee. It's simply *cafecito.* Or *café con leche.* Would you like a cup?"

"I would love one, thanks."

Maria went to work grinding beans and loading a very sophisticated espresso maker.

Veronica winked at Eli, and he moved beside Maria and spoke to her while she worked.

"What you said about the email was very helpful, Maria."

"I saved it and printed it out. Do you need to read it yourself?"

"I do, thanks, but that can wait. Can you tell me the last time you actually saw Almario?"

"Three days ago."

"Where?"

Maria ground the beans and loaded the filter. After she pressed a series of buttons, the coffee began to boil. With nothing to occupy her hands, she began fidgeting again. She started fiddling with the spice rack, rearranging the bottles that were out of place.

"Maria, I do not care if Almario was drinking or associating with people he shouldn't have. Just tell me where you last saw him."

"I'm very mistrustful, Mr. Sharpe." Maria poured coffee into a tiny espresso cup, added steamed milk, and a lump of sugar. She picked up the cup and handed it to Eli. "I saw Almario here, but I think he went to the Burly Earl. He's been going there for several months now. The bartender lets him drink without ID."

"Do you know the bartender's name?"

"I know what he looks like. Black. Bald. Muscles. He has an earring, but in his lip. Do you know the kind?"

"Unfortunately, I do." Eli sipped his coffee and told her how wonderful it was, and then got out his pocket-size leather notebook and copied down her description of the bartender as well as a few observations about Maria. "Can you think of any other reason why Almario would go to this bar? A teammate invited him, perhaps?"

Maria shook her head. "Not his teammates. Almario doesn't get along with most of the other ballplayers."

"How come?"

"My brother is sensitive."

"That's true," Veronica added as she tossed a pinch of salt into the sauce pan. "Almario doesn't care for the macho locker room atmosphere. I suspect the other players were jealous of Almario's talent."

"And his hefty signing bonus, no doubt. Do either of you think one of his teammates might have something to do with his disappearance?"

"Highly unlikely," Veronica said. "Even during games and practices, Almario doesn't associate with any of them. He hardly speaks to the coaches."

Maria said something else in Spanish.

Eli said, "Maria, you speak English so beautifully. Tell me what you just said to Veronica."

"I told her that Almario might have a—how do you say it?—a substance abuse problem. Two months ago, I found liquor bottles in his bedroom when I was cleaning. That's why he went to the bar that night."

Eli finished his coffee. As he wrote in his notebook, the caffeine coursed through his veins, obliterating any lingering effects from the previous night's whiskey intake. "Maria, can you think of anyone else I should talk to about Almario? Anyone who might be able to help me locate him?"

Maria said, "You should talk to Christine Lovatt. She's Almario's girlfriend and my tutor. I got an A minus in English one-oh-one with her help. She's a student at UNC-Asheville."

"Maria will enroll there next fall," Veronica said proudly.

"If my grades stay good. Is it good or well, Mr. Sharpe?"

"It's good, and call me Eli, Maria." Eli wrote down some new information in his notebook. He put away the notebook and asked to have a look at Almario's bedroom, alone. The two women stared at him. Maria nodded.

"Third door on the left," Veronica said. "Please be careful."

Along the hallway off the kitchen were four doors, and Eli entered the last one on the left, figuring Almario may have put the luxury apartment in his sister's name, but wouldn't have given up the master suite, too. When he opened the door, a life-size cutout of Rafael Palmeiro in an Orioles uniform smiled at him from the corner of the bedroom. *A liar and a cheat*, Eli thought and then remembered he had an office full of Nixon memorabilia. Eli scanned the rest of the room. A massive platform bed with a thirty-two-inch flat screen TV built into the bed frame dominated the space. Burned DVDs and an iPod sat atop sheets that had to be pushing the limits of thread count. The DVDs were all labeled similarly. Gato Batting Session, June 1st. Gato Batting Session, June 8th. Eli scrolled through the iPod playlists. No music or videos. Just audiobooks, mostly self-help stuff about positive visualization, setting and achieving goals, and maximizing human potential. There were a few sports psychology titles that Eli recognized from his own playing days.

"Hope they work for you," Eli said, glancing up at the high ceiling, the sunlight streaming into the room and reflecting off the marble. "I really do."

Drifting toward the attached bathroom, Eli studied a row of framed pictures hanging on the white marble walls. In every photograph, Almario was center frame. There were pictures of Almario with his parents: his mom was a tall, svelte, light-skinned woman—Almario got her genes—and his dad was short, stocky, dark-skinned man with menacing eyes—Maria got his. There were pictures of Almario in Little League uniforms, Almario carrying books, Almario playing stickball on the streets of Havana. In most of the pictures, usually in the background, Eli saw shabby apartment buildings with corrugated metal and tin roofs. Maria was absent from the pictures on the wall—except for one. In the photo Almario wore a sharkskin suit, his mop of black curls perfectly tousled, his smile five hundred watts. Standing in the crook of his arm in a beige, ill-fitting dress, Maria looked camera-shy and uncomfortable. Behind the happy, dressed-up siblings was the American Airlines logo. Eli slipped the picture out of its frame and pocketed it, moved on to a MacBook Air sitting on a glass desk facing the window. Opening the computer, Eli waited for it to come to life and double-clicked on Internet Explorer. The homepage: the Asheville Travelers' website. Eli scrolled down to Player Bios and skimmed Almario Gato's stats for the season. Subpar.

A check of the internet history brought up fifteen websites. Some of them had filthy names with "cock" or "pussy" in the URL. The rest were harmless. Eli clicked one of the harmless ones—Almario's bank: Wells Fargo—and found the password already stored. He took a look at Almario's debit purchases for the past few days. El Chapala's. Local ABC Store. Ingles on Merrimon Avenue. All of them were in the Asheville area. A good sign: Almario hadn't fled. He was hiding somewhere in town. But why hang around? Eli closed the laptop and made a quick sweep of the room, looking in drawers and closets and behind the mirror in the bathroom. Nothing interesting. Time-traveling back to the early nineties and the year he turned seventeen, Eli recalled filching one of his old man's joints and stashing it under his mattress. He chuckled as he remembered how long and hard he'd coughed after the first drag. Eli lifted up Almario's mattress. Two back issues of *Playboy* and a small bag of pot, maybe an eighth of an ounce. Wouldn't have lasted Eli's old man a day, but he pocketed the weed anyway and left the room as he'd found it.

In the kitchen, Veronica and Maria were sitting at the island, eating *achiote*, wonderful garlic smells filling the room.

Veronica asked if Eli had found anything useful, and he pulled out the picture he'd taken off Almario's wall.

"I'm going to borrow this, Maria. I have enough to start with, but I had a few more questions. Do you and Almario share the same cellphone plan?"

Maria looked at Veronica.

"Yes," Veronica said. "They do. Verizon. I helped them set it up over a year ago."

"I need to have a look at the phone records for both Almario's number and Maria's. That'll be the easiest way to track him down."

Maria got up and hurried down the hallway. She came back holding her latest Verizon bill. Maria handed the bill to Eli.

"This has our account number and a list of charges. I will call and have them release our records."

"Maria handles all the household bills," Veronica said. "And she's on the Dean's List. I don't want to tell you what I was doing at her age."

"Good," Eli said, "then I won't have to disclose my own youthful indiscretions. Maria, I just need a copy of that email."

"I'll get that for you," Veronica said and stood up. "Walk me to the elevator."

Eli shook Maria's hand, promised to do his best to find Almario, and Maria's pupils widened.

"Do your best, Mr. Sharpe, and find him."

Eli followed Veronica to the elevator, where she reached into her skirt pocket and handed him a folded piece of printer paper. Eli tucked the paper into the pocket of his pants and pressed the elevator button.

"You really care about Almario and Maria. I can see why they trust you."

"And I can see why your exes take your phone calls."

"If you're trying to make me blush, I'm too old. I'll call you later with an update."

"Don't you need a ride?"

"Nah, my next stop is close by."

CHAPTER 3

The offices of DMSI Investigations were on College Avenue, one block over and two blocks up from 23 Battery Park. Despite the near ninety-degree heat, Eli covered the distance from Maria Gato's apartment in less than ten minutes. What made this feat even more miraculous was that Eli had to plow through a crowd of thirty or so people that had formed around the doo-wop group on the corner. While Eli excused his way through the audience, the group was doing a spirited rendition of "The Book of Love."

The office building occupied by DMSI was an unassuming, three-story brick square sandwiched between a microbrewery and a greasy spoon. The building sat across the street from Magnolia Park. Asheville being a Mecca for free spirits, the park was one of many places downtown where street artists and college dropouts gathered to protest against the super-wealthy and swap Phish tapes. When they weren't smoking hand-rolled cigarettes or burying their noses in Chomsky, they politely pestered the millionaire bankers and real estate developers on lunch or coffee breaks. As Eli approached the office's revolving door, a park dweller with a gray beard and a golden retriever at his side asked Eli for a dollar. Eli handed the man a McDonald's gift card—payment from a ten-year-old girl in Eli's neighborhood who hired him to find her missing stuffed animal, a purple bear named Gus.

"That card has thirty dollars on it," Eli said. "I like the double cheeseburgers, no pickles."

"But I'm a vegetarian."

"They have salads." Eli patted the retriever's bullet-like head, went inside, rode the elevator to the third floor, and walked through a glass door with the word INVESTIGATIONS painted in white letters on it.

The third floor was a wide-open space, three thousand square feet of drab beige carpet and putty-colored walls, cubicles and fake ficus plants, copiers and computers all requiring logins and passwords to use. The cubicles belonged to the ten or so private investigators DMSI kept on salary, but catching one of them at his or her desk was like catching a marlin in the Sahara. Eli had been offered one of those cubicles on numerous occasions and declined, preferring to set his own schedule and take or leave cases according to his whim. Also, the thought of wearing a suit and tie to work and staring at those putty-colored walls every day made the mercury fillings in his teeth quiver. He glanced down at his well-worn blue jeans and buttoned his tan seer-sucker sports jacket, conscious of the sweat produced by his sprint outdoors.

Striding past the sad cubicles and sadder plastic plants, Eli stopped before an unmarked wooden door. Without knocking he entered and shut the door behind him.

"Jesus, Sharpe, were you born in a barn?"

"The parking lot at Red Rocks Amphitheater, actually. According to my old man, it was a very special night. The Dead did a fifty-three minute version of 'Truckin.'"

"Swell." Carpenter, a sixty-five-year-old man with a face like a Saint Bernard and thinning gray hair, aimed an unlit cigar at a director's chair buried beneath a pile of papers, folders, invoices, receipts, and Dunkin' Donuts coffee cups. Eli filled his arms with Carpenter's detritus, dumped it on the floor, and sat down. The room smelled of good tobacco and aftershave.

"You look fit, goddamn you."

"As do you."

"Quit studying my hair. When you get to be my age, you don't care what color it is as long as you got some."

"Ernest, you want the truth?"

"Hardly ever."

"The truth is you've added some wrinkles since last I saw you."

Carpenter stroked his thick gray mustache, asked about Eli's trip to Seattle. Then he embarked on a rant about being a homicide detective on the Asheville Police force for twenty-three years and a rat-shit private in the Army before that. He pointed to a framed picture on the wall of a clean-shaven and much slimmer Carpenter in an Army uniform, a Marlboro Red dangling from his lip and an M-16 in his hand. Beside the picture was one of Carpenter crouching beside a bloodstain on the concrete. He wore a ratty sport coat, and his necktie was tucked into the breast pocket of his shirt. In his latex-gloved hand he held an empty evidence bag.

"Uncle Sam snatched me up right out of high school. *This* is supposed to be my retirement gig." He lit his cigar, puffed until his cheeks turned a deep shade of crimson, and peered at Eli through a dense cloud of gray smoke.

"You'll get no sympathy from me," Eli said, always delighted to hear his mentor and friend whine. "You've got a view. On a clear day you can see all the way to Tennessee."

"Been to Tennessee," Carpenter snorted. "Didn't think much of it."

While Carpenter admired the view, he drew on his Arturo Fuente. Eli thought of cracking a joke about the old man's garb—a purple Hawaiian shirt with three different colors of Hibiscus and a pair of cargo shorts. But he thought better of it. Old guys were, in Eli's experience, a sensitive lot and could only take so much abuse. Eli's mentor was no exception. They'd first met at UNC-Asheville. At twenty-five, Eli found himself out of baseball and in a college classroom with a bunch of shaggy-haired eighteen-year-olds. Like the other freshmen, Eli had only the vaguest notion of what he wanted to do with his life until Ernest Carpenter came to speak to his Criminal Justice 101 class. Dressed like a TV cop in a colorless suit and a tie stained with barbecue sauce, Carpenter lectured on the art of criminal investigations and tracking down murderers, and Eli was enthralled. Afterward, he walked up to Carpenter and told him what a lousy public speaker he was. The old man laughed. Carpenter, who never had a son of his own, bought Eli a beer, and they talked, mostly about detective work, which had fascinated Eli since he was a boy. Over time, they developed a mutual admiration society. Carpenter, an avid baseball fan, admired Eli for making it all the way to the Big Leagues. Eli admired Carpenter for putting criminals behind bars. Carpenter helped Eli with papers and research, and later, helped him get his private investigator's license. Even bought him an S&W revolver and taught him to shoot.

"I took the Gato case," Eli said. "My first day."

"Gato? Refresh my memory."

"It's gah-toh. Almario Gato. The missing ballplayer. Plays shortstop for the Travelers."

"Hang on a minute. I'm having a senior moment." He shuffled some papers around his desk, rearranged three different coffee mugs until he found a sheet of yellow notebook paper. He held the paper a quarter of an inch from his face, squinted, and read while cigar ash fell onto his desk. "Of course, how could I forget? The kid's agent called me last night, grilled me something awful about you and your résumé. I gave her names and numbers to call. Then she demanded that I see her at six in the a.m. Almario Gato is her client."

"Gah-toh."

"Right. Eighteen. Missing. Lives with his sister. Veronica Craven, the agent, is tall, smart, and demanding."

"That's her to a T."

Carpenter handed over the piece of paper, and Eli read it. It actually said "Veronica Craven. Tall. Smart. Demanding."

Eli asked if Craven had connections.

"Her old man does. Don't tell me you've never heard of Martin Craven."

"Should I have?"

"Kids today, no respect for the past."

"I turn thirty-five in August. I'm hardly a kid."

"Until you pluck your first nose hair, you're a kid in my book. Besides, you still have all your own hair and most of your teeth. By the way, my wife misses you at our dinner table. Just said the other day what a pretty face you have."

"Not as pretty as Almario's." Eli grinned. "May I ask what you had to say about my face?"

Carpenter grunted. "I said, 'Sure, the kid's Robert Redford handsome, but he's never had to shave a day in his life.'"

"Enough, you old fart." They both laughed. "Tell me about Martin Craven. I need to brush up on my history. It might be important to the case."

"Ol' Marty was one of the first hotshot sports agents. In the mid-eighties he signed that what's-his-name football/baseball star to the first million-dollar contract. Kansas City Royals paid one-point-one million dollars. Memory serves, Craven had half a dozen Hall of Famers as clients."

Eli got out his pocket-size notebook and jotted the new information down, brought the old man up to speed (minus the pot he'd found in Almario's bedroom), and then showed him the picture of Almario Gato in a suit. The old man grunted, "Handsome," as if the word were an insult and not a compliment. He passed the picture back, blew a smoke ring the size of an orange. He got up and lumbered over to a four-foot filing cabinet. Reaching into the top drawer, he pulled out a fifth of Maker's Mark and two Dixie cups. He poured two fingers of bourbon into each cup and passed one to Eli.

Carpenter raised his cup, Eli raised his.

"To finding Almario Gato," Carpenter said.

"In one piece."

"A-men."

They drank.

Carpenter said, "About Gato. He's young, he's good-looking, and he's got money. Add those up and what do you get?"

"Women troubles."

"Women. Or drugs. Maybe both. That's where I'd lay my money. Talk to the girlfriend first."

"Sounds like a plan to me, but first I need to read over my notes, use a computer to do some research. Can you spare one?"

"You kids and your computers. Shoe leather solves cases, not bandwidth."

"I wear Chuck Taylors, no leather. Work smart, not hard. That's my motto."

Carpenter ashed his cigar into one of the empty coffee mugs on his desk and then turned and slapped Eli on the leg. "Whatever works for you, kid. Since you're such a handsome protégé, I'll let you use my computer. Even let you sit in the ergonomic chair my wife bought me."

"No, thanks, Ernest. That cigar is killing me almost as fast as it's killing you. I'll use Rita's computer."

"Suit yourself, but do me a favor."

"Name it."

"Don't make Rita fiancée number six. Some of us have to work here every day." Carpenter mumbled something else about kids and clean air. He waved Eli away, and Eli left the office.

Rita Cline was a part-time investigator, and a damn good one, but she spent a majority of her time babysitting Carpenter and his business. Paying bills. Organizing client records. Limiting Carpenter to six cigars a day. She had her own cubicle near the kitchenette, away from the other detectives whose personal habits she took exception to. She kept a much cleaner work station than the old man. Neat piles of folders, all of them clearly labeled and dated. Dust-free keyboard and computer monitor.

Framed pictures of her four-year-old daughter: a cute-as-a-button blonde with sparkly blue eyes. On the corner of her desk sat a scented candle—peach. His eyes still burning from the cigar smoke, Eli breathed deeply and sat down, pulled out the email Almario supposedly wrote to his sister. He laid it carefully on the desk and slipped on his glasses, remembering Veronica Craven's comment about preferring men who wore contacts, not spectacles. He smiled, concentrated.

Maria,
Dont want you to worry. Decided to take some time off. Need to clear my head. With friends but dont worry Ill be okay. About our fight. I wish I hadnt said those things to you. Youre probably right I do need to cool it but you dont know what Im going through. Things havent been right since my knee. Please dont worry and dont look for me, Ill come back when Im ready.
Love,
Almario

Aside from the poor grammar and punctuation, Eli took note of the tone. Frustrated, but thoughtful. Self-effacing, but desperate. The concern for Maria's well-being, the oblique allusions to Almario's drinking and drug use, the knee injury: everything in the letter jibed with what both Veronica and Maria had said about Almario.

So why did Maria believe someone else had written the letter?

Surely she wasn't basing that belief solely on grammatical errors? Eli put the picture of Almario in a sharkskin suit beside the email and read it a second time. After some reflection, he decided that if Almario hadn't written those words, then somebody who knew him (and probably knew him well) had.

Removing his glasses, he put the note and the picture away and logged onto Internet Explorer, ran a Google search on Almario Gato that yielded one hundred fifty-nine hits. He skimmed several articles until he found one entitled, "Go Go Gato." According to an ESPN blogger named Kent Rosenbaum, Almario's story was a compelling one. It went something like this:

In January, 2007, Almario's parents handed over three thousand dollars (their entire life savings) to a boat captain to smuggle fourteen-year-old Almario Gato out of Cuba and into Puerto Rico. With nine people in one tiny speed boat, its motor barely functioning, the journey was incredibly dangerous, but they made it to Puerto Rico. From there, Almario was taken into Miami, where he stayed with friends of the family. After almost a year of legal battles, those same friends were granted custody of Almario, and Almario was granted temporary U.S. citizenship. Three weeks later, in March of 2008, a man named David Lash discovered Almario playing in a Pony League baseball tournament. After watching Almario hit six triples and two doubles and steal eight bases over a two-game stretch, Coach Lash offered Almario a full scholarship to the prestigious Asheville Country Day School.

Almario spent the next two years at Asheville Country Day during which time he carried a three-point-six GPA and led the varsity team to two state championships. During his junior year, 2009, Almario received scholarship offers from several collegiate powerhouses: Florida State, Oklahoma, Miami, and Cal State-Fullerton. In May, Almario met Veronica Craven, daughter of the legendary sports agent Martin Craven. In June, Almario was drafted in the sixth round by the Toronto Blue Jays, but decided to finish high school—on the advice of his agent, Veronica Craven.

Eli skimmed the rest of the article, which recounted the last year of Almario's life. Drafted fourth overall by the Colorado Rockies. Collected one-point-two million dollars. Assigned to the Single-A club, the Asheville Travelers. Tore his ACL after a lackluster debut. Eli scrolled down a little farther and found a link to a related story entitled, "Gato Defection Inspirational." He clicked on the link and read about how two months after

Almario cashed his signing bonus check, he flew to Miami, found a boat captain, and paid him twelve thousand dollars (amount not confirmed by the author of article) to go pick up his parents, José Molina Gato and Manuela Gato, and his twin sister, Maria Gato, from the Port of Havana and bring them all back to Miami. Only Maria Gato and the boat captain made it. José and Manuela drowned somewhere in international waters off the coast of Cuba. Details were sketchy, but the author did confirm that Maria Gato spent time in a mental health facility in Miami where she was heavily medicated and didn't speak for almost two months.

Eli shook his head in amazement at what that poor girl had been through to get to America. And now the only family she had left was missing.

The rest of the article was an inflammatory screed on the availability of public information. Apparently, the author was unable to access the Gatos' death certificates or the coroner's reports or police reports.

A tragedy.

Jesus Christ.

Eli checked his Seiko: 12:36 p.m. He removed his glasses, picked up Rita's phone and called his ex-fiancée in the county recorder's office.

"April Clemmons, I need one more favor."

"I sent you a fax this morning. Didn't you get it?"

"I did. And thank you. You're a beautiful and intelligent woman." Eli meant it, too. His brain flooded with memories. Long debates over who made the best sushi in town. Whole days spent in bed, cursing at the *New York Times* crossword, watching idiotic rom-coms on cable, and making love. The memories led to a brief but acute stab of regret. "I still care about you, April."

"You say that to all your exes."

"And I mean it."

Deep sigh. "I know you do. Which is why I'm going to help

you out. Again. Tell me what you need, Sharpe."

"I need you to resend that fax to DMSI."

"Is that all?"

"Another shot with you would be much appreciated, but that ship has sailed."

"Actually, you sank that ship. I say again: what do you need?"

"How about you see if Almario Gato has a registered will? Also, since I'm already in your debt, find out if a Christine Lovatt, L-O-V-A-T-T, has a marriage license?"

"It'll take me a minute."

"For you I'll wait."

April put him on hold, and he got to listen to an elevator music version of "Street Fighting Man." Appalled at the massacre of a classic, he mouthed the lyrics anyway and smiled at the picture of Rita's little daughter. She had hair like golden wheat and big blue eyes and looked like Rita on a twenty-seven-year delay. Eli wondered what type of man a woman like Rita would go for. The strong, silent type? A wimpy hypochondriac? Either way, Eli didn't fit the bill.

"All right, Magnum PI. I got your information."

"I was never worthy of you, April."

"You're annoyingly cute, Sharpe. That's a no on the Gato will, and as for Miss Lovatt, she isn't planning on getting married anytime soon, at least not in Buncombe County. Satisfied?"

"Not since we parted ways."

April laughed. "Maybe you're not so sweet, talking to a married woman that way."

"Probably why I wasn't invited to your wedding."

"Yeah," she laughed, "that was the reason."

"Thanks again, April."

"Stay out of trouble, Sharpe."

Eli hung up, and Rita's fax machine spat out Almario Gato's marriage license. Under the bride heading was the name Sharon Stuckey. Eli added the new information to his notebook, folded the fax into quarters, and tucked everything into his jacket pocket.

His next call was to David Rubio, a narcotics detective assigned to the Adam 2 district in West Asheville.

"Rubio speaking."

"Davey, it's your old teammate."

"Eli Sharpe, my friend, what can I do for you?"

David Rubio grew up in a dirt-poor section of the Dominican Republic, but baseball got him off the island. Eli played on various minor league teams with Rubio until Rubio's knees made him quit the game. After doing some Division II coaching for a year, Rubio met his wife-to-be and entered the police academy. He'd worked his way up the ranks, and now he was a narcotics detective whose star was on the rise.

Eli said, "For starters, you can actually accept one of my invitations to drink with me. I have no one else to talk about the horrors of Astroturf and the abomination that is the designated hitter."

"You drink me under the table every time. Besides, women run my life. My beautiful wife. My lovely daughters. You should come by some time. I have good tequila and one room where my girls let me be." Radio chatter. Rubio copied and then silenced his radio. "Have you ever watched a ballgame on a fifty-two-inch plasma TV?"

"No, I haven't, but it sounds great. Listen, I need a favor."

"For my old double-play partner: anything. Anything legal, that is."

"I'm working a missing persons case. The client doesn't want police involvement."

"Shameful how no one trusts the police in this country. Not even in a safe city like ours."

"I trust you, Davey. I got a lead on a guy. A bartender at the Burly Earl on Tunnel."

"Do you have a name?"

"I have a description. Black. Bald. Muscles. Lip piercing. Can you run a search on him, see if he's got a sheet? Maybe see if any other employees at the Earl have records?"

"Of course, but it'll take a while. Give me your cell and I'll call you within the hour."

"You're not too busy?"

"It's a light day, my friend, knock on wood."

Eli recited his number, said thanks.

"I'll call you soon. My friend, do you still think about the Bull?"

"Sure, I do, Davey. And thanks for reminding me." Eli hung up, leaned back in Rita's chair, and stared at the putty-colored office walls.

The Bull.

The fucking Bull.

In '99 Eli had a cup of coffee with the Tampa Bay Devil Rays, and after failing to hit, was sent back to the Triple-A team, the Durham Bulls. After striking out five times in the first game of a doubleheader sometime in late July, Eli, the starting second baseman, was benched for the second game and snuck a fifth of George Dickel into the dugout. During the seventh inning, plastered and bored senseless, he stole the team bus and drove it into the three-story-high bull that guarded the left field wall. That little stunt got him a few days in the Durham County Jail. His baseball career declined steadily thereafter.

Eli disinfected Rita's keyboard and phone and exited the building. He didn't have time for regrets. He had a case to work. And he liked to work. Kept him from sitting around dwelling on the past.

CHAPTER 4

A new Blue Bird taxi wound its way around the UNC-Asheville campus and stopped before an ivy-covered brick building. Eli paid the driver, tipping him three singles on a nine-dollar fare, and exited the cab.

Slipping his sunglasses into place, Eli quickly adjusted to the midday heat and glanced around his alma mater. The administration had wisely minimized the concrete and maximized the plant life. Purple, red, white, and yellow chrysanthemums lined the newly paved roads. Oaks and pines and magnolia trees dotted the lush green quad, providing plenty of shade for serious afternoons with Kierkegaard while still allowing ample room for tossing a frisbee or juggling a hacky sack. Ivy crept up the sides of the academic buildings surrounding the quad. After making friends with Ernest Carpenter in Criminal Justice 101, Eli used to imagine himself an investigator and the other students as his suspects. While he sat alone in the quad dutifully plowing through his reading list, he would pick a specific subject and make observations about his or her appearance and wardrobe, body language and mannerisms, and later that same night, he would record as many details as he could remember in his red leather notebook. He got good at it. Really good.

Eli spotted a group of students milling around the bronze statue of a bulldog that guarded the entrance to Highsmith Center, the campus cafeteria. He slung his seersucker jacket over his shoulder and headed in that direction, hoping one of them might know where Christine Lovatt could be found. The sidewalk was made of brick, and each brick had an alumnus's name and date of graduation on it. Wondering if he might stumble upon his own, Eli read some of the names as he walked. Douglas, '86. Everett, '94. Taylor, '69. When he looked up, he realized that he had invaded the turf of a trio of attractive girls of different shapes, sizes, and colors. Eli apologized and asked if anyone knew Christine Lovatt. He put on his jacket to make his question seem more official.

All three girls exchanged glances before the tallest and least attractive of the group—a brunette wearing a royal blue and white volleyball jersey—asked who he was.

"Forgive me," Eli said and extended his hand, the brunette shaking it without hesitation. "The heat has evaporated my manners. My name is Eli Sharpe. I'm a private investigator."

The other two girls got out their cellphones, either to demonstrate their annoyance with Eli's intrusion or to call campus security. Eli figured he'd find out soon enough.

"Go on without me," the brunette said to the other girls. "I'll catch up."

"Are you sure?" a strawberry-blonde with a tattoo on her wrist asked, glaring at Eli.

The other one, a pretty black girl with her hand on her iPhone, said, "We'll totally stay with you, if you need us."

"No," said the brunette. "I'm all set."

iPhone girl hugged the brunette first, then the strawberry-blonde hugged the brunette. The strawberry-blonde walked past Eli, bumping his shoulder. Halfway down the sidewalk the girls spotted a group of boys they knew and stopped looking over their shoulders. Eli had to smile.

"Your friends are very protective," he said turning his attention to the brunette.

"Teammates look out for each other."

"Is Christine Lovatt a teammate?"

"No, she's a friend. Which is why I need to ask you some questions before I take you to her. If I take you to her."

Eli removed his sunglasses, tried to look trustworthy à la Eddie Haskell minus the schmuck grin. He asked if she wanted to walk to a nearby stone bench, in the shade of a large willow tree.

"I proposed to my third fiancée under that tree," Eli said. "That time she said no."

"Smart girl."

"You have no idea."

"Look, you can reminisce on your own time. We'll do this out in the open."

"You're wise beyond your years, Miss?"

"Courtney Mullins. I'm too young to be wise. I'm suspicious, highly so. A cute stranger in an Atticus Finch jacket asks to see one of my closest friends, of course I'm going to give him the third degree. For all I know you could be an internet perv."

"I could be, but I'm not."

"Give me your driver's license and your private investigator's license. Now." Eli showed her both without taking them out of his wallet. "Dude, do you really have a Velcro wallet? Like seriously?"

"I'm comfortably un-hip."

"Whatever, just take the IDs out. I'm nearsighted." Eli obeyed and she examined them up close. Then she pocketed them.

"At some point, I'll need those back."

"Answer my questions first. Why do you want to talk to Christine?"

"I'm looking for Almario Gato. I've been informed that Christine is his girlfriend."

"Do you think Christine had anything to do with his disappearance?"

"Who said anything about disappearance?"

"I did. Just now. Don't jerk me around. Christine is a wreck, so answer my question."

"Yes, I am looking for him, but that's all I'll say. Almario's sister claims Christine is a sweet girl and a positive influence. Being highly suspicious myself, I need personal confirmation of superlatives like those."

"Christine is a sweet girl, but she's in a bad way right now, for obvious reasons. She lives on my hall in Mills." The brunette looked Eli over from head to toe, as if he were a horse she was thinking of buying and wasn't sold on yet. She felt the fabric of Eli's jacket, told him the shoulder pads made him look even skinnier.

"I shop at thrift stores. You get what you pay for."

"You're weird. Are you weird harmless or weird dangerous?"

A fat, bearded man in tweeds stopped beside Courtney, looked Eli over, and said, "Miss Mullins, this man is far too old to be your paramour."

She forced a smile. "He's not my boyfriend, Professor Lynch. He's a private investigator."

"Really? How splendid! I'm an avid fan of the gumshoe genre myself. Never met a sleuth in the flesh. I'll have to tell my wife the exciting news. Carry on, Miss Mullins." The professor wished Eli and Courtney a pleasant afternoon, sucked on his inhaler and disappeared into the cafeteria, whistling Dixie.

"Pretentious," Courtney said and looked back at Eli. "I'll take you to see Christine on one condition: I'm in the room while you question her."

"You wouldn't by any chance be interested in going to law school, would you?"

"Maybe. After I spend a few years in the Peace Corps. If you don't accept my condition, I'll go straight to the Administration, see how they feel about you questioning their students."

"So it's not a condition, it's an ultimatum."

"Pretty much. We all good?"

"It would certainly appear so."

It was a short but pleasant walk to Mills Hall—more trees, flowers, grass, and ivy-covered brick buildings. More students, too. Lots of them. The quad was especially crowded for a summer term. Bronzed girls in peasant skirts pedaling bicycles. Shaggy-haired boys sans shoes toting Frisbees and environmentally-friendly water bottles with catchy political slogans on them. The air was laced with patchouli and irises, and Eli chastised himself for not joining in the merriment during his own college days. They walked across the quad and between two buildings and onto a parking lot filled with hybrids and convertibles and vintage Volvos. As they neared a four-story building, they encountered a giant black man wearing an honest to goodness smoking jacket and a purple cravat. He tipped his Rex Harrison hat and bid Eli good afternoon.

"Provost," Courtney said.

"Is that a job title?"

"Liberal arts universities should be classified as separate planets." Courtney sneered at an acne-faced kid carrying a skateboard under his arm, and then quickened the pace.

As they entered Christine's dorm and walked up two flights of stairs, Eli tried not to stare at a pretty brunette's hairy legs and said, "A lot of free spirits at this school, eh?"

"Only the boys shave here," she snorted. "Well, some of them."

They knocked on room 317, and a striking redhead wrapped in a towel swung open the door, spitting curses.

"Oh, hi, Courtney. I thought it was those simpletons in 306 again."

"Nope. It's just me. And this harmless weirdo looking for Almario."

"I'm Eli Sharpe. I was hired to locate Almario."

Christine's cheeks flushed. "Tell me you have leads. Tell me you know where he might be."

"I have leads, but it would help if I could speak to you. Your friend volunteered to stay while we talk. Could you get dressed and join us?"

"He's harmless, C-Lo. He tries anything and my first call is campus security. Put on some clothes. We'll wait in the rumpus room."

Christine disappeared into the bathroom, but the scent of her body wash lingered. Something citrusy, not too overpowering.

Courtney took Eli by the hand and dragged him into the "rumpus room," a ten-by-ten room with a blue carpet, white brick walls, and one window decorated with Hello Kitty stickers. Courtney let go of Eli's hand. They sat on a black futon.

"Somebody likes Bob Marley," Eli said, noticing the many posters on the wall.

"C-Lo's roommate is gaga over Marley and Hello Kitty. Her presence is obnoxious to me. In a civilized society I would be allowed to beat her daily with a rubber mallet." She grabbed Eli's knee, the one he'd had scoped by an orthopedic surgeon some years prior, and squeezed. Eli groaned. "Don't fuck around, okay? Christine loves him. They met in high school, and he's always been good to her, and she to him. It's actually *nice* to see two people who genuinely care about each other, and I can't stand to see her hurt again."

Eli removed her hand from his knee.

Christine entered the room wearing a thin blue pointelle cardigan with a white camisole underneath, beige twill pants, and flip flops. Her toenails and fingernails were painted to match her cardigan, and her hair was dark red and wet and redolent of tropical fruit. Judging by the way she stood with her back slightly arched, she was the type of girl whose body had matured at an early age and was, Eli surmised, aware of how to stand just so to optimize her best features.

"My name is Eli Sharpe. Please sit down."

"I'll stand. What do you know about Almario?"

"You look haggard, C-Lo. Why don't you sit down and we'll gab?"

"Of course, I look haggard. My fucking boyfriend is fucking missing. He could be in a gutter somewhere, or lying in a fucking alley with his fucking throat cut. So yes, Court, I look haggard and don't exactly feel like gabbing. If you ever get a boyfriend and he goes missing, you'll look haggard, too." Her breathing turned rapid, and she clutched the wall, ripping down a poster of Marley plucking an acoustic guitar with a joint stuck between the strings and the fret. Courtney sprang off the futon, wrapped her arms around Christine and stroked her hair, all the while whispering into her ear. Christine calmed down, hugged Courtney, and apologized. She stood slowly, carefully. She breathed deeply.

"You should go back to your room, Court. I'll talk to him alone."

"Are you sure? You're fried. I should stay."

"I need to do this myself. You have that Chem midterm, anyway. Do you still have my notes?" Courtney nodded, and she no longer seemed so tough. "Good, use them. I'll come down after I finish here and quiz you. Now go."

They hugged once more, and Courtney yanked open the door.

"Courtney?" Eli waved. "My IDs. I need them back."

Courtney threw them. They separated midair. Eli caught one with the left hand and one with the right.

"Nice coordination. For an old dude."

"I was an athlete. A long time ago."

"You look more like a chess player to me," Courtney said. "A very cute, very old chess player."

With her friend gone, Christine wiped away the remaining tears from under her eyes. She took a deep breath and sat down on the futon, folded her hands demurely in her lap.

"I've been such a bitch lately."

"It's understandable. You're under a lot of stress. Can you tell me the last time you saw Almario?"

"Saw him or spoke to him?"

"Tell me the last time you saw him."

She rubbed her hands together and put her feet side by side. "Last Saturday, I think. He knocked on my door at like four in the morning. He wasn't wearing a shirt and he had scratches on his chest and arms. And his pants...he was wearing a pair of black chinos I bought for him at the Gap. They were ripped. Cost me eighty bucks, those pants. He didn't smell like himself."

"What did he smell like? Alcohol?"

"Yeah, but it wasn't that. He just, I don't know, it's hard to explain. I've always loved the way he smells. I don't wash the sheets for a week after he spends the night. But last Saturday, when I saw him, he smelled different. Like, I don't know, fear or something."

"So he was scared?"

Nodding now. "It was in his eyes. Usually, I look in his eyes and I think of the Caribbean and all those cruises I took before my parents split up. His eyes look like the Caribbean just before a storm." She shivered at the thought, even though it was stuffy in the room. "He's tall and built and I love his body, but his eyes are what make him beautiful. That night, they were bloodshot and shifty. His hands shook, too."

"Was he hurt?"

"I don't think so. He left like five minutes after. I couldn't convince him to stay, and I'm very persuasive."

Eli wrote in his notebook. *Saturday night. Shirtless. Ripped black chinos. Bloodshot eyes. Drunk? Stoned?* "Did he mention where he'd been or who he'd been with? Anything that might help me track him down?"

She shook her head, and a teardrop fell in a straight line from the middle of her left eye. Turning to a blank page, Eli handed her his leather notebook and pen, asked her to write down the names of the places she and Almario liked to go on dates.

"Go on," Eli said and placed the pen in her trembling hand. "This will really help."

As she wrote, Eli said, "Four years ago I was hired to find this guy by the name of Kent Fisher. Ever heard of him?"

"The name sounds familiar. Who is he?"

"Kent Fisher was a middle-reliever for the Atlanta Braves.

Owns three Subway sandwich shops now. Has two sons and two daughters, but I digress." Eli glanced at what she'd written. "Anyway, when Fisher's wife came in to see me and told me Kent was missing, she was a wreck. Lines on her face. Disheveled hair. Stains on her clothes."

"I'm guessing you're telling me this story for a reason."

"I am and here it is: I found Kent Fisher within a week, and I had much, much less to go on than I do with Almario."

Christine stopped writing. "That's all I can think of right now."

"You did good." Feeling a nagging pang of ownership, Eli took back his notebook and pen. "I can't say I'll find him, but I can promise to try my best."

"You're corny. Are all old dudes corny?"

"To a man."

"Then I'm glad Almario is young. Is there anything else I can do? I'll literally do anything."

Eli removed the bag of pot from his jacket pocket and placed it on the futon between them. "I found that in Almario's bedroom. Do you smoke?"

She raised her chin. Her eyes flashed defiance. "I carry a three-point-nine GPA. I'm a member of the student government and sometimes I need to unwind. That isn't a crime."

"Unwinding? No. Smoking dope? Yes, it is a crime."

"Don't be an asshole. You know what I mean."

"Did you give this pot to Almario?"

"No, I didn't."

"I know you care for him, which is why I'm asking these questions." Eli looked over the list of places Christine had written down. The Burly Earl on Tunnel Road was at the top of the list. "How often did you and Almario go to the Burly Earl?"

"When the team was in town, a couple times a week. Me, I hate the place. A lot of creeps hang out there. Frat boys slumming. Hippies. Biker-types."

Years ago, in between fiancées two and three, Eli had frequented the Burly Earl. It had been his favorite watering hole, but he kept that to himself. He asked about the creeps instead.

"The bartender is definitely weird. Talks funny, like an aristocrat in a British movie."

"So he has an accent?"

"I'm not a hall monitor or anything, far from it, but this bartender didn't card anybody. He gave away free Jell-O shots to anything with muscles and facial hair and ignored everyone else. He had a thing for Almario, and one night I had to set him straight. Explain to him Almario was taken."

"Did the bartender have a name?"

"I can't remember. I can tell you what he looked like."

"Black and bald? Muscles? Lip pierced?"

"That's him. Is he involved in Almario's disappearance? Tell me. I deserve to know."

"Don't worry, I've got a friend in the police department doing a background check on this guy and others at the bar." Eli picked up the bag of pot, put it in his pocket, and handed Christine a printout of the email Almario allegedly wrote to Maria Gato. She read the first line and burst out laughing.

"You're joking, right? Almario didn't write this. He's not an illiterate. He was on the Dean's List at Asheville Country Day. He got like a 2150 on his SAT."

"Maria doesn't think he wrote it either."

"Maria's smart. Could definitely use a makeover and lose a few pounds, but she has a good heart and takes care of Almario. She's coming here in the fall. We've talked about rooming together, Maria and me. Courtney will be devastated."

Eli put away his pen and notebook. He glanced out the window. Hello Kitty stickers blocked the view.

"Christine, I think I can use your assistance."

CHAPTER 5

Christine Lovatt drove a candy-apple red BMW convertible with vanity plates that spelled LUVME. Sitting apart from the half a dozen other vehicles in the parking lot, her car was waxed to a high-mirror shine, and the top was down, presumably so the surface temperature of the white leather interior could exceed two hundred degrees.

Christine pressed a button on her keychain, and the car's engine turned over. She flung her purse, a Gucci bag that could be used to smuggle a Great Dane onto an airplane, into the backseat. "What are you waiting for?"

"Air conditioning."

"Doesn't work. Get in, you baby. It's not that hot out."

Eli applied hind quarters to burning seat leather, mopped his brow, and did a deep breathing exercise. He inhaled through his diaphragm and exhaled through his mouth, remembering the day his mother demonstrated this breathing technique. It was just after Eli's old man had blackened his eye for coming home an hour late from school. After the fireworks, his mother sat him down at the kitchen table, applied ice to his throbbing eye, and put her hand on his stomach. "Suck in air until your belly is full," she'd said, "and then let it go. Slowly." Eli did as he was told, and the pain transformed from an ear-piercing scream to a tolerable background noise. When he opened his eyes, his mother patted his belly, told him to breathe from his diaphragm whenever he needed to take his mind off pain. Even at age thirteen, Eli knew full well she'd had plenty of practice.

Christine adjusted the rearview mirror and peeled out.

"A damn shame about the AC," Eli said, his ass almost fully adjusted to the scorched leather.

"Daddy won't give me the money to fix it because I got a D-plus in Statistics. I'm re-taking it now during summer session. Was your dad strict?"

"That's one way of putting it. Sadistic is another."

"Struck a nerve, did I? My bad, it's none of my business." Her cellphone buzzed. She typed a text and steered the car with her knees, narrowly missing a masochistic jogger who chose the hottest part of the day to work on his cardio. Fastening his safety belt, Eli prayed to a God he'd rarely spoken to and never seen.

Mercifully, Christine put the phone away and gripped the wheel with her manicured hands. "What about your mother?" she asked. "Was she nice?"

"On occasion. She was more pretty than nice."

"Pretty, huh? Yeah, I can see that."

"She taught me two very important things: how to break into houses and how to take a punch."

She peered over at him. Shook her head. Turned her attention back to the road. "You must have had a shitty childhood."

"Eventually, my old man turned his life around. He moved us here when I was thirteen, and I haven't been homeless since. Or listened to a Grateful Dead album."

"I hate hippies."

"They're peace-loving," Eli said, his mind still on his formative years. "And I wouldn't call my childhood shitty."

"Courtney was right. You're weird." At the edge of campus, Christine blew through a STOP sign and turned onto Merrimon Avenue heading south toward I-240. "If it wasn't shitty, what was it?"

Eli scrolled through a mental thesaurus. "'Instructive' is the word I'd use. Go to the Verizon Store on Tunnel Road. I need to check out some phone records."

"Almario's?"

Eli pointed to an elderly pedestrian in a gabardine suit, and she swerved just in time. Eli asked to hear how she met Almario, and Christine sped through a yellow light and turned onto I-240 heading east. As she weaved in and out of the midday traffic—the hot summer breeze playing havoc with her dark red hair—she explained how she met Almario at Asheville Country Day when she was sixteen and he was fifteen.

"I remember, I was sitting in Geometry when Principal Hale walked Almario into class. He was lanky with horrible posture. Had these big soulful blue eyes and the cutest curly black hair. I must have outweighed him by twenty pounds when we first met, but oh my god was he adorable. Pure Latin sexiness. Don't get me wrong, I'd been on a few dates, and I wasn't a virgin before Almario, but this was different. I was, I don't know, *drawn* to him. Do you know what I mean?"

"Yes, I do."

"I thought you might. By the way, one of my roommates is into salt-n-peppers. If you're interested."

"I don't have any gray hair. I'm thirty-four, not eighty."

"Don't be so insecure. You're a good-looking older man."

Eli blushed, remembered the first time a woman made his cheeks red. A middle-aged librarian in Tupelo, Mississippi. Orange scrunchie in her auburn hair. "I could get lost in those dreamy brown eyes," the librarian had said and pinched his nine-year-old cheek.

"Tell me more about Almario," Eli said, hoping Christine hadn't noticed his reaction.

"Asheville Country Day is pretty small and a bit cliquish, so of course we all knew that Almario had come over to America in a boat from Cuba. We all knew how horrible our baseball team had been and that that was why they gave him a scholarship. But I think knowing his story, and imagining how scared he must have been leaving behind all his family and friends, made me love him even more. It may sound, I don't know, adolescent or whatever, but I think I loved him before I even met him. Is that insane?"

"Not even a little bit. I once dated a truly horrible woman simply because she'd lived near the Salton Sea for a year and had shown me all these pictures she'd taken."

"Holy shit, you're a romantic."

"Shhh, don't tell anyone."

As Christine squealed off the highway and onto Tunnel Road, she went on to say how sweet Almario was, how he took her out for ice cream and let her win at miniature golf and how she used to take off one piece of clothing for every math problem Almario did correctly when they studied for tests. She whipped into the Verizon Store parking lot and killed the engine. Eli thanked her for the ride, and for not killing him. She took off her sunglasses.

"On our first date, Almario turned to me all serious and said, 'I am going to play in the majors.' You know what he said he would do with his first paycheck? Bring his family over from Cuba. He did it, too. Or he tried. I guess you know what happened to his parents." Her voice sounded sad. Her eyes welled up. "I know I'm a spoiled brat, but Maria needs Almario almost as much as I do. Just find him and bring him back to me, okay? I'm fucking lonely here without him."

Eli got out of the car, nauseated from the jostling car ride.

"Do you want me to stay? I can give you a ride to your next clue?"

"No, thanks. I've escaped unscathed. Don't want to press my luck."

"But I want to help," she whined. "I need to, really. I'm going crazy at the dorm. Just between us, Courtney is driving me batty. Honestly, she needs a man."

"Is there any chance Almario left town?"

She shook her head. "No chance. Almario grew up in a section of Havana called Old Havana. He showed me pictures. Kinda poor, but normal. Modest, I guess would be the word. His school, his family, his friends: everything was within a few blocks. When he moved here, he loved it right away—the mountains, the people, the school, the safety. He never wanted to leave. I tried to get him to go with me to Hilton Head or Atlanta for a getaway when he was injured last year, but he wouldn't do it."

What she said made sense. Almario was seeking stability, especially now that his parents were gone. Maybe that's why he wanted to marry Sharon Stuckey. Whoever she was.

"Do you know if Almario was seeing another woman?"

She laughed heartily. "Are you serious? Not to be conceited, but I'm gorgeous. He's gorgeous. We match. Just look at me."

Eli did as she asked. Red hair. Womanly curves in the right locales. The kind of clothes women pay outrageous prices for to ensure that they were not made by little Cambodian slave children.

"Do you need anything else? I'm totally good at research."

"I need you to get back to school. You've done more than enough already."

The Verizon Store teemed with customers arguing over bills and late charges. Employees in Verizon shirts and khakis were trying to sell smartphones and computer tablets to anyone with a pulse. There was a line twelve-deep at customer service. The air conditioner was on full-tilt. Someone had a terminal case of B.O. The wait gave Eli time to organize his impressions of the women in Almario Gato's life.

Veronica, the tall blonde, was sexy, tough, and sharp, an alluring combination; she seemed to care about Almario as well. Maria was shy and dutiful; her black eyes were hard, had seen things most people hadn't, but there was a sweetness reflected in them, a vulnerability. As for Christine, the buxom redhead, she was self-absorbed, whip-smart and trapped in that odd time between post-adolescence and womanhood. Eli found her story of how she met Almario endearing though, and he could certainly see why Almario was attracted to her.

The only real problem: all of them were, in some way or other, dependent on Almario. Which worried Eli, made him wonder who else in this kid's life might be dependent on him. Like, say, his future wife, Sharon Stuckey.

When it was his turn, Eli stated his business. The elderly woman behind the counter shuffled into the backroom and came back out with the store manager, a dark-skinned man with dreadlocks and bags under his eyes. In a Midwestern accent that Eli found charming, the manager introduced himself as Garrett and asked Eli to step into his office: a nondescript near-closet with cardboard boxes stacked up to the drop ceiling. There was a student desk in the middle of the room with a thin stack of papers on it. The stack of papers had a Post-it note on top that read GATO, ALMARIO.

Garrett pointed to the desk. "Miss Craven called. She said you needed access to Mr. Gato's records immediately. She said you should look them over here."

"Oh?"

"Yes, sir. She thought you might need our assistance. She informed me of the situation, in a very general way."

"What exactly did she inform you of?"

"Just that you were investigating, and that you had police connections. I just thought if we at Verizon could be of assistance in solving a crime—"

"No crime has been committed."

"No, no, of course not, I didn't mean to imply such. It's just, well, you see, I'm being considered for district manager, which is quite a step up in pay. There'd be more traveling involved, and I'm not sure my girlfriend would approve, but with my new salary I could buy her an engagement ring and maybe things could change."

"Women aren't as superficial as men. Trust me, Garrett, if she loves you she won't give a damn about a ring. Or being in a higher tax bracket."

"Yes, you're probably right. If we at Verizon, or, more specifically, I, the manager of store number four-sixty-one, could assist you in any way, that might go a long way in getting me that promotion."

Eli promised to do what he could. Garrett left the room.

First, Eli combed through Almario's phone calls for the past two months and highlighted any repeating numbers. There were six of them, four with 828 area codes, one 901, and one 310. He scanned the page of text messages as well. There were only three, and each one said nothing of consequence.

Next, Eli went through Maria's phone calls for the past two months and highlighted any repeating numbers. There were six of them, four with 828 area codes, one 901, and one 310. Maria, like her brother, didn't text much, so there wasn't much there either. Eli got out his leather notebook and wrote down the repeating numbers for both Almario and Maria. He opened one of the desk drawers and found a framed picture of Garrett and his girlfriend, a large but handsome black woman with a shaved head and long painted fingernails.

Eli's cellphone rang. Checked the caller ID. Asheville Police Department.

"Sharpe here."

"Eli, my friend, I have that information you requested."

"David Rubio, you're a gentleman and a scholar. What do you have for me?"

"The name of your bartender is Dantonio Rushing. He has a sheet."

"Give me the highlights."

"Misdemeanor. Possession of a controlled substance. To wit: marijuana. Suspended sentence. Paid fine. Misdemeanor. Public intoxication. Paid fine. Eighty hours of community service. He has some moving violations, too. Nothing to write home about. As criminals go, Mr. Rushing is a novice."

"Mr. Rushing's offenses against the state, they took place

right here in Buncombe County?"

"All but a few of the moving violations, which were in Memphis."

Eli wrote everything down and asked about incidents at the Burly Earl.

"According to our records, Asheville's Finest have been called to that location some three times in the past two years. All the calls were simple noise complaints, no assaults or robberies. For a dive bar, they keep it fairly quiet."

"What about the employees? Anybody besides Rushing have a sheet?"

"It looks like two others have records. One Sharon Stuckey, also known as Sheri Stuckey, and one Dale Walters. Miss Stuckey was arrested on minor drug charges and passing bad checks in the amount of four thousand dollars. Mr. Walters, who is also the owner of the Burly Earl, was arrested for indecent exposure. In 1972."

Eli took down the names Rubio mentioned and asked for a physical description of Sheri Stuckey.

"Five-one. One-hundred pounds. Dirty blonde hair. Hazel eyes. She is divorced with one child. A daughter."

"Good stuff, Davey. Thanks."

"Do you need anything else, my friend?"

"Home addresses on Rushing and Stuckey would be greatly appreciated."

Eli wrote down the addresses, thanked Rubio again, and promised to come to his house for dinner later in the week.

Garrett stuck his head inside the door.

Eli put away his cellphone and wrote down the repeating numbers he'd found in Almario's records. He handed the paper to Garrett. "Look in your database and tell me who these numbers belong to."

Garrett took the sheet of paper. His face went slack. "I'm fairly certain phone records are private, Mr. Sharpe. We would need permission. Authorization."

"Miss Craven informed you that I was working with the police?"

"She did."

"Miss Craven hired me on behalf of Almario's twin sister, who is anxious to have her brother back where he belongs. If she loses him, she has no one. Do you understand me? No one." As he said the words, he realized he wasn't acting. The thought of Maria Gato alone in that cavernous, cold apartment, cooking huge Cuban meals for no one...

"Whoa, that is truly awful. Just dreadful. I would be a wreck if my sister was missing, and we don't even get along. It's just, I'm not sure—"

"I might also mention Miss Craven is licensed to practice law."

Garrett put his hands in his pockets. "You're not threatening me, are you, Mr. Sharpe?" His voice had lowered an octave, maybe two.

"Not at all. I'm offering to help you. If you get the information I need, I'll see to it that Miss Craven writes a glowing letter of recommendation to your boss and your boss's boss. If you get the information I need and get it fast, I'll speak to your boss as well, tell him what an amazing job you're doing here at store number four-sixty-one, Garrett." Eli opened the desk drawer and handed Garrett the picture of his smiling girlfriend. "Maybe I was wrong. Perhaps if you get the district manager job this lovely lady might agree to be your lawfully wedded wife."

Garrett looked at the picture and then Eli.

Seven minutes later Eli was in the parking lot, leaning against a yellow SUV while reading the printout Garrett had given him. Eli scanned the numbers and names twice. According to Verizon, Almario had called four 828 numbers with great frequency in the past two months. The names corresponding to those numbers were Christine Lovatt, Maria Gato, Herbie McClure, and Brad Newman. The first two names were no surprise—Almario's girlfriend and his sister. Eli knew Herbie McClure, too. He was the manager of the Asheville Travelers, Almario's ballclub. It was the last name on the list, Brad Newman, that didn't connect.

The 310 number turned out to be Veronica Craven's cell-phone number; 310 was a Beverly Hills area code. The 901 number belonged to Dantonio Rushing, the bartender at the Burly Earl. Eli wrote down the name Brad Newman in his notebook, starred the name Dantonio Rushing, and looked at Maria's numbers. The four 828 numbers belonged to Almario Gato, Christine Lovatt, Homer Hodge, and Brad Newman. The 310 number belonged to Veronica Craven, and the 901 number—a Memphis area code—belonged to Dantonio Rushing. Rushing. So Maria had been in contact with Almario's bartender (and possible drug connection) too. Interesting.

Eli glanced up from his work. A man in a suit walked toward him.

"Get off my car, guy. It's new."

Eli finished scribbling in his notebook and put it away. He removed his sunglasses and looked the guy over. The man's suit was tan and tailored to his pear-shaped body, but it was the gin blossoms on his face that spoke to Eli. "My apologies," said Eli. "Perhaps I could buy you a drink to make amends. I know a place nearby. I'm buying."

"Are you serious?"

"Sure, I'm serious. Who would refuse a drink in this heat?" Eli straightened his posture, squared his shoulders and showed his teeth.

"Nice jacket, guy. Thought Atticus Finch was the only man to wear seersucker."

Eli joined the man for a laugh. The man checked his watch, which was gold and much nicer than Eli's Seiko.

"What the hell? So I take three hours for lunch instead of two."

The man's laugh was repulsive, his teeth capped and white as polished bone.

"Perhaps you could give me a ride in your shiny new Escalade?

I'd be much obliged."

The man sucked his teeth. "Sure, I'm always willing to help the less fortunate. Where to?"

"I hear the Burly Earl is decent."

CHAPTER 6

As a semi-reformed barfly, Eli Sharpe categorized all drinking houses in the Asheville metropolitan area as either Establishments or Dives. Establishments were upscale and typically located downtown. They were the kinds of places where mixologists used top-shelf liquor to make complicated cocktails while obscure jazz recordings played on a state-of-the-art sound system. Establishment patrons wore designer clothes and made six-figure salaries and talked about skiing in Vail and golfing in Hilton Head. Perfectly nice places. Just not Eli's cup of tea.

The Burly Earl was definitely a Dive.

And an old hangout of Eli's back in the day.

Across the street from Walmart, the Burly Earl was a modified log cabin with a wraparound porch and a tin roof. Guarding the entrance was a five-foot-tall fiberglass statue of a corpulent English gentleman in a plaid suit and a top hat. Locals called him Early Burl because of his roughed cheeks and landlord's smirk.

Patting Early Burl on the cheek, Eli held the screen door open, and the man in the suit stopped in his tracks, his face contorted in horror. Eli looked at the man in the suit and then looked inside the barroom. Half-century old jukebox. More pool tables and spilt beer from the night before than paying customers, none of whom was wearing a suit or tie.

"Come on," Eli said, "time's a wasting."

"What the fuck is that smell?"

"Decade-old grease. They do a nice Monte Cristo here. I'm buying."

"It smells like vomit in there."

Eli stuck his nose in the air. Undercurrents of vomit—vomit and stale beer and regret. All the earmarks of a truly good Dive Bar. After almost eight years of private investigations, Eli had a sixth sense about places like the Burly Earl.

"Can't be that bad," Eli said. "They're playing the Stones on the jukebox."

"Keith Richards is a dinosaur."

"You don't like the Stones?"

The man in the suit shook his head like a child refusing to eat his vegetables.

"Thank you very much for the ride," Eli said and slammed the door in the man's face. Enduring all manner of character flaws was an occupational hazard, but mocking the greatest rock-n-roll band to ever walk the planet was a deal breaker.

Eli bellied up to the bar, ordered a tomato juice. A hefty woman with pigtails and pasty white arms covered in colorful tattoos served him. He sipped, had a look around. No Dantonio Rushing. No Sheri Stuckey. Just a trio of unemployed construction workers drinking domestic beer on tap and munching free tortilla chips in a booth by a sign that read TOILETS. When Eli turned back to the bar, he shifted his weight and realized his pants were wet. Someone had spilt beer in his chair.

"Sorry about that." The bartender retied the purple bandana wrapped around her head. "Some asshole overturned a Newcastle during lunch."

"No worries. These pants were cheap."

"You wear them well enough. I'm into skinny dudes. Just throwing that out there."

"You like them enough to give me some information?"

"That depends. Smile for me first." Eli obliged. She tilted her head, squinted. "You have nice teeth. Not too nice though. Your upper bicuspid is misshapen, and the whole lower row is crooked. I like that. I'm saving up for dental school. I like teeth, I know it's weird."

"That's not weird at all," Eli said. "A few years ago I tracked down this guy who was convinced a neighbor's boxer was his dead brother reincarnated."

"What was he...on drugs, a psycho?"

"Neither, as best I could tell. He was a highly paid athlete. He just happened to really miss his brother. After three days of searching, I caught up with him on a cotton farm in South Carolina. Him and his boxer/brother were sharing a pup tent. My point is, you're not weird for wanting to devote your life to teeth."

She smiled, revealing a very white and even set of teeth. "No, I'm a weirdo. But you have a gift for slinging bullshit. Bet it goes over with the ladies. What kind of information are you after?"

"The scheduling kind. I just need to know when Dantonio and Sheri are working."

"Collection agent?"

"I'm insulted." Eli flashed his private investigator's license.

She arched an eyebrow. "Dantonio and Sheri. I should have known."

"Why do you say that, if you don't mind my asking?"

"I don't mind you asking, I mind answering."

"Are they dangerous?"

Another non-starter. Shaking her head, she picked up a dirty rag and wiped down the bar top. She had a sleeve of tattoos on her left arm: a wizard with a monocle and a cane. A big-bosomed pin-up girl from the fifties.

"Excellent detail work. Your ink is art." She blushed. Eli took off his jacket, showed her his right forearm: Frosty the Snowman throwing stacks of one-hundred-dollar bills onto a bonfire. She pulled his arm closer, ran her soft fingertips over Eli's tattoo.

"Skinny, good teeth, cool ink: you're a lady killer."

Eli took his arm back and put on his jacket. "My name is Eli Sharpe."

"I'm Summer. You seem like an all right guy, Eli. Are you an all right guy?"

"I think I'm an all right guy. So help me out. Dantonio? Sheri?"

One of the working stiffs pulled his chair back quickly, which made a scratching sound on the hardwood floor, and Summer jumped, held her hand to her large chest.

"Summer, it's important. I'm looking for someone. Almario Gato. Some people call him 'Go Go.'"

"Light brown skin? Curly hair? Always looks wrecked?"

"Don't know about the wrecked part, I've only heard rumors. I know he comes in here, and I'm trying to track him down."

"He used to come in a lot. I don't serve jailbait, though. Since you're not with the Alcohol Control Board, I'll tell you Dantonio'll serve anybody, men especially. Come check him out tonight. He works the ten to two shift. He definitely knows Almario."

"What about Sheri Stuckey? Does she know Almario?"

"Unfortunately, that's his girlfriend. They both know him." She tapped her nose three times and sniffed. "They know a lot of people, wink-wink. Definitely not my scene."

Eli finished his tomato juice. Almario Gato. Drugs. Infidelity. Professional failure. Some of the puzzle pieces were beginning to fall into place, and Eli didn't care for the picture. A sense of urgency propelled him off the bar stool.

"Thanks for the chat, Summer. Maybe I could buy you a drink some time."

"I have a man right now. Two, as a matter of fact."

"Are they as skinny as me?"

"No, but I'll starve them." She winked. Then her smile vanished. "Be careful with Dantonio. Sheri, too. I've heard things."

"Such as?"

"They're crafty, is all I'm going to say."

"Funny, my old man used to say the same about me."

Eli called a cab, and when it pulled into the parking lot, he stepped outside. Heat index aside, it was a Chamber of Commerce day. The sky was robin's egg blue, the mountains green and fertile.

"McCormick Field," Eli said and climbed into the backseat.

Home for the Asheville Travelers was a brick and concrete band box at 30 Buchanan Place, just on the edge of downtown proper. Built in 1924 on a section of flat ground halfway up one of the city's many hills, McCormick Field was nostalgia-inducing and unassuming, plus a few other adjectives that wouldn't come to Eli's mind while the taxi driver's right-wing radio show blared through the speakers. Eli paid the driver, tipping him ten percent, all the while trying to remember the last time he voted.

Peering through the ticket gate and over the turnstile, Eli saw an inter-squad scrimmage in progress and instantly forgot his failures on the diamond. His stomach somersaulted at the smell of lime chalk and freshly mowed grass. The fielders chatted up the batter while pounding their fists into their gloves. The third base coach flashed signals to the batter and then clapped three times. The pitcher, a tall lefty, shook his head twice, nodded, checked the runner on first, wound up, and fired—the *thwok* of the catcher's mitt slicing through the humid summer air. The blood coursed a little more quickly through Eli's veins. He listened to the sounds of the game, remembering. He admired the dented outfield fence that advertised everything from Ingles Grocery Store to Barbara's Pet Grooming Boutique to Hough, Nicks, and Sutton, Attorneys at Law. His trance was broken when the infield turned a shaky but successful four-six-three double play, and Eli pumped his fist, remembering all the times he'd stood in the hole at second base with his heart galloping, praying for a hard grounder up the middle, so he could dirty up his uniform.

Crossing the parking lot he saw the team Greyhound being loaded for an extended road trip. Sweaty men in khakis and collared shirts loaded equipment into the rusty bowels of the bus, while pretty young women of all hues stood around, talking and texting. One of the bench coaches, a baseball lifer with leathery skin and eyes like hollow points, stood next to a burly black man in a bus driver's uniform. The two men were smoking. The whole scene brought back memories of Eli's years in the bus leagues. Playing to half-empty crowds more interested in buying a fifty-cent beer and chasing women than the game. Riding in cramped buses and sleeping in fleabag motels and taking batting practice with brown, scuffed-up baseballs. Standing there, sweating in his seersucker jacket and blue jeans, Eli would have given a year or two of his life for one more season playing ball.

Eli yelled at the bench coach chatting up the bus driver.

"Burns, isn't there a mandatory retirement age?"

Coach Burns turned and squinted through the sunlight. After shaking hands with the bus driver and returning the man's silver Zippo, Burns flicked his cigarette, which landed on the hood of a black Mustang. He limped toward Eli, cupping his hands around his mouth to yell back.

"Hope you're here to suit up." They shook hands. Burns gripped Eli's shoulder blade with his free hand and grimaced, flashed his nicotine-stained teeth. "Arthritis in my knees."

Eli nodded, knowing better than to offer sympathetic noises of any kind.

"I'm serious, son. Shed the seersucker and borrow a jock from one of those Barbie dolls. Our infield has made thirty-five errors in thirty-one games."

"They looked good to me," Eli said, gesturing toward the scrimmage.

"Don't believe everything you see. I swear I'm ready to take a flamethrower to this place. At this point I don't give a blue fuck, I really and truly don't."

Eli laughed. Burns cared. The man loved baseball and his Barbie dolls. And loved them both deeply. Eli had never been to Iowa farm country, but he'd often wondered if all corn farmers cursed like Burns.

"I'm sorry to hear you're so miserable, Coach."

"The hell you are. You come here for two reasons: to hear me bitch and listen to me brag on you. Speaking of which, you remember ninety-eight?"

"Sure, I do. Batted lead-off for you in Durham."

"Only All-Star I had in three seasons with the Bulls. What'd you hit that year? Three-seven-five?"

"Point-three-two-four. Came down to earth after mid-season. Somehow I remember ninety-nine more clearly."

"Yeah, I hate it that things ended the way they did. But it was awful damned funny, you steering the Greyhound right into the goddamn Bull. You forgot the Golden Rule: skinny pissants can't hold their liquor."

Eli cut his own laughter short. "I'm here on business, Coach."

"Need to see the Cripple, huh?"

"I do. McClure in his office?"

"This about Gato?"

Eli nodded.

"Almario's making the same mistakes you did, son. Find him and bring him back to me, you hear? He needs a Come to Jesus meeting."

"I know you're the man for that job."

"You bet your ass." They shook hands again, and Burns crunched Eli's knuckles with his grip. "You were a damned good ballplayer, son. Nothing to be ashamed of. Not a thing."

"That's not exactly true, Coach. I appreciate the sentiment, just the same." Eli, in fact, had plenty to be ashamed of. Faking injuries so he could avoid long road trips and drink instead. Playing drunk and hung-over. Countless unpaid bar bills and IOUs, many of them to women. Not to mention all the money the Tampa Bay Devil Rays organization wasted on one Eli

Sharpe. Wasted time, wasted talent. Eli wondered if Almario Gato was already that far gone. The thought burned in his gut, lit a fire under his ass to find the kid before it was too late.

Drifting past the bus and the players' girlfriends and around the back of the stadium, Eli entered a door marked RESTRICTED. The concrete hallway tunneling beneath the bowels of the stadium was painted purple and white to match the Travelers' uniforms. The air was redolent of sweat and leather, ointment and desperation. Eli knew the scent well. Too well. All bus league locker rooms smelled that way, almost as if the baseball gods knew you weren't going anywhere. The fluorescent lights overhead gave the narrow hallway a crime-scene feel, and Eli quickened his pace, scanning the framed photos on the walls of big leaguers who once played at McCormick Field. Through some mystical combination of luck, talent, and work, they had made it out. Todd Helton. Eric Anthony. Bobby Abreu. Eli muttered curses that sounded an awful lot like prayers.

At the end of the hall, next to an open closet stuffed with empty kegs and boxes of peanuts, was a purple door with HERBIE McCLURE, MANAGER painted in white letters. The purple paint had footprints all over it. Burns' temper, no doubt. Eli removed his sunglasses, knocked on the door.

A familiar scratchy voice said, "Come in."

Eli turned the knob and caught his breath. No windows, no furniture, and a very odd smell: a mix of aftershave and glove leather and cat piss. In the middle of the room sat Herbert McClure in an electric wheelchair. He was surrounded by baseball equipment and stacks of Travelers' programs and empty cans of Copenhagen and sunflower seeds. What little hair McClure possessed was thinning and sherbet orange and could be found on the sides of his head and coming out of his ears and bulbous nose. His face was bloated and covered in liver spots and freckles. Like many baseball lifers, he had the leathery skin of a dirt farmer and the eyes of a prophet: pale blue with flecks of gray. Partially paralyzed due to polio, the man everyone called Herbie was pinned to his wheelchair like a butterfly to a wall. In the corner Eli spotted two litter boxes, both in need of emptying.

After exchanging an awkward hug with his old coach, Eli asked why Herbie was wearing his uniform. Herbie's smile widened. His freckles glowed orange.

"Need a game changer. We've lost eight of our last nine. We can't hit, catch, or throw."

"You always were superstitious. Burns'll give you shit all the way to Kinston."

"You know I was hired as the manager here on the same day the Durham Bulls fired him. When I brought him here, I told him he needed to cool his jets. Maybe work on his people skills. 'This is A-ball,' I told him. 'Ninety-eight percent of these guys will never make it to the Big Leagues.'"

"I'm betting you remember his response."

Herbie smiled. "Said I was a 'gutless cripple' who needed his 'balls reattached.' The man's meaner than a hungry cobra. Underneath he's got a good heart."

"Nobody knows the game better. Except you, Herbie."

Herbie, a nostalgic Irishman, couldn't resist talking about the glory days when all three of them—Burns, McClure, and Sharpe—were with the Durham Bulls and going places. In '98, before the incident with The Bull, Eli was still a hotshot prospect on the Tampa Bay Devil Rays radar, Burns was an up and coming manager, and Herbie was going to make it to the Show as a pitching coach—the first physically disabled manager in the Big Leagues. Didn't work out.

"Well-laid plans," Herbie said good-naturedly, "but I can throw a pity party anytime. You came here for information about Almario."

Eli got out his leather notebook and pen, found a two-foot high stack of programs to sit on. "When was the last time you actually saw him?"

"It must have been last Saturday."

"So you haven't seen or heard from him in four days?"

"Right. We played two against Winston-Salem that day. Hot as Hades. And humid, too, like breathing soup out there. Almario struck out four times in the first game and made three throwing errors in the field. I had to bench him for the second game. Didn't want to, but you know the drill."

"All too well. Did you notice anything strange about him that day? His behavior? Something he might have said?"

"He was quiet in the locker room afterward. Was reading a book, just like you used to. That's just how he is. Doesn't say much to the other guys. It's just, 'yes, sir' or 'no, sir' to the coaching staff. Hand me that score book." Eli did. McClure opened it to the official score for the last game Almario played. He shook his head. "I do remember Almario's timing was off that day. Of course, when you strike out, your timing is off, but this was different."

"How so?"

"When he got in the batter's box, he seemed keyed up. Digging in the dirt with his cleats even as the pitcher was in motion. Messing with his batting gloves. Tugging on his uniform. Almario has a calm, confident presence at the plate. Even when he's slumping, he keeps his bat steady behind his right ear, but that day he was wagging and wiggling it around. Our hitting instructor told me after the game that on three pitches Almario swung before the pitcher had even released the ball. Never seen anything like it."

Eli removed the bag of pot from his pocket.

Silence.

Then, "Baseball's a rough game," said Herbie. "You get a hit three times out of ten, and you end up on a baseball card. Two out of ten, and you're bagging groceries. That gnaws at you. It can poison your mind, especially the mind of a young man used to succeeding. Then there's what you do when you leave the ballpark."

"Almario was taking his failures to heart?"

"And then some. He was usually the last one to leave the stadium. Spent hours watching video of his at-bats, dissecting his swing, and then spent a few more in the batting cage. All ballplayers obsess. The ones that want to succeed, anyhow. You know that." He chucked the official score book against the wall. His smile vanished. "Damn it, Almario passed all five drug tests we gave him. He's a good kid."

"Everyone I've talked to confirms that. I've also got some other information."

"Tell me now."

"For starters, it's been confirmed that Almario frequents a dive bar on Tunnel Road called the Burly Earl. The bartender there has a criminal record. There's also a waitress named Sheri Stuckey who has a history with drugs and passing bad checks."

"Almario is mixed up with these people?"

"I pulled his cellphone records. Almario called the bartender seventeen times last month, the waitress—who may or may not be his fiancée—nineteen times."

"Do you think they have something to do with his disappearance?"

"I'm going to find out. In the meantime, anything else you could tell me about Almario would be helpful."

Herbie pressed a button on his chair and rolled toward the open office door. He whistled and an orange tabby came out of the hallway and jumped into his lap, her neon green eyes fixated on the stranger who had invaded her turf. Herbie put the chair in reverse until he was even with Eli once more.

"She's been with me for sixteen years."

"That can't be the same cat."

"Her name's Lady."

"The same one you used to keep on the bench?"

"The same one. Lady is a scary judge of character. I mean, uncanny."

"What does a cat have to do with your starting shortstop?"

"Almario brought his agent and his sister to practice one day.

This must have been sometime in late April. Almario introduced them to me, and Lady just happened by. Lady immediately took to both of them. Aside from being a good judge of character, Lady is also highly suspicious—she never approaches strangers—but she rubbed up against Maria and even let Veronica pet her. That never happens." His voice was shaky, excited. Sweat poured down his face, and Eli wondered if Herbie was sick and not telling anyone. Or, worse, going senile.

"I'm confused, Herbie."

"Let me finish. A couple of weeks ago Almario brought another visitor to practice. A woman. Lady scratched her leg up, but good."

"Did you get a name?"

"We weren't formally introduced."

"What did she look like?"

"Small. Sandy blonde hair. Cute, in a trashy kind of way, forgive me for saying. Plenty of makeup. Tight clothes, what little she was wearing. As soon as I saw her standing behind the batting cage, my first instinct was to give her a coat to cover up. She looked underfed, sickly. I told Almario to take her to Two Guys and get her a corned beef sandwich."

"So she was skinny?"

"Too skinny. Short, too."

"Did you notice anything else about her?"

"She had worried eyes. Lightish brown, hazel maybe. And she never looked anywhere other than at Almario. She couldn't look away from the boy."

Eli wrote the information down in his notebook and thought for a minute. The description Herbie gave matched the description of Sheri Stuckey. Five-foot-one-inch tall. Dirty blonde hair. One hundred and one pounds. Hazel eyes. Eli checked his Seiko: 3:37 p.m. He stood up. Lady purred.

"You see," Herbie said. "Good judge of character."

Eli rubbed the cat's belly. "I have a way with women. So Almario, he's a good kid? You give him your seal of approval?"

"You know about his parents and his twin sister, what he did for them? Your average eighteen-year-old millionaire wouldn't do that. Forget about baseball. Forget about the drugs. Both are phases he'll grow out of. The kid has a brain and a heart. He can do great things with his life once the game is through with him."

The old man's eyes watered. Eli knew. This wasn't '98. Herbie wasn't counting on Eli to drop a suicide squeeze to bring home the tying run. Herbie was counting on Eli to find an eighteen-year-old kid. A kid who, the evidence suggested, was in trouble.

They shook hands. Eli asked when the bus was leaving.

"Four o'clock sharp. Why?"

"I was hoping for a ride back to the office."

The scrimmage was still in progress when Eli emerged from the tunnel with Herbie rolling beside him, his sherbet-colored hair damp with sweat.

"Bus leaves in fifteen," Herbie barked, and the pitcher held up his thumb.

Eli stood beside Herbie in the first base dugout while the pitcher, a tall black kid with his hat on backward, carved up two batters on six pitches.

"Nice velocity," Eli said.

"We clock him in the low nineties."

"Has a deceptive delivery, too. Can he go all the way?"

"Grab a bat and see for yourself. We got time."

Surge of adrenaline. Eli's hands buzzed. Conflicting thoughts. Fear of failure coupled with supreme confidence. In his mind he saw the ball connecting with the bat, the ball whizzing over the pitcher's head at top speed. Laughter from the other players on the bench brought Eli out of his trance.

A voice said, "He looks like a computer programmer, Coach." More laughter. Spitting of sunflower seeds.

Herbie turned his wheelchair around, faced the bench warmers, and said, "Twenty bucks my friend here gets a hit off Jackson. Any takers?"

"Who is he?" a skeptical voice asked.

"He ain't a computer programmer," Burns said and spat tobacco juice on the dugout steps. "Take the bet, rookie. I'm in for ten."

After the bet was arranged, Eli put on a helmet and selected the lightest bat on the rack, a black Louisville Slugger with Derek Jeter's signature on the barrel. He gripped the handle and strode to the batter's box, the fielders jeering him along the way. He removed his jacket, folded it neatly, and placed it on the grass behind home plate. Eli took two practice swings, made a show of wincing. More heckling. More jeers. Shouldering the bat, he tentatively placed his right foot in the batter's box and looked at the pitcher, who wasn't smiling like the others. He'd turned his cap around, had a menacing gleam in his eyes. Eli placed his left foot in the box, fully in character now, really feeling the blood pumping in his arms and hands. It was all coming back to him. The fear disappeared, replaced with a total sense of calm. He switched off his brain, as it was no longer needed. He allowed his body to remember.

"Go easy on me," Eli said.

The pitcher rocked back and fired.

Swing and a miss.

Eli's shoulder smarted from the force of his swing. He tapped the end of the bat on home plate three times, did two deep knee bends, and aimed the barrel of the bat toward centerfield.

The pitcher rocked back and fired.

Pop-up foul ball. Barely reached the stands behind the first base dugout.

Stepping out of the box, Eli wiped the sweat from his eyes and surveyed the infield and outfield, looking for a chink in the armor. Any hole to slap a seeing-eye grounder through. Some vacant territory between shortstop and left field where he could safely land a bloop single. As a former lead-off hitter, it was his job to get on base, no matter what. The big egos were in the middle of the order, but the lead-off man got on base however he could. He dug his heels into the batter's box, his heart thundering in his ear, confident. Ready.

The pitcher got the ball back from the catcher, and Eli made eye contact. He winked. The pitcher spat. The pitcher wound up, fired, and Eli quickly squared around, dropped a bunt, and legged it down the line, beating the third baseman's throw by a half step.

As the team's Greyhound snaked down Patton Avenue, Eli regaled the young players with tales from his thirty-four games in the major leagues. After explaining the proper way to give someone a hot foot—attach matchbook to the back of victim's cleat with chewed bubble gum and set fire—Eli asked Almario's teammates a few questions, but learned nothing he didn't already know. Nothing except that he missed being in a uniform.

CHAPTER 7

The Greyhound honked twice and inched away from Eli's apartment building, the pitcher giving Eli the thumbs up and then covering his bald head with oversized headphones.

Standing in the middle of his office, Eli yanked on the cord before realizing the ceiling fan was still broken. He glanced around the office, thinking. Seven years ago, Eli Sharpe took a month-to-month lease on this six-hundred-square-foot office/apartment at 917 Patton Avenue. Armed with a healthy savings account, a degree in criminal justice, and a laminated copy of his North Carolina private investigator's license, he bought some secondhand furniture, installed his collection of Nixon memorabilia on the walls, and opened up shop.

Eli began by cold-calling the general managers of all thirty major league teams and explaining what investigative services he could provide. When that didn't work, he called on Don Trader, a scout for the Devil Rays, who had recommended the club draft Eli in the first round of the 1996 amateur draft. The timing of the call was fortuitous. After recommending a string of wash-outs, Don was in danger of losing his job and asked Eli to "look into" a prospect down in Montgomery, Alabama. Beau Wade was an outfielder for the Montgomery Biscuits Double A team, and Don suspected he was abusing drugs and consorting with "lowlifes." Eli followed Wade around for three days before catching him in a dank hotel room with a woman of questionable morals and an eight-ball of cocaine. Wade had cried for nearly an hour, begging Eli not to call his momma or tell his coach. Instead, Eli told Wade his own cautionary tale, and Wade agreed to seek outpatient treatment while remaining with the team. For three weeks, Eli stayed in sweltering Montgomery—in June—and drove Wade to and from his appointments with a substance abuse counselor. In the meantime, Wade passed his daily drug tests and began to produce on the field. Don was so grateful he spread the word about Eli Sharpe, ballplayer turned private investigator. Later, Carpenter called the general managers himself and let them know Eli Sharpe was a subcontracted investigator for DMSI Investigations, and it worked.

Seven years, Eli thought as he emptied his pockets on the desk. Leather notebook, pen, cellphone. Wallet, cash, keys. Almario's picture. Dime bag of pot. Eli removed his jacket and tossed it on the swivel chair. To break the heat, he poured himself a glass of tap water and looked out the window.

Across the parking lot sat an abandoned body shop that specialized in Swedish cars. Che Guevara, Jimi Hendrix, and Martin Luther King, Jr., were painted on the side of the brick building, the work of criminals with artistic talent. A rusty Saab with three flat tires and FAQ spray-painted on the hood guarded the entrance. Two white boys were playing whiffle ball in front of the car, using it as backstop. The pitcher, the taller of the two, threw the ball, and the hitter, a lefty, swung and missed and fell backwards into the Saab. The pitcher pointed and laughed. The lefty chucked the bat at the pitcher's head and took off running in the opposite direction. Insults were hurled.

Eli looked over his case notes.

The second thing Eli had learned on the job: find parallels between your own experience and the person being investigated. Eli had blown his shot on alcohol. Almario was doing the same. Eli had failed, and it damn near finished him. Almario was in danger of suffering the same fate. And Eli had to stop it, no matter what. The more he investigated, the clearer the narrative of Almario "Go Go" Gato became. Here was this talented, good-looking kid, in a country not his own, playing a kids' game for big money. But for the first time in his life, the kids' game didn't come so easily and now, when he stepped on the field, he felt panic, not relief; pressure, not joy. With his parents dead, he felt the tremendous weight of responsibility, for he had a twin sister to look after as well; he had coaches and scouts and general managers and agents whose future employment rested on his shoulders. It was easy to see why he would want to escape into alcohol and drugs, why he'd get involved with people like Dantonio Rushing and Sheri Stuckey.

What wasn't easy to understand was why Almario Gato didn't just split town.

In 1996, Eli, just nineteen, was drafted in the first round by the Tampa Bay Devil Rays and assigned to their Double A team. After starting thirteen games at second base and failing to get a single base hit, Eli panicked and rented a jet-black Mazda sports car. For three days, he drove west, stopping each night at rest stops and crying himself to sleep. On the fourth day, he drank a fifth of Popov vodka and woke up in a pool of his own vomit and shit. The next day one of the bench coaches tracked him down and brought him back. Had the coach not found him, Eli probably would have kept right on running. And drinking.

"Why didn't you split town?" Eli held the picture of Almario Gato up to the light, studied the kid's eyes for an answer. There was kindness in Almario's face, a capacity for joy. Eli unfolded part of the picture so he could see Maria Gato as well. Her eyes were like polished marble, black and scared. The two of them had a bond. Almario was The Protector, Maria, The Protected.

Eli's cellphone rang.

"Sharpe here."

"Is that really the way you answer your phone?"

"Veronica, I was going to call you later. I've made progress."

"Give me the highlights."

"I've spoken to Christine Lovatt and Herbie McClure. Both provided me with solid information. I have some leads to follow up. It sounds like you're in the car. I can call you back when you've stopped."

"My hearing is acute." Flick of lighter. Exhalation of smoke. "Did you check Almario's phone records?"

"I did. Maria's, too."

"Why check Maria's records? She's not missing. She's sitting in her apartment as we speak, waiting patiently for you to locate her brother."

"How is Maria?"

"Riddled with anxiety. As am I. Tell me about the phone records."

Eli did. Told her about the numbers Almario and Maria called frequently. Brad Newman. Dantonio Rushing. Homer Hodge.

"Those names mean nothing to me."

"Newman and Hodge I'm still working on. Rushing's a bartender. Deals on the side."

Exhalation of smoke. "How does he know Almario?"

"From the bar where he works. I'm heading there tonight. This is a solid lead."

"I wasn't aware Almario went to bars." More inhaling, exhaling. "This is unfortunate."

Eli heard a car door open and shut. "Look, narrowing down the locations where a missing person could be is half the battle. We're doing that."

"That is extremely comforting." Her tone suggested otherwise.

Eli decided not to tell her the name of the bar where Rushing worked or about the Sheri Stuckey connection. At least not until he could get harder information.

"Look, Rushing works tonight, and I'll be there when his shift starts. In the meantime, I'll figure out who Brad Newman and Homer Hodge are. Let me call you tonight."

"No," she snapped, "I'm on the phone all day long. I want to meet face to face."

"I'm not sure where the Rushing lead will take me. It could be very late."

"That's not an issue. I'm staying at the Renaissance Hotel, room five-one-five. Call me when you are on your way. Bring good news."

"I'll do my best. Was there anything else?"

Another exhalation of smoke. "Just an apology. For my tone. I've been on the phone with one of the Rockies' executives for the last half hour. He's in town with his PR man and a security consultant. They know about Almario, and they want answers."

"For the record, I spoke to Almario's coaches, and none of them informed the Rockies about his disappearance. As for his teammates, they think he's got the flu."

"I appreciate that. The executive's name is Frank Waring. He received an anonymous call claiming Almario was missing. Waring flew in an hour ago."

"What did you tell him?"

"The truth. Or part of it."

"Which part? In case I need to back up your story."

"I told him Almario was missing, but only for two days. I said I had a private detective, a very good one, on the case. 'He will find him by the close of business tomorrow,' were my exact words."

"I wish you hadn't said that."

"I wish Almario was batting lead-off for the Rockies instead floundering in the bus leagues." She took a deep breath. "Christ, I'm behaving like a child. Maria is an emotional wreck. She wanted me to stay with her in the apartment, but I have a low tolerance for weakness and crying. Don't misunderstand me; I care for Maria a great deal, but I do not have a maternal bone in my body. Not one."

"No apology necessary." Eli considered the words *weakness* and *crying*. As a kid, he'd felt weak and cried a lot, wondered why his parents weren't like everyone else's, why they didn't seem to want him around. As an adult, he rarely cried. Eli told a therapist once that he'd just reached a lifetime limit on tears and couldn't shed another one. Now, he channeled his emotions—anger, sadness, insecurity—into his work. "I'll see you later."

Eli dialed David Rubio's extension at police headquarters.

On the third ring, David answered, "My friend, you have impeccable timing. I'm in the middle of filling out reports. Save me."

"I'm no savior, just a mooch in need of another favor."

"As long as it does not involve putting pen to paper, I will do it."

"I've got two more names for you. Homer Hodge and Brad Newman."

"*Uno momento por favor.*" Music began to play, top forty crap from the sound of it. Rubio interrupted the second verse of a teenybopper pop song about love and high school. "Who do you want to hear about first, my friend?"

"Proceed alphabetically."

"Excellent choice. Hodge, Homer James. African-American. Sixty-four. Five-five. One hundred and eighty-five pounds. Eight arrests, all for disturbing the peace. Political protests mostly."

"Sounds like somebody I'd like to meet. And the other one?"

"Newman, Brad. Caucasian. Forty-one. Five-eleven. One hundred sixty pounds. No arrests. No traffic violations. He is squeaky clean."

Eli wrote down the information in his notebook. "Since I'm already pestering you, can you give me their addresses, too? Save me the trouble of looking them up in the Yellow Pages?"

"I never knew you to let others do your work for you. Do you need a partner, by any chance?"

"Davey, if you were my partner, who would I call at police headquarters for favors?"

"When you put it that way."

Eli thanked Rubio and checked his Seiko: 4:28 p.m.

Eli showered and changed into a light green button-down

and fresh blue jeans. He sat behind his desk and had a gyro and a ginger ale delivered from the Grecian Corner down the block. He ate and drank while looking out the window. The two white boys used their combined strength to throw a cinderblock through the Saab's rear window.

Team work, Eli thought and made two calls. Brad Newman didn't answer. Homer Hodge did.

CHAPTER 8

Tired of hustling rides and paying for cabs, Eli drove his light brown Nissan pickup truck through the winding campus of AB Tech on Victoria Road. Students crowded the sidewalks. The older ones wore normal clothes, while the millennials donned basketball jerseys and flat-brimmed ball caps and pants a few sizes too big. The lot of them milled in front of the three- and four-story buildings smoking cigarettes and sipping energy drinks and texting.

After nearly clipping a skateboarder with humongous headphones on, Eli eased into a parking space in front of the Humanities Building and checked his Seiko: 5:47 p.m. His appointment with Homer Hodge, long-time instructor of psychology and criminology, was at six. Punctuality was like breathing to Eli, and to be tardy, even a couple of minutes late, was a kind of suffocation. A death most vicious. Shortly after ending things with his fifth fiancée, a hotshot paralegal at Asheville's largest law firm, Eli made an appointment with a therapist, an Asheville-by-way-of-Yonkers Jew who made oil paintings of the Blue Ridge Mountains and ended each session with a dirty joke, some that would have made Larry Flynt blush. According to Dr. Kurtzbaum, Eli's obsession with punctuality and his short but substantial relationships with women were all reactions to his chaotic upbringing. As Eli watched the students hustle to and from class, he remembered the doc's diagnosis almost verbatim.

"Your parents were nomadic criminals," Kurtzbaum had said. "For years, they were allergic to responsibility, and now you seek the opposite. Responsibility. Stability. Why do you think you've proposed to so many women? Marriage equals stability. It is also means you'll be married, just like your parents were, and you've seen the results of that union. And what about the profession you've chosen for yourself?"

The doc's questions ping ponged around Eli's head as he got out of the truck and hustled into the cool, canned air of the Humanities Building.

Hordes of students swarmed around the elevator, quizzing each other with flash cards. Eli ducked into the stairwell, climbed to the third floor and found a whiteboard on Hodge's office door with a message block-written in black Expo marker: YOUR EMERGENCY IS NOT MY URGENCY. Eli checked his Seiko: 5:53 p.m. He knocked three times.

"Mr. Sharpe, I presume."

"That's me. We spoke on the phone an hour ago. I have a six o'clock appointment."

"I'm not senile." Hodge's voice was thunderous, like a stage actor's. "I'm rather busy at the moment. Would you classify your visit as urgent?"

Eli tried the knob. Locked. "Yes, I would. As I said on the phone, I'm investigating the disappearance of Maria Gato's twin brother."

Squeaking chair. Shuffling of papers. "Maria *was* a student of mine. A bright young woman. But she is not currently enrolled in any of my classes, nor am I acquainted with her sibling."

"Professor Hodge—"

"*Instructor* Hodge. Professors possess doctorate degrees. I completed all my course work, but alas, never finished my dissertation."

"Instructor Hodge, you agreed to speak with me." Eli pressed his ear to the door. Typing. Clicking of a mouse. "You said six o'clock. It's now four till. If you didn't want to speak to me, you should have said so on the phone."

The door flung open, and a short, stocky black man in a pink and brown sweater vest, cream-colored trousers, and flip flops appeared at the threshold. He had deep-set eyes and dark, acne-scarred skin.

"It is impolite to stare," Hodge said. "I cultivate an eccentric image, which allows me to maintain a certain distance from both students and administrators."

"I can relate." Eli took a step forward, and Hodge blocked the path, his hands clasped behind his back. "We have an appointment. Are you going to honor it?"

"You're awfully young to be giving lessons in etiquette, especially to a senior citizen."

"I'm older than I look. Care to guess my age?"

"I'm an educator, not a carnie."

"The two occupations have many similarities."

"That's comical," he said without showing any outward sign of amusement.

Eli fired another joke that landed like a Nerf bullet. Hodge extended his right hand. Eli shook it and made for a cushioned armchair in front of a cherry wood, L-shaped desk about two sizes too big for the space. He got out his leather notebook, inventoried his surroundings. Stacks of yellowed newspapers—some dating back to the mid-eighties—were everywhere. Magazines, most of them political or psychological in nature, covered the windowsill and bookshelves. On the wall opposite the desk was a faded flag of South Africa. On the other walls were framed pictures of Hodge standing in picket lines and marching with scores of other black men. If the pictures, handwritten notes, and other souvenirs on the wall were any indication, Hodge knew—or had met—Martin Luther King, Jr., Mike Tyson, Al Sharpton, Samuel Jackson, Terry McMillan, and Condoleezza Rice.

Hodge settled behind the desk.

"How may I assist you, Mr. Sharpe?"

"Start by telling me what Mike Tyson was like."

"That's interesting, you inquiring about a boxer and a convicted rapist when there are other important figures on my wall. Most strangers in my office ask about Dr. King."

"We're not strangers, Instructor Hodge."

He crossed his arms. Slowly. Tried on an all-knowing look and liked the fit. "I've been questioned by police many, many times, young man. Suffice to say I'm aware of the 'try to bond with the suspect to get information' technique."

"I'm not a cop, and I wasn't trying to bond with you. I've seen every one of Tyson's fights. As a former athlete, I was simply curious. Primary sources are more informative than secondary ones."

Hodge smirked. A bit of white spittle appeared at the corner of his mouth. "So you are aware of how to perform basic research, I take it."

Eli let the condescension bounce off him and ricochet around the room. The sun came out from behind a cloud and sunlight spilled through the lone window. When the light hit Hodge's mottled face, his eyes flashed bitterness, contempt. His smirk faded.

"I thought I was the one sizing you up."

"Tennis," Hodge said. "You played tennis in college."

"Baseball. Professional. College came later."

"You're a bit thin to bat clean up. A leadoff hitter, perhaps? Why aren't you still playing?"

"Had trouble with the curve. Which drove me to drink. I dried out and went to college."

"College, indeed. I've been employed by this institute of so-called higher learning for twenty-seven years. I applaud you for wading through all the petty bureaucracies and arbitrary courses to complete your degree."

Hodge complained about his college's policies. As well as the lack of diversity on the faculty. And the apathy and underdeveloped work ethic of the student body.

"So," Eli interrupted, "Maria Gato called you more than a dozen times in the last two months."

"I don't believe we spoke that many times. Not telephonically."

"Cards on the table. I don't need to know the nature of your relationship with Maria. I just need to know if she ever spoke to you about her brother, Almario."

Another smirk. "First, to the 'nature' of our relationship. It seems to me you were implying something untoward was going on, which wasn't the case. As you can plainly see, I am elderly and began collecting Social Security two years ago. Also, my wife is very ill." He paused for effect. "To your second point, no, Maria and I never spoke of her brother."

"What you did talk about?"

"Her studies, obviously. She was my advisee. I was counseling her on which courses to take. Her goal was to enroll next fall at UNC-Asheville, another flawed institute of higher learning, but one with some color on the faculty at least."

"Did Maria ever discuss anything besides academics?"

"Rarely. She was a focused young woman. Very determined. Remarkable really. Her main focus was getting into university. She wanted to major in psychology. To graduate with honors, one would need to write a book-length thesis, and she had already chosen her subject and begun research."

"What was the subject?"

"She wanted—or wants, I should say—to study the relationship dynamics between parents and twins, more specifically, the relationship between parents and fraternal twins. You see, her own parents drowned while fleeing Cuba. Although she only mentioned it once, my sense was that her parents' tragic deaths haunted her. In my clinical opinion, her choice of research subject was a tribute, a way of continuing her education and exploring the dynamics of the parent-child bond. Beyond the grave, so to speak."

A productive tribute, Eli thought. Certainly more constructive than when Eli lost his mother, the petty burglar/old man's punching bag, and Eli went on a three-week bender that culminated with a brief stint in St. Joseph's for severe dehydration. Eli was twenty-eight at the time and not especially close to his mother. He couldn't imagine what Maria must have felt when her parents died.

Eli wrote in his notebook. He asked if Maria ever mentioned Christine Lovatt, Dantonio Rushing, Brad Newman, or Sheri Stuckey. Hodge shook his head, began leafing through a stack of papers on his desk, impatient now that the conversation had steered away from the psychological.

"What about Veronica Craven? Did Maria ever mention her?"

"Yes, that name is familiar to me."

"Do you recall what Maria said about her?"

"Veronica was someone Maria trusted and respected. Now that the subject has been broached, my memory is working overtime. I recall on more than one occasion Maria talking about how accomplished and beautiful Veronica was. Maria was enamored with Veronica's toughness, too. That was, if memory serves, the word she used. *Toughness*."

"Can you think of anything else Maria might have said?"

"Los Angeles. Aside from this Craven woman's beauty and accomplishments, she lived in L.A., and Maria talked about wanting to move there someday. She made a L.A. collage once with pictures of Rodeo Drive and the Hollywood sign. She asked my opinion. I told her she was a scholar, not an artist. Now, I have a prior engagement soon. Do you have any other questions?"

Eli put away his notebook and pen and stood up. "What was Mike Tyson like?"

"Droll, Mr. Sharpe. Very droll."

Eli drove away from AB Tech thinking about Maria and Almario Gato and L.A. He turned onto Biltmore Avenue and headed north, back toward downtown. Stopped at a red light in front of McCormick Field, Eli called Brad Newman's cellphone number a fifth time and got no answer or voicemail. He hung up, veered on I-240 east and took the Tunnel Road exit.

Kenilworth was a hilly neighborhood with tree-lined streets and houses ranging from humble to extravagant. Brad Newman's home, a bordering-on-decrepit bungalow sitting at the top of a steep driveway, sat at the end of a cul-de-sac that backed onto a thick forest.

Not wanting to risk the near-vertical driveway, Eli parked on the street and hiked up to the front door. He rang the bell. A neighbor gave Eli the stink eye while he waited on the sagging porch. Eli waved. The neighbor disappeared into a much nicer bungalow next door, muttering to herself. Eli rang the doorbell again, peered in the window. Stained carpet. One couch sans cushions. Six laptops sitting atop a scuffed coffee table. Eli rang the bell a third time.

The disapproving neighbor, a middle-aged woman in a gardening hat, was standing on Newman's porch beside a heavyset man in head-to-toe denim.

"If you're looking for Newman," said the heavyset man, "he's not in there."

"We've been trying for three days," the woman added and rang the doorbell herself to make her point. "We own this place, and it was lovely before *him*. We put our sweat and money into it. Now, in this neighborhood, it sticks out like a sore thumb."

"I can understand your frustration. Do you—"

"Mr. Newman, he is not a good tenant. Or father. He leaves his little girl home alone."

"My husband is putting it politely. Mr. Newman is a slob. He pays his rent late every single month, and worse, he won't even let us come inside for repairs."

"That would grate on my nerves as well. Tell me, do either of—"

The husband interrupted, "When he signed the lease, he agreed to mow the grass once a week. Hasn't happened. I'm a contractor, you see. This is an investment property. I need to repair things in the house. He called a lawyer on me the last time I went in."

"My husband is a good man. He only went in to check on a leak he spotted outside. We're not snoops. We're just trying to keep the neighborhood property values up."

"My wife is frustrated. This lawyer said I can only go inside under two conditions."

"If the man invites us in, or if there is a serious problem, like a fire. A fire. Can you imagine? My husband is no snoop. Nor am I."

"The man still has four months left on the lease. I can't kick him out; the little girl would have nowhere to go. What can we do? " The frustrated couple looked at Eli as if he might be able to answer the question. Eli showed them his private investigator's license.

"Maybe we can help each other out."

The man took his hands out of his pockets for the first time. He put his arm around his wife, who looked as if she might shed tears.

Eli called the police. Fifteen minutes later two officers arrived on the scene in a black and white patrol car. One officer wore sunglasses and the other one didn't. Eli introduced himself, flashed his private investigator's license.

"I'm working on a case involving Brad Newman," Eli said. "We heard a noise inside."

"I'm Donna Rogall, and this is my husband Hank. We own the house. The noise: it was groaning." Mrs. Rogall imitated the fictitious noise, and Eli fake-coughed to avoid laughing.

"We were worried someone might be hurt," Mr. Rogall said.

The officer not wearing sunglasses asked the couple if they had a key.

Mrs. Rogall unlocked the front door.

The officers told everyone to wait on the porch while they checked the house.

"May we go inside?" asked Mr. Rogall when the officers returned.

"Of course," the officer not wearing sunglasses said. "You're the owners."

"Mr. Newman brought a lawyer around the last time my husband went inside to check on things."

"Maintenance," Mr. Rogall said.

"That's right," Mrs. Rogall said. "Maintenance. We're not snoops."

Sunglasses officer said, "It is a bit complicated, ma'am. You do have the right to do scheduled maintenance on your property. You just have to give the tenant advance notice."

No-sunglasses officer said, "Otherwise, the tenant has a right to privacy. Most rental contracts come standard with a scheduled maintenance clause. Does your contract have that clause?" The couple looked at each other, shamefaced. "Don't worry, ma'am. Just have your attorney look over the contract. In the meantime, you should have a look at the bathroom off the front hallway. There appears to be some water damage. That would definitely qualify as an emergency repair."

The officers left in their squad car.

Eli followed the couple inside.

"I better take a look at that bathroom," Mr. Rogall said and lumbered down the hallway.

"I'll make sure the kitchen isn't in shambles. By the way, what kind of a name is Sharpe?"

"The kind my father thought amusing. I'm going to look around for a minute. I'll be out of your hair soon, Mrs. Rogall."

"Be my guest. It's not as if you could mess the place up."

Which was true. Stains covered the beige carpet. Fast food wrappers and lottery tickets and dirty laundry were strewn about the couch and loveseat. The entertainment center, TV, and DVD player hid beneath a thick layer of dust. The living room wallpaper—dark blue with a Mallard duck border across the top—was bubbling and peeling. And the smell... Aside from the musky clothes lounging on the furniture like houseguests who'd overstayed their welcome, the room reeked of cat urine. And pot, a scent Mr. and Mrs. Rogall seemed to be unfamiliar with. In the corner by the front door were three litter boxes, each in dire need of being emptied. Whoever Brad Newman was, whatever his connection to Almario Gato, he didn't place any value on order or cleanliness.

Eli cleared out a place on the cushion-less couch and sat down. He opened up one of the six laptops on the coffee table and checked the internet history. Two websites. Facebook and an online gambling site called paradisebet.net. The login and password to the gambling site were stored in the computer, and Eli examined Newman's betting history. Texas Hold 'Em. Pot Limit Omaha. Five card stud. High-ball, low-ball. Newman's gaming account contained eleven hundred twenty-five dollars. He'd opened the account five months prior with fifty-one hundred dollars. As gambling habits went, Eli had seen much worse, especially among the potential free agent ballplayers he'd investigated. But those guys were affluent, and Newman, judging by the state of his rental house, was not. Newman was losing an average of twenty-six-fifty per day, which made Eli's stomach churn. No doubt, Eli had his problems—reclusive/obsessive-compulsive tendencies, bouts with binge drinking, and commitment issues, to name a few. But being responsible with money was never one of them. Instinct, as well as his childhood experiences, taught him to be fiscally conservative, and during his almost seven years of professional baseball, he'd saved two out of every four dollars he'd earned, not including per diems he'd often banked in lieu of spending them on food.

Eli checked the bookmarks. Newman played fantasy baseball, football, and hockey and also bet on both college and professional sports. Eli checked the other computers' histories. More of the same. Gambling websites. A bit of porn. Eli hit the home button and Yahoo! popped up. Newman had four unread emails. The first three were spam. The last one had the word ASSHOLE in the subject line. It was from sparklygirl13. Eli wrote the address down in his leather notebook and read.

> im getting married very soon hes twice the man you are. our arrangement is going to change. starting with crystal. i want her back i know you leave her home alone every chance you get. one other thing pay the cell asshole! ive gotten calls for disconnection.

Eli forwarded the email to his own address.

"I don't think you're allowed to look at those." Mrs. Rogall was holding a jar of peanut butter in one hand and her gardening hat in the other. "Are you really a private investigator?"

"I showed you my license."

"You could have gotten that off the internet. You can get anything on the internet. Or so I've heard."

"Sad, but true. No, I'm trying to track down a missing ballplayer. A teenager by the name of Almario Gato. Mr. Newman may have some information."

Sighing, she sat the peanut butter on Newman's kitchen table, a cinderblock with two two-by-fours on top. She sat down on the couch.

"I don't know about any missing teenager. I do know Mr. Newman has the cutest little girl, and I worry about her. You see, Mr. Newman is *divorced*." She said the d-word as if it scorched her tongue. "He has an odd relationship with his ex. She comes around here to pick up the daughter, and she yells. Loudly. In front of the whole neighborhood. I think I've heard things I probably shouldn't have."

Eli told Mrs. Rogall a little about the case he was working on, and how Newman might fit in. He asked if she knew Newman's ex's name.

"No, we were never introduced. Mr. Newman does try to

call her names when she yells at him, but he stammers, you see. He stutters. If he wasn't destroying our house, I would feel sorry for him. My cousin used to stutter. Awful to see. Just awful."

"Can you tell me what she looks like? Newman's ex?"

"Difficult to say. I always see her from a distance. I'd say she was short, or shorter, with dirty blonde hair. Always wears tight clothes. I shouldn't think she eats very much. She's teeny-tiny, as my mother used to say."

Eli checked his notebook. The description Rubio gave of Sheri Stuckey matched Mrs. Rogall's description. In the anonymous email the author referenced Crystal (a daughter) and demanded that Newman pay the cellphone bill. The author also mentioned she had a new man, and she was getting married. It clicked. Almario had obtained a marriage license and was going to marry Sheri Stuckey. The woman who worked at the Burly Earl. The woman who'd been arrested for drugs and passing bad checks. The woman who used to be married to a man with a gambling problem. There were too many threads to unravel at once.

Eli cross-referenced a few more things in his notebook and came to a tentative conclusion: Maria Gato knew about Almario and Sheri Stuckey; she'd been calling Stuckey's cellphone, which was registered under her ex-husband's name.

Eli wrote down his cellphone number on a scrap of paper.

"I need a favor, Mrs. Rogall. Next time you see Mr. Newman, give me a call."

Eli left in a hurry before she changed her mind.

With more than three hours to go until Dantonio Rushing's shift began at the Burly Earl, Eli wanted a second interview with Maria Gato. He sped down I-240 west and took the Merrimon Avenue exit. Heading into downtown, he constructed a narrative for Almario's disappearance. *Almario's struggling at the plate and needs an escape from the pressure. So after a rough game, he goes out for a drink at the Burly Earl. Enter Sheri Stuckey. She bats her eyes at him, and before he knows it he's doing things no eighteen-year-old should do. Like hanging out with a drug dealer named Dantonio Rushing...*

Eli raced through a yellow light and turned onto College Avenue, parking in front of 23 Battery Park. A new valet attendant—an elderly white man in a black suit and tie—opened Eli's door.

"How are you today, sir?"

"Worried," Eli said and hustled in out of the heat.

The concierge called the head of security, who called upstairs and got permission before unlocking the red box on the elevator and sending Eli to the penthouse. The elevator doors opened onto the fifth floor and Eli stepped inside, following the sound of men's voices in the white marble living room.

There, sitting on the red velvet couch, sat Maria Gato in a tie-dyed T-shirt and blue jeans. Her eyes were downcast, her arms crossed at the chest. Two official-looking men in dark suits sat on either side of Maria while a third stood near the floor-to-ceiling window, his hands clasped behind his back. Clean-shaven with disappearing hairlines, all three men looked prosperous in the way many white, middle-aged men in suits look. But as Eli drew nearer, he recognized the man standing by the window. Frank Waring, an executive with the Colorado Rockies. Waring, the oldest, widest and most expensively-dressed man in the room, had a face like a relief map of Afghanistan, complete with pockmarks and busted blood vessels. He made a show of adjusting his solid red tie, making sure everyone in the room caught a glimpse of the National League Championship ring gleaming on his right hand.

"You must be Eli Sharpe."

"Judging by girth, you must be in charge here, Mr. Waring."

"Call me Frank, please." Grinning like a Cheshire cat who just disemboweled a baby mouse, Waring let go of Eli's hand. Waring introduced his "associates," neither of whom had a name or a championship ring. The associate seated to the right of Maria had a cauliflower ear and a granite jaw. His suit bulged. He wore no necktie. The one to Maria's left was thin and pale, and his tie had an American flag pinned to it.

Waring said, "We're delighted you're here, Eli. Maria has just apprised us of the situation with Almario. Upsetting."

"Extremely upsetting," said American Pin Man. "Attendance spiked twenty-six percent when we drafted Almario. The Latino community in Colorado is clamoring for this young man to make the big league team. Our offices get calls every day asking about Almario." American Pin Man gripped his Indian red leather briefcase with both hands, while Cauliflower Ear projected an air of malice.

Waring said, "The organization is confident that with a little guidance, Almario could be a productive major league player."

"Extremely productive," American Pin Man added.

"Give us an update on the case," Cauliflower Ear demanded.

"Come now," said Waring with a bland smile on his face. "We can be polite. Eli, we would *appreciate* an update on the case."

Eli looked at Maria. There was something different in her marble-black eyes now, something he couldn't place. Urgency? Sadness? Disappointment? With her hands grasping her elbows, she seemed more angry than nervous.

"I need my brother back," Maria said.

"I understand," Eli said.

"No, Mr. Sharpe, you don't. No one does. I didn't want to call these men. I don't want to drag Almario's name—"

Both Waring and American Pin Man assured her she'd done the right thing in calling.

Cauliflower Ear said, "We're wasting time. The first forty-eight hours in a missing persons case are the most important. Almario's been missing for going on four days already. We need to move." Cauliflower Ear stood, crossed his hands in front of his generous waist. With his dark suit and menacing jaw, he looked like the pit boss at a mob-owned casino.

Waring placed his hand on Cauliflower Ear's shoulder. "We all are working for Almario's safe return. After all, your client contacted us. Isn't that right, Maria?"

Maria's eyes lowered. Her shoulders quaked.

"Maria, maybe you might like to splash some water on your face." She walked out of the room, head down and muttering in Spanish.

Eli said, "I'm aware of how *valuable* Almario is to you and your organization, Mr. Waring. However, Maria isn't technically my client. Veronica Craven is. She is the one who hired me to find Almario."

Waring said, "I'm aware of who hired you. I spoke to Veronica Craven earlier today, and she lied to me. A man in my position, a man with my responsibilities, does not appreciate being lied to."

"Mr. Waring doesn't like liars," Cauliflower Ear said. "Not one bit."

"Lucky for me, I haven't lied to Mr. Waring or anybody else. I'm simply doing my job, and part of that job demands that I get permission from my client before divulging case information to you or anybody else."

"Is authorization really necessary?" American Pin Man asked, his knuckles white from gripping his briefcase. "Surely there's no state or federal law that prohibits you from providing us with information."

"I need no state or federal law to tell me what's right or wrong."

"All you need is a high horse to climb upon." Cauliflower Ear rumbled with laughter.

Eli smiled. "I figured you for an ex-cop. And given the way you grimaced when you got up off the couch, I'd say you have knee trouble. That, and the state of your left ear...a football player in college? A northeastern college, if your accent is any indication?"

"Wrestler. I was an Olympic alternate. Dean Gifford. Vermont University, class of ninety-one."

"Nice to meet you, Gifford. You must be Security." Eli

turned to American Pin Man. "And you're the Numbers Guy. I'll bet there is a detailed spreadsheet in that briefcase of yours that shows Mr. Waring just how much money Almario's disappearance is costing the Rockies."

"Short and long-term," he said. "And I, too, have a name. It's Roger Caulder. I'm head of public relations, in addition to being a 'Numbers Guy.' A missing ball player, particularly one with such a compelling back story like Almario, is detrimental to the club's image."

"Excellent," said Waring. "Now that we're all acquainted, how do we resolve this situation?"

"The easy way," Eli said. "Call Veronica Craven. If she signs off, I'll read you into the case. If she says no, I'll tell you to back off and let me do my job."

"Let's say I promise to keep you employed for the next say eight months, and you just assume Miss Craven has given the necessary authorization."

"I will assume nothing."

"Think about it first. As I'm sure you know, there are some big free agents looming out there in the coming off-season, and it is company policy to run a thorough background check before signing any long-term contracts. I could guarantee steady work. You'd have an expense account, stay in luxury hotels, first class travel, ample resources."

"I believe," Caulder said, "we could even arrange for Mr. Sharpe to sit in the owner's box during as many home games as he cares to see."

"Absolutely. Denver in July is much more pleasant than here in the South. I'll even put Mr. Gifford at your disposal. You'll find him a capable investigator. What do you say, Eli?"

"I say call Veronica Craven and get permission."

Gifford grunted.

Caulder tightened his grip on the briefcase.

Waring put his tongue in his cheek while Maria re-entered the room, eyes clear and calm.

"Make the call," Maria said. "Miss Craven will do the right thing."

Caulder, a stoop-shouldered man, stepped into the hallway and made the call to Veronica Craven. Eli asked if Maria had any more *café con leche*, and her face lit up. As he waited for the coffee, Eli kept within earshot of Caulder and his phone call. By the time the coffee was finished brewing, Caulder had finished with Veronica Craven. In the living room, Caulder slipped his iPhone into his suit pocket, ran a hand through his thinning black hair.

"She said Mr. Sharpe could give us an update on the case, but that we couldn't interfere in any way."

"What about involving the police?" Waring asked.

"No go, sir. I told her we wanted to file a missing person's report. She said she had every confidence in Mr. Sharpe. I said it was a deal breaker. She said her detective should have at least two days to locate Almario before we go to the police."

"You didn't agree to that horseshit, did you?" Gifford looked like he wanted to pin Caulder to the marble floor and choke him out. "The police have databases, resources. They can go places, see and do things your average citizen can't."

"I had to agree to her terms," Caulder said meekly. "What choice did I have? If I may, sir, taken from a PR standpoint, not involving the police has its advantages."

"Enough," Waring said. "Eli, where are we with the case? Give me the highlights."

Eli asked that Maria come out of the kitchen and join them in the living room. When everyone but Frank Waring was seated, Eli got out his notebook and brought them up to speed. More or less. He left out a few crucial details that would have painted an unflattering portrait of Almario Gato, and more importantly, would have upset Maria. Eli also had plans to talk to her alone and didn't want the present company to influence her in any way.

"So that's all you've got," Gifford said. "Phone records and a marriage license? If your interviewing skills are to be trusted, no one you've talked to has seen the subject—"

"Almario," Maria interrupted. "His name is Almario. My brother is not a subject."

"Apologies, Miss Gato. An old habit. I just meant no one has seen Almario in three or four days now. He has the means to leave town. Christ, he could be halfway around the world."

"Despite his bulldog attitude and crude vocabulary, I have to agree with my colleague," Caulder said. "Almario could be anywhere."

"He could be, but he isn't. I have a pretty good idea Almario is mixed up with a woman named Sheri Stuckey. I have her home address. I also know where she works and that she has a police record. I have confirmed that Sheri was or is Almario's girlfriend. As for the possibility of Almario lying on a Tahitian beach: unlikely. Almario has used his debit card exactly four times in the last three days. All charges can be traced to local shops and restaurants. He's close by."

Gifford asked if Almario was mixed up with drugs.

"I can't confirm that," Eli said.

Caulder asked about Sheri Stuckey and her criminal record, and Maria stood up.

"Mr. Sharpe, after you left this morning, I went through some more of Almario's things and found something."

"He's passed every drug test," Caulder said, nervously.

"There are ways around urine tests," Gifford said. "The league needs to use hair tests. No getting around those."

"Those are marvelously expensive, and some studies have shown, not as reliable as originally believed. Mr. Waring, I assure you—"

Waring said, "How long has Almario been using drugs? I want to know what kind and amounts, and I want to know now."

Maria's eyes flashed hatred before she walked down the hallway and returned with a brown paper bag, which she tossed onto Caulder's lap. Gifford snatched the bag, dumped the contents on the glass coffee table in front of the couch. A prescription bottle. Gifford whistled.

"Boss, this is Oxycotin. A Schedule II narcotic. Potent stuff."

Waring's bloated face reddened.

Eli read the name on the prescription bottle. Gladys Hodge. He looked at Maria, who looked away.

Eli said, "Gentlemen, I understand you're very concerned about Almario's well-being."

"He's a very valuable asset," Caulder said as he opened and shut his briefcase. "Castro will not live forever, nor will communism in Cuba. A talented young player like Almario will increase the Rockies' exposure in that country. He is extremely valuable."

"So you've indicated. I need to speak with Maria. Alone."

Gifford and Caulder turned to Waring, who checked his Rolex.

"I have a conference call to make," he said. "Eli, I will need an update in four hours and I expect to be impressed with your progress. You say Almario is still in town; then find him. For this young lady's sake." Clutching his briefcase to his chest, Caulder followed Waring to the elevator, Gifford taking his time adjusting his cufflinks and tie before doing likewise. Gifford brushed up against Eli's arm as he cut his own slow, lumbering path to the elevator.

When they were gone, Maria stared at the prescription bottle on the coffee table. She choked off a sob at the throat. The defiance, the shame, the anger she'd exhibited mere moments earlier had vanished. Facing the possibility her brother was mixed up in things he didn't understand, she was a scared teenager once more. Watery eyes. Slumped shoulders.

Eli took the prescription bottle from her hand.

"Come on," Eli said. "We are going to do some leg work."

CHAPTER 9

Maria Gato gripped the steering wheel at nine and three, double-checked her blind spot, and pulled into dinnertime traffic on College Avenue while Eli tried not to squirm in the passenger seat. He'd owned this Nissan pick-up truck since '96, bought it with his signing bonus check and used the rest to purchase the only house he'd ever lived in with his parents, one now dead, the other very much alive. In more than fifteen years of ownership, he'd never ridden in the passenger seat, and now that he had he wished he hadn't. There was no useful place to put his hands. Every dip and divot in the pavement caused stomach discomfort. He longed for control.

As they passed the main stretch of hip bars and hipper restaurants, he saw a power couple enter a sushi bar with a red neon sign out front that read FISH! He turned on the radio. NPR. The seven o'clock run down.

"Maria, do you have a driver's license?"

"Why? Am I driving poorly?"

Melissa Block, a commentator on *All Things Considered,* recited the latest unemployment numbers, and Eli turned off the radio, angled the vent so air blew directly in his face. After several blocks, they'd yet to be involved in a catastrophic crash and Eli leaned back in his seat, taking note of the intense look of concentration on Maria's face.

At the corner of Biltmore and Patton, a father and son crossed the street, and the son reached up for the father's outstretched hand. Only then did Maria threaten to smile. The light changed from red to green. A cacophony of car horns. Curses. All traces of Maria's smile vanished as she stomped on the accelerator, snapping Eli's neck backward. A sharp pain shot up his spine and settled at the base of his skull.

"I'm sorry, Mr. Sharpe."

"No worries. I enjoy being a passenger."

"You tell a lie. But I thank you for letting me drive your truck. I needed something to do with my hands."

"I know the feeling. Why did you steal the Oxycontin from Hodge's office? His wife is very sick and needs that medication."

Maria gripped the wheel even tighter and changed lanes.

"Maria, I know you stole the pills."

"Then I won't deny it."

"Just tell me why you stole them."

"No, you tell me about a time you stole."

"That's easy, I stole this morning. A bag of pot from Almario's bedroom."

Her mouth opened and closed. She honked at kid on a skateboard, muttered something in Spanish. "I know what you're going to say, Mr. Sharpe. You didn't tell me about the pot because you were protecting me, trying to help me."

"Not exactly. I did it to help *me* find *your* brother."

A red light. She drummed on the steering wheel. "Mr. Sharpe, you were a ballplayer once. Were you ever injured?"

"Broke my collarbone when I was twenty-three. I thought my career was over."

"Then you should understand why I stole those pills. Ever since the knee injury, Almario has been in pain. And not just physical pain. Do you understand?"

"I do. Your brother is worried he'll lose his job."

"No," she snapped, "he's worried he will lose everything."

The light changed, and Maria stomped on the accelerator, speeding past a minivan clogging up the right lane.

Everything. Eli remembered what it was like to be young and carry the weight of the world on his shoulders every time he stepped up to the plate. He remembered how food had no taste after going oh-and-five, how whiskey had no effect when he was slumping, how sex seemed like the ultimate lie and money the biggest fraud when nothing was going right on the baseball diamond. Even the fresh air was poison to his lungs when he wasn't playing well, and the only thing that brought rest to his weary mind was the thought of inching his toes up to the cliff's edge.

As Maria swerved in and out of traffic, Eli put his hand on his gut, remembering the bouts of diarrhea he'd suffered during his own playing days. Spastic colon, the team doctors had told him. Brought on by high levels of stress.

"I had to take them," Maria said. "I owe Almario everything. He brought me to this country. He pays for my school, my apartment, my life. Without him, I have nothing."

"I understand you want to help. But those pills, stealing prescriptions for Almario: nothing good can come of it. Turn left at the next light. Get on 240. Head east."

"I know where the highway is. When I arrived here, I looked forward to Almario's first road trip. I wanted to be alone, so I could explore the city, really get to know it. Now, I know where everything of importance is. Police. Fire. Library. School. Everything."

"Tell me where Almario gets his drugs."

"I don't know where everything is."

"If you don't know, why did you call Dantonio Rushing so many times? You knew when I went to get the phone records I'd find out about the calls. That's us coming up. The Leicester Exit."

"Where are we going?"

"Stakeout."

For the next five minutes, they rode in silence.

Off the highway, Eli guided Maria to a large apartment complex called The Meadows, told her to park in front of Building C. The building had gray aluminum siding and windows with blue shutters; the aluminum siding was covered in dirt and grime, and the blue paint on the shutters was peeling. There were no lights on in the apartment windows, no kids playing or women smoking on doorsteps. But the parking lot was almost full. Maria had to parallel-park between a compact car and a beat-up station wagon the size of an aircraft carrier. After several tries and some swearing in Spanish, she managed to squeeze the truck into place.

Eli checked his Seiko: 7:10 p.m. The sun was yellow and pink and hung low in the sky.

"What are we doing here, Mr. Sharpe?"

"Staking out Sheri Stuckey's apartment. Getting you out of your house."

"Who is Sheri Stuckey?"

"You need to work on your poker face."

"Poker? I don't gamble." She crossed herself, kissed her fingertips.

"Maria, call this your first lesson in lying."

"But I'm not lying."

Eli ignored her and continued. "Most people think that when you lie you should maintain eye contact with the person you're lying to until he or she looks away first. Kind of like a staring contest. But that's not true. You should look at them, count to three Mississippi and then look away."

"I wasn't lying. I've never been here before."

"I know you haven't been here before. But you do know Sheri Stuckey. According to Verizon phone records, you called 828-433-3312 ten times in the last month. Brad Newman, Sheri Stuckey's ex-husband, pays her cellphone bill. I went to his house and found an email from Sheri on his computer saying he needed to pay the overdue bill. It also said that she was planning on marrying Almario."

"Marrying?" Maria leaned her head against the window. "He didn't tell me."

She sounded mildly surprised. Or disappointed. Or judging by the way her lower lip arched into an almost grin, she might even be amused. Eli couldn't tell. Someone came out of Building C, and he craned his neck for a better view. An obese man in a windbreaker jogging suit. He continued, "I had a friend run a check on Stuckey. She's been arrested for drugs and passing bad checks. In the email I found on her ex-husband's computer, she hinted at possibly coming into some money soon."

"Not Almario's," Maria said defiantly. "Miss Craven set him up with an accountant. His investments are safe. Both he and I stick to a monthly budget, and I handle all the bills myself."

"Okay, his money is safe, but he may not be."

"I don't know what you mean."

"You're a bad liar, which is a good thing. I know you've been calling Stuckey and Rushing, trying to get them to leave Almario alone. Maria, you have to let me handle this."

Maria slouched in the driver's seat, crossed her arms like a petulant child. A tear rolled down her right cheek, crested a large pimple, and continued trickling down her neck.

"I told that whore to leave my brother alone, and she laughed at me. She said she loved him, as if she knew what that meant. No whore could ever understand what love is."

"What exactly did you say to her?"

"I don't remember. I just know I was very polite and didn't call her names." Another tear fell. She wiped it away. "Stuckey is a whore. She fucks the black one, too. I just know it."

"I think you're mistaken," Eli said. "It's my understanding Rushing is gay."

"Whatever he is, he's hurting my brother. When I found out he was selling drugs to Almario, I called him and told him to leave my brother alone. He acted like I was crazy, like he had no idea what I was talking about. I offered him money. I even went to the bank and withdrew two thousand dollars. But when I got home and looked at myself in the mirror, I heard my father's voice." She muttered some things in Spanish, curse words probably, and began sobbing. "I couldn't do it."

Eli rubbed Maria's shoulder, disturbed by the tenor and tone of her words, but impressed with her gumption. How many eighteen-year-old girls would attempt to bribe their brother's drug dealer? How many would threaten their brother's toxic fiancée? When the sobbing abated, Eli brushed the hair from her face, told her she did the right thing and was surprised by the fatherly tone in his voice. As much as Maria had been through and as tough as she seemed, she was also fragile, in need of protection. At that moment, Eli remembered his mother, who once upon a time also needed protection. Only this time Eli wasn't a frightened little boy with a worried mind and a shaky hand. This time he was a capable man who saw clearly what needed to be done: to protect Maria Gato. From everyone. Including herself.

"Maria, this is important. What else did Rushing say?"

"I don't know. He only pretended to be polite. That horrible man. He'll burn in hell." She muttered something else in Spanish that sounded like a prayer and stared out the window, licking sweat off her lips. "I haven't been to confession since I came to this country."

"That sounds like a confession to me."

"It doesn't count. You're not a priest."

They sat in silence for a while, Eli watching Building C for any signs of Stuckey. Of the four units in the building, Stuckey's was on the ground level. Two windows with the shades drawn. Weeds sprouted up through cracks in the brick walkway.

Eli got out his leather notebook and reviewed the information Rubio had given him about Sheri Stuckey. Five-one. About one hundred pounds. Dirty blonde hair. Eli considered breaking into her apartment, having a snoop around. Wouldn't be the first time. Or the last. He had the skill; his mother had taught him how to get in and out of any place in under two minutes. But it was too risky. Too many unseen eyes about.

After ten minutes, Eli grew impatient. On any other type of case, forcing the action was a monumental error. But a missing person case, especially one as fraught with complications as this one, was time-sensitive. Eli checked his Seiko: 7:21 p.m. He took the keys out of the ignition and pocketed them. He got out. Through the open passenger side window, he said, "Wait here."

"I have somewhere to be."

"Don't worry, I won't be long."

"I can't be late."

"Trust me."

With his hands in his pockets, Eli wandered down the brick walkway and past the edge of the Building C, taking note of the drawn shades in the front window. Behind the apartment building there was a quarter acre of overgrown grass, past that a thicket of brush followed by a drop-off. At the bottom of the forty-foot drop-off was a four-lane road with miniature cars inching along the asphalt. He turned and walked toward the rear of Stuckey's apartment building. He peered in a window. Dirt and grime. The only sound was that of a window-unit air conditioner. On the little concrete patio were girls' toys. A pram. A deflated kiddie pool with smiling crocodiles painted on the side. A headless Barbie covered in dirt. He walked past the building next door—Building D—and wandered onto a tennis court with no fence around it. The court itself was once green, but time and weather had faded it to a non-color. Where there should have been a net, there was an uneven row of Budweiser bottles, some broken.

Maria waved from the truck.

Eli held up a finger. Propelled forward by instinct and restlessness, he weaved through the broken beer bottles and headed toward the parking lot adjacent to Building A. As he stepped off the tennis court and onto the cracked asphalt, he heard a rhythmic thumping sound and moved toward its source. In the overgrown grass between Building A and Building B was a man in black clothes and a black ski cap. A sledgehammer rested on his shoulder. Standing in the shade of a pine tree some thirty yards away, Eli could only see the man's back, but he could tell he was well-built. Eli watched the black-clad figure examine the head of the sledgehammer and then set to work, raising the heavy tool above his right shoulder and striking the top of a wooden post. The post was no more than two feet tall, and as the man swung the sledgehammer over and over and over again, the post began to sink into the ground, millimeter by millimeter. When mere inches of the post were sticking up out of the ground, he got down on all fours. With a Herculean effort, he pulled it out of the ground and placed it in a different spot. Then he picked up his sledgehammer and began pounding all over again.

After three minutes, the man raised the sledgehammer but couldn't get it passed his waist. He dropped it and like a marionette whose strings had been clipped, fell to the ground, sucking wind, his chest heaving. When his breathing steadied somewhat, he rolled over on his back and started to hum a tune Eli couldn't place.

Eli moved toward a different tree for a closer look, stepping on an aluminum beer can in the grass.

The man stopped humming. He sat up, looked around like a baby deer who'd wandered into a strange field. Eli saw the man's face and was struck by it. The pictures he'd seen didn't do it justice.

There had always been something anti-climactic about the moment Eli found a missing person, something uninspiring like when a magician, in a moment of professional impropriety, reveals how a trick was performed. But this was different. Profound somehow. Defining even. The man slowly stood up, dusted off his black pants, and began stretching his legs and arms. Eli waved. The man sprinted toward a path in the woods behind the apartment. Eli's brain gave orders to move; his legs and feet disobeyed. His brain gave orders to speak; his vocal cords refused to cooperate. His brain gave orders to wave, or jump up and down, or scream. Nothing. It was too late anyway. The man was gone.

A full minute later, Eli had regained the use of his legs and followed the man's path through the woods. Only footprints remained. And steadily lengthening shadows.

Eli walked back to where the man had been hammering the fence post. He picked up the sledgehammer and struck the post, cursed as he did it. He struck the post again, again, again, again. He dropped the sledgehammer, his arms and hands burning. The pink and yellow sun began its descent behind the mountains.

Maria was sitting in the passenger seat when he got back to the truck.

"I saw your brother," Eli said and started the car.

Maria gasped. Once. "He ran away, didn't he? When he saw you?"

"He's fast."

"He runs. That's what he's always done."

"I think we should wait."

"He won't come back. He knows you're after him."

"He was wearing all black. Even had on a black ski cap. In this heat."

"The black attracts heat and makes you sweat more. It makes you work harder. Get fitter."

"He was working a sledgehammer."

"He's trying to stay in shape for the rest of the season." Maria put her face up to the vent, let the cool air chill the beads of sweat on her face. "Our father was a professor and a disciplinarian. He was also fat like me. He tried to build muscle and lose weight by swinging a sledgehammer. Along with a change of clothes, that sledgehammer is all Almario brought to this country. Did you see him run? He's a beautiful runner."

Maria asked what the next move was.

Instead of answers, Eli had questions. Should he sit on Stuckey's apartment and wait for Almario to show? If he truly intended on marrying Stuckey, if he was truly in love with her, sooner or later he would come back, right? Or show up at the Burly Earl to see her?

Too many questions.

"Maria, we should go to the police. They could circulate his name and picture. They'll find him before midnight."

"No," she snapped. "We can't indulge him. He's being immature. This is a test, Mr. Sharpe. Don't you see? You have to find him. No police."

She was angry, and for the first time, the anger was directed at her brother. A test? A test of what? Eli felt angry, too, but at himself. For freezing up. He handed his cellphone to Maria.

"Call him," Eli said.

"You don't know him."

"I ran away once. For some of the same reasons Almario did. When I was holed up in a shitty motel room, drinking warm beer from a can and crying into my pillow because I couldn't get a hit and couldn't figure out why my talent had deserted me, I wanted someone to call me. I stared at the phone and prayed."

"Calling him won't work."

"You need to try."

Maria dialed the number, let it ring. "Voicemail," she said.

"Say something. Convince him to see you. Tell him how you feel."

In Spanish, Maria left him a rambling, sob-interrupted message and handed the cellphone back to Eli.

"Take me home," Maria said. "I have somewhere to be."

Eli checked his Seiko: 7:49 p.m. He drove Maria back to 23 Battery Park.

"Find him," she said and walked through the revolving glass door.

By 8:15 p.m., Eli was sitting at his office desk replaying the scene with Almario. Each time he replayed it, new details emerged. A strand of curly black hair peeking out of a ski cap. A steel sledgehammer with an aqua blue handle. Soft, damp earth. The smell of sweat and fear. Eli clenched his eyes shut, commanded his brain to reach some reasonable conclusion based on these details, something that would lead him to Almario while simultaneously loosening the knot of failure in his stomach. But a fact is a stubborn thing, and the fact remained: Eli had frozen; he had failed.

Covering his stomach with one hand, Eli retrieved the bottle of George Dickel with the other and drank, but did not swallow. As he held the liquor in his mouth, his teeth quaked and his heart thumped and he counted one Mississippi, two Mississippi, three Mississippi, and then spat the whiskey into the sink and stood up.

He paced along the wall of Nixon memorabilia, stopped before his favorite piece: a poster of Nixon in silhouette with the quote, "A man is not finished when he is defeated; he is finished when he quits." Fragments from his old man's profanity-laced screeds about Tricky Dick came back to him. *Boy, he's a goddamn lying bastard...the devil in an expensive suit...special wing reserved in hell for politicians like Nixon...if you vote for a Republican, you ought to be drawn and quartered.*

As a kid, Eli didn't think anything was wrong with having a hippie father who worshipped the Grateful Dead, smoked marijuana laced with pesticide, and broke into houses. Because they lived on the road, Eli rarely interacted with other children, and he thought it was normal that his father didn't have a job. Or a home. Or medical insurance. But when the family finally settled in Asheville and Eli enrolled in school and saw his mother smacked, slapped, and punched regularly by the old man, Eli began reading Nixon biographies and covering his bedroom walls with posters of the thirty-seventh president. Partly to piss off the old man. Partly because Eli found Nixon to be a fascinating study in contradictions.

Eli wiped a fingerprint smudge off of the frame of his favorite poster. His heart rate slowed. He checked his Seiko: 8:21 p.m. Still an hour and a half before Rushing's shift at the Burly Earl. Way too long to wait. He needed to move. Needed action.

He called DMSI, and Carpenter answered midway through the first ring.

"Frank Waring called."

"What did he want?"

"To threaten me, mostly. Said if you didn't find Almario and quick he would tell the other GMs not to hire DMSI. He spouted all sorts of malarkey. You look like a high school kid, you manipulated Maria Gato, blah, blah, blah."

"Sounds like Waring, all right. What did you tell him?"

"I told him to piss off, pardon my French. Frank Waring's comb-over doesn't run this outfit, I do. And as for you, I brought you along since you were a pup. I trust you. End of story."

The knot in Eli's stomach loosened. A bit. But the only way to untie it completely was to tell his mentor what really happened, to admit his failure. Which Eli did.

"You there, boss?"

Carpenter cleared his throat. "You fucked up, kid. No two ways about it. What matters now is what you do next."

"Which is why I called. Almario hangs out at the Burly Earl, knows the bartender and one of the waitresses pretty well. I'm going to check it out. Maybe he'll show."

"When do you need me?"

"Ten o'clock."

"Fill me in on the details first. I hate being unprepared."

Eli gave him a rundown of the last ten hours, including a more detailed description of what happened at The Meadows with Almario.

Eli said, "He was driving a wooden fence post into the ground with a sledgehammer. Maria said the hammer belonged to their father. He was black from head to toe. When he saw me, he bolted. Now I know why they call him 'Go Go.'"

"Almario, he's into something, isn't he?"

"Looks that way."

"Drugs?"

"All signs point to." Eli filled him on the Rushing and Stuckey connection, and why they were going to the Burly Earl.

Carpenter cursed.

Four years ago Carpenter had lost his youngest daughter to heroin. An overdose. Her name was Rachel. She was twenty-eight. A sheriff in Okaloosa County Florida found Rachel's emaciated body in a flea bag motel with a needle sticking out of her foot. Except for the black eye, her face was as blue as a glacier. Eli helped Carpenter track down Rachel's dealer/boyfriend, a handsome Guatemalan with neck tattoos. Carpenter, like any devastated father, wanted blood, but Eli talked him down, came up with an alternative plan. After a week of surveillance, pictures, and a well-timed anonymous tip to local police, the Guatemalan got popped with two kilos of pure cocaine, his third strike. He was now doing a mandatory fifteen-year prison term. A small consolation prize, but Carpenter had always been grateful for Eli's help.

They made plans to meet at the Burly Earl. Eli made two more phone calls, the first to Frank Waring. Straight to voicemail. Eli brought him up to speed (without mentioning the Almario sighting) and called David Rubio next, asked if Davey could make some calls and get some information on the deaths of José and Manuela Gato.

"The usual stuff," Eli said, his nostrils burning from the smell of spilt whiskey. "Death certificate. Coroner's report. Police file. Whatever you can get a hold of."

"It'll take some time, my friend. A few days maybe."

"Whatever you can do, thanks."

Eli slipped the cellphone in his pocket, feeling the near-quiet and emptiness of his office. His mind raced. Action. Movement.

He opened the closet, found his lock-picking kit and checked his Seiko: 8:31 p.m.

At 8:43 p.m., Eli tiptoed into Sheri Stuckey's apartment and shined a tiny flashlight around the living room. Mouse traps and beer cans on the floor. Water damage on the walls, ceiling stained nicotine-yellow. The world's oldest TV—a twenty-inch Super Zenith—sat atop a wooden milk crate. On a weathered coffee table sat a purple Graffix bong with a fire-breathing dragon painted on it, a hamburger wrapper jammed down into the smoke chamber. The couch, an L-shaped thing with foam and springs poking out of the cushions, was made up for Stuckey's little girl, Crystal. Dora the Explorer comforter and pillowcase. A Barbie with fright-wig hair lying atop the blanket. Eli swallowed his anger and moved down the hallway, side-stepping dirty clothes, pizza boxes, and plastic grocery bags. The whole apartment was an allergy sufferer's nightmare, and he breathed through his mouth, wondering what species of mold were lurking about.

Taking in only shallow breaths, Eli entered the first door on the right, flashed his tiny light around the room. A queen-size mattress on the floor, no bed sheets or pillows. A secondhand dresser with two drawers missing. Stick figures and houses with chimneys scribbled in crayon on the wall. Thumb-tacked to the closet door was a picture of Almario, Sheri, and Crystal, the three of them sitting Indian-style atop a pile of brown leaves. They looked happy. Eli opened the closet door and aimed the light inside. Women's clothes. Skimpy skirts and blouses. Cheap jeans and high heels with MADE IN CHINA written on the sole were piled two-feet high on the floor. He kicked the middle of the pile and connected with something hard. Underneath the clothes lay a brass Boston Terrier. It had a coin slot on its head. Crystal's savings. He put it back on the floor and covered it with clothes.

Next he searched the bathroom across the hall. In the vanity he found makeup, an unopened box of dental floss, an empty box of Trojan condoms, and a bottle of Prozac with Stuckey's married name Sharon Newman on the label. The prescription had exceeded its expiration dates; there were five pills inside. He shut the mirror door and looked under the sink. Lady Gillette razors. Dove deodorant. Tampons. Some unopened cleaning supplies that Eli was tempted to use on the whole apartment.

He saved the kitchen for last, hoping to find some evidence Almario was living there, some evidence Sheri Stuckey kept some semi-nutritious food in the house for her daughter's visits. All he found was a trail of ants that started from the cabinet and ended in a turned-over box of Fruit Loops on the counter. He found a quarter-empty bottle of Popov vodka in the freezer and a pitcher of radioactive green Kool-Aid in the refrigerator. No fruit. No eggs. No bread. He looked in the pantry. Empty shelves. More unpleasant smells. The only edible item in there was a pyramid of Oodles of Noodles. He knocked over the pyramid of noodle packages, and most of the packages fell to the tile. After knocking the rest to the ground, he spotted something else and shined the light: a stack of clothes. Eli reached inside and pulled the stack of clothes closer, inspected it under the light. There were several articles of clothing and each article was folded. He began unfolding them. Three pairs of black pants. Three black shirts. Six pairs of boxer briefs. All fresh-smelling. Using the flashlight as a stick, he shoved aside the underwear and inspected the shirts and pants. No names on any of the tags. Nothing revealing in any of the pockets.

He went back into the living room, flashed the light here and there, and settled in on the couch. Upon closer inspection, he saw rust on the metal springs. Which made him think of tetanus. Which made him anxious to make the acquaintance of one Sheri Stuckey.

CHAPTER 10

All fourteen parking spaces at the Burly Earl were filled when Eli pulled into the gravel lot at 9:50 p.m. He lapped the lot, pulled back onto Tunnel Road, parked at Walmart, and jogged back, taking note of Carpenter's shiny black Cadillac parked near the bar's dumpster.

Inside, the barroom was loud, crowded, and smoky. Attractive coeds, bored with the 'pay nine bucks for a watered-down drink and get hit on by an investment banker' scene downtown, were hogging the booths. And the jukebox. How they found Shania Twain on an ancient Wurlitzer filled with baby boomer icons—Jagger, Joplin, Jerry, and Jimi—was anyone's guess. Ditto how they talked Summer—the fat, tattooed bartender who liked skinny guys—into making them Alabama Slammers. Their tables were filled with Pepto-pink concoctions and packages of clove cigarettes, and big purses. Meanwhile, on the opposite end of the barroom, scruffy-faced, shaggy-haired boys in Widespread Panic T-shirts played pool against biker types sporting bandanas. The Scruff Faces were giving the Bikers hand-rolled cigarettes and buying them draft beers, so all was well with the world.

Not interested in shooting pool or learning the difference between a hog and a crotch rocket, Eli took a second look at one of the co-ed tables and recognized two faces—Christine Lovatt and Courtney Mullins, her brunette, overprotective friend. They were wearing skimpy dresses and too much makeup and singing out of time with the jukebox music, something about men being unimpressive and not worth shaving your legs for. Eli slid into their booth.

"It would appear," he said, "that the whole world is three drinks behind."

Courtney tugged at her dress strap with one hand and slurped her umbrella drink with the other. She belched and one of the scruffy faces playing pool yelled "Manners!" She gave him the finger, crunched ice between her teeth.

"Court, I'm drunk," Christine said and lunged across the table, made a big show of kissing Courtney's neck. Christine was wearing a black and white striped T-shirt dress and a diamond tennis bracelet. Her hair was wavy, the color of a fire engine just back from the car wash. In a dive bar like the Burly Earl she couldn't have been more out of place if she had a third head.

"Courtney, I'm drunk. And depressed. You know why? Because I'm here with the wrong guy. I am here with Sharpe when I'm supposed to be with Gato, the man of my dreams. The sexy Latin ballplayer with a big—"

"Please don't finish that thought," Eli said.

"'Please don't finish that thought,' says Mister Sharpe. Says Mister Eli Sharpe. Mister Nice Button-Down Shirt and Parted hair. Who dresses like that when they come to a bar?"

Courtney said, "You really do look like a nerd. The nerdiest of private investigators."

"I can live with that. What I can't live with is allowing either of you to drive home. Why don't I call you a taxi?"

"Spare me the disappointed father routine, will you? I'm depressed. My fucking boyfriend is missing. He could be in danger."

"And you came here to do what exactly?"

"Help," Courtney yelled over the loud music. "We came here to help. Tell him, C-Lo."

Christine took another drink. Mercifully, the Shania Twain song ended and The Doors "Hello, I Love You" came on. Christine leaned closer to Eli and said, "Almario had me cop here once. I got the stuff from this skanky-looking blonde with no tits."

"Sheri Stuckey?"

"I didn't ask her name. Improper etiquette during a drug deal."

Eli wondered whether a standup guy would tell Christine who Sheri Stuckey was and how Stuckey knew Almario. While he mulled it over, he asked Christine about Rushing.

"He supplies the skank with blow. They're partners, I think. He's smart, stays away from the actual selling."

"I thought you said he was 'creepy'?"

"The two aren't mutually exclusive. He's smart and creepy. With huge muscles."

"Muscles gross her out," Courtney added.

"Shut up, Courtney." She stared down her friend, exhaled slowly, and faced Eli. "The muscle-y one talks like a professor wannabe. Kinda like you, Mister Eli Sharpe, but like thirty percent more annoying."

"More like fifteen percent," Courtney giggled.

"Why didn't you tell me all this sooner?" Eli asked.

"She's telling you now, aren't you, C-Lo?"

Eli asked if Christine or Courtney saw Rushing, and Courtney pointed toward the bar. Eli looked at Christine. Christine winked. Eli turned toward the bar. Rushing was changing one of the beer taps. From a distance, he matched the description. Black. Bald. Muscles. His lip, however, wasn't pierced. Dressed like a prep though: light pink button-down shirt and tight tan pants. Nice watch. As he changed the tap and let the excess foam out into a chilled pint glass, he talked with Summer and two other patrons awaiting cold beers. He smiled easy, laughed heartily. He didn't look like any drug dealer Eli had ever known. And he'd known exactly five. And known them well. Too well.

Carpenter, who was sitting at the end of the bar and had a better view of Rushing, caught Eli's attention, ashed his cigar, and turned the page of his newspaper. Jim Morrison began to yell as Eli exited the booth.

Courtney said, "The skank is on a smoke break out back."

"You've been on stakeout?"

"Since nine."

"Drinking," Christine yelled and everyone in the barroom cheered. Christine raised her glass and drank and when all eyes returned to their drinks and games of pool she handed Eli her glass. "A secret," she whispered. "We're virgins."

Eli sniffed the glass. No alcohol. Courtney grinned. Christine, still feigning inebriation, whispered in Eli's ear.

"We're under age," she said, her lips moistening Eli's ear. "Besides, the fat bitch wouldn't serve us."

"Watch it. Summer is a friend of mine."

"We don't care about your friend," Courtney said. "We want to help. The skank and big bald guy will be more likely to talk to us."

"We could be customers," Christine said. "Casually ask some questions about Almario."

"C-Lo's already bought from the skank. We have a plan here."

"No chance."

"Why not?" Courtney whined.

"Because I'm a standup guy. Now go home, girls. Cab's on me." Eli dropped a twenty on the table.

Courtney called him another name, and Christine told her to please, pretty please, shut the fuck up. They slammed the rest of their virgin drinks and shouted and everyone cheered. Eli watched them pay Summer and leave before he bellied up to the bar.

"Like 'em kind of young," Summer said. She poured a non-alcoholic beer and slid it across the bar. "Those two had the worst fakes I've ever seen. When I refused to serve them, the redhead with the tits asked if I knew who her father was."

"My apologies for that. Hubris of the young. Where's

Stuckey now?"

"She's out back. He's about to take a break. Neither of them carry, not their style. But be careful. I'd hate to see that skinny body of yours get messed up."

Eli winked at her and sipped his faux beer. Cold. Flavorless. Rushing went into the kitchen, and Eli counted one Mississippi, two Mississippi, three Mississippi and got up, leaving Summer two bucks on a free drink. He passed Carpenter without making eye contact, pushed through the swinging door.

The kitchen was fragrant. Fryer grease. Body odor. The line cooks were too busy frying buffalo wings and goosing each other to notice Eli, who pushed through the EXIT door and walked behind the dumpster.

There, under the pale yellow streetlight, were Dantonio Rushing and Sheri Stuckey, leaning against a red Prius, smoking cigarettes. Stuckey had stringy, longish blonde hair and the gaunt face of a lifetime smoker. She had been pretty once, Eli decided, and she could be again were she to go on an all-steak diet and wear less blue eye shadow and crimson lipstick. Maybe ditch the pink velour hoody and tattered acid-washed blue jeans, too. As Eli stared at her sunken cheeks and bloodshot eyes, a word popped into his mind. *Victim.* She looked like a victim, the kind of wounded-bird woman you see on the six o'clock news far, far too often.

Rushing, by contrast, was the ideal poster boy for natural selection. He reminded Eli of the beefed-up, well-dressed, well-groomed ballplayers who kept themselves in peak physical condition long after their careers were over, more out of vanity than anything else. But whatever the reason, he was an impressive physical specimen. His head was bald, smooth, and spherical, his face handsome, his skin the color of thick molasses. His shirt, a light pink Oxford button-down, was pressed, and his sleeves were rolled neatly to the elbow, exposing his thick forearms.

"Nice evening," Eli said, and Stuckey moved closer to Rushing.

"Are you looking for anyone in particular?" Rushing asked. "Or do you require a cigarette and a view of the stars?" Smiling like a Baptist preacher passing the collection plate, Rushing removed a pack of Lucky Strikes from his breast pocket and held the pack in Eli's direction.

"The former, not the latter."

"What'd he say?"

"What the gentleman said, Sharon, is he is indeed looking for someone. May I inquire as to who you are looking for?"

"I'm looking for you, Dantonio Rushing. And her, Sheri Stuckey."

Stuckey's eyes went turgid with panic. Rushing blinked once, smiled. "I see," he said.

"I don't," Stuckey whined. "Why are you guys talking like that, D? I won't deal with crazy. No way."

"Nonsense," Rushing said and stubbed his cigarette out on the hood of the Prius. "The gentleman is not crazy. Nor do I think he requires your professional services, Sharon. Unless I'm mistaken, he wishes to speak with us about a certain individual, which we would be happy to do provided he removes his shirt and pants first."

"I'm not a cop," Eli said.

"Of course you aren't. Not in those clothes. No, my concern is Big Brother."

"A reasonable precaution. Orwell himself would be horrified with today's lack of privacy."

"Nothing is sacred."

"Agreed."

"We find common ground. And yet your shirt and pants remain."

Eli flared out the lapels of his jacket. Turned a circle. He turned out his pockets. Nothing. "I'm not wearing a wire or carrying a digital recorder."

"Don't trust him, D. He looks like a cop. A good-looking cop, but a cop just the same."

"Thank you for the compliment."

"Hey, don't make fun of me." She tugged on Rushing's shirt like a petulant child. "Get rid of this asshole," she said, but there was no confidence in the command, no oomph. Here was a woman familiar with disappointment. She had a whiny voice, the kind that brought to mind all manner of offensive sounds—squeaking dog toys and nails on chalkboards. "But D, I don't trust him. Don't trust him at all. Kick his ass for me, D. Please. Come on."

"Sharon, you are embarrassing yourself. And this is not a matter of trust. This is a matter of courtesy. If Mister... I'm sorry, I did not catch your name."

"Eli Sharpe. I'm a private investigator." Eli showed Rushing his investigator's license. Rushing showed it to Stuckey. Stuckey spat on the ground.

"Looks fake to me." She used one butt to light another.

Rushing scrutinized the license a bit longer, nodded his approval, and gave Eli his wallet back.

Rushing put his hands behind his back. "Mr. Sharpe, as a courtesy to Sharon and myself, kindly remove your shirt and pants, but not the underwear and turn around slowly. Do this and I'd be happy to talk. I believe you'll find we have similar interests in a certain individual."

"And if I refuse?"

"D will kick your skinny ass." She laughed. Not a pleasant sound.

"Sharon is excitable. Two, she is overstating the case. You've no doubt ran a thorough background check on me and found no history of violence. Should you choose not to comply with my request, I assure you there will be no hard feelings. My offer of a cigarette is still valid, but alas, I will not answer any of your questions, nor will my partner."

"Damn straight."

Creepy and smart, indeed. Eli looked them both over. An odd pair. A bulky, polite, educated coke dealer and an underfed, chain-smoking single mother. Eli thought of Maria. Without Almario, she had no one. He thought of his failure at The Meadows.

"Atonement," he muttered.

"A-what?" Stuckey asked.

"Just a novel by a writer I admire." Eli took a deep breath, removed his shirt and pants and rotated once, slowly.

Rushing said, "You have a swimmer's build, Mr. Sharpe. Very lean and aerodynamic. I thank you for this demonstration of good faith, and I apologize for the precaution. What can I do to help you?"

Eli put his clothes back on. "Almario Gato," he said. "He's missing. I've been hired by his agent to find him. I know he drinks here at the Earl. I know he's engaged to her, Sheri Stuckey, and she supplies him cocaine through you, Dantonio Rushing." Eli paused. Rushing appeared neither surprised nor angry. Quite the opposite: his shoulders were relaxed, his eyes calm but alert. He seemed engaged, as if he were playing a game of chess with a worthy opponent—but one he was confident he would beat in the end.

"We don't have to tell you nothing. Right, D?" Stuckey brought her latest cigarette to her lips with a trembling hand.

"I know that Almario is staying at your apartment, Miss Stuckey, the one off Leicester Highway. I saw him there earlier tonight."

"See, D, I told you he's crazy because I haven't seen Almario in more than a week."

"I'll rephrase. Was Almario staying with you?"

"No, he wasn't with me. I haven't seen him in a week. You deaf?"

Rushing put a finger to Stuckey's lips. "Calm down, Sharon. Let the man finish what he has to say."

"I saw Almario outside Building A. He was wearing all black. He was pounding a wooden post into the ground with a sledgehammer. He ran when I spotted him. Do you know where he went?"

"Go-Go," Stuckey whimpered. "The sledgehammer was his daddy's." She covered her mouth, sobbed. Rushing eyeballed Stuckey like she was a lame horse he might have to put down. She tossed her cigarette and hugged her chest. Crying, she looked more appealing. Her face was prettier, more feminine, less like a talking scarecrow's. After several false starts, Rushing touched her hair, stroked it, said "Shhh." He reached into his pocket and pulled out a white pill.

"Open up, Sharon. Wider, please. Good girl." He placed the pill gently on her tongue. She swallowed. The sobbing abated, and he turned back to Eli.

"Sharon is heartbroken. I wonder if we might speak privately for just a moment."

"I need to ask her a few more questions first."

"Such as?"

"Let me ask her. Miss Stuckey, Almario is not staying at your apartment?"

"No, he's not staying with me. I want him to, but he ran off."

"Does he want to wait until you're married?" Stuckey hugged herself tighter. "Sharon, I know Almario and you filed for a marriage license two months ago."

"Only D can call me Sharon. Not you."

"I suppose you weren't aware that Almario had three pairs of black pants, three black shirts, and some underwear stashed in your kitchen pantry."

She lowered her eyes. "He keeps some things at my place. But he won't live with me. Not now."

Eli dug his hands deeper in his pockets, trying to figure out the game Stuckey and Rushing were playing with Almario, trying to figure out why they were answering his questions at all. "Miss Stuckey, Almario has another girlfriend, a really lovely redhead. She is a topnotch student, and she drives a red BMW. Her father has money and she, well, she doesn't deal drugs or have a daughter she neglects like you do."

"Shut your goddamn mouth," she said flatly. "I'm a good mother. I love Crystal."

"If you love her so much, why do you leave her all alone in your apartment?"

"D, I don't. Honest, I don't."

"I believe you, Sharon." Rushing steadied her trembling by putting his hand on her shoulder. "Mr. Sharpe, you've been inside Sharon's apartment without her knowledge or permission."

"Proving that will be difficult. That said, I can tell you there is evidence of child neglect. Very little food in the kitchen. Mildew and mold everywhere. Drug paraphernalia. Crystal, who Miss Stuckey claims to love so dearly, sleeps on a couch with rusty springs poking out of the cushions." Eli's pulse quickened, and his breath became shallow and rapid. He counted backward from twenty, his mind flashing back to the one and only conversation he'd had with a case worker from Child Services. Short sleeves. Stained tie. Bad breath. Eli had lied, said he got the shiner from a playground dustup. Although his old man eventually sobered up and stopped punching his wife and son, Eli still indulged in revenge fantasies on occasion. Tying the old man to a tree, covering him with honey, and releasing an army of red ants. He also indulged in other fantasies: his parents and him around a table filled with Thanksgiving treats—turkey, stuffing, cranberry sauce.

Normal breathing restored, Eli continued. "I can see why a judge granted your ex full custody of your daughter. Suppose I just make an anonymous phone call to Protective Services... You wouldn't even get visitation rights. And, of course, the police would be interested as well."

Panicked eyes. Quivering lower lip. "You won't do that, will you?"

"Depends. Tell me where Almario is."

"If I knew, I'd be there myself. I love him, I want him to get help, I want us to get help." A fit of shaking overtook her. She sobbed some more, and Rushing fireman-carried her over to a chair that was keeping the backdoor open. He placed her in the chair, gave her another white pill, whispered in her ear. She nodded. Rushing came back.

"Mr. Sharpe, walk with me a moment. Please."

Eli followed him. Rushing stopped three cars down from the red Prius. The light was still good, and out of the corner of his eye Eli spotted Carpenter crouched behind his Cadillac, .38 drawn just in case. Eli stood three feet behind Rushing. Rushing moved his hands to his pockets. His eyes went cold.

"I'm afraid I must insist you put your cards on the table, Mr. Sharpe."

"For the record, I don't care what activities you are involved in, so long as it doesn't involve Almario. My only concern is locating him. Quickly and safely."

"I appreciate your candor. Honesty is a rare commodity. But what assurances do I have that if I provide you with information you will leave me and my activities out of your investigation?"

"You have my word."

"That's insulting."

"I'm crushed."

Rushing tilted his head to the left, and his neck cracked. He tilted it to the right, and his neck cracked again. "Look at the way I dress, Mr. Sharpe. Listen to the way I speak. I'm college-educated, I've held respectable jobs and done well for myself. My father was a pediatrician, my mother a nurse."

"And my parents were Deadheads and petty criminals, so what?"

"So I want you to understand, I grew up in an affluent suburb of Memphis. If you think I would simply take the word of a private investigator, one that I've heard has police contacts all over town, one that is seemingly already aware of my activities, then we are not operating on a level of mutual respect."

Eli straightened to full height. Crossed his arms over his chest. "Cards on the table: I don't respect you. I don't respect the way you're using that poor woman to peddle drugs. I don't respect the way you corrupted Almario. The only thing about you I respect is your size."

"That's wise. I would hurt you badly in a fair fight."

"Who says I fight fair?"

"I would advise you not to underestimate me. The criminal file, my arrest record: that's a memoir, not a biography."

"With your preppy clothes and perfect elocution, I'm sure you've fooled more than your share of cops and criminals in your time. And, for right now, so long as you provide me with good information, you and I can part ways amicable enemies. Now, what did you want to talk about?"

"Making an accommodation. Would that be possible?"

"All depends on the details."

Rushing grinned. "Then allow me to fill you in on a few salient ones. I can see you're a competent investigator, but I'm willing to bet a considerable portion of my nest egg you didn't know about Sharon's true intentions with Almario."

"Now who's not showing respect? Almario earned over a million dollars just for signing his name to a piece of paper. He earns high six-figures in yearly salary, too. Of course I'd considered her true intentions."

He held up his hands, his Baptist preacher grin widening. "While it's true, Sharon does feel some affection for Almario, she holds money in much higher esteem. Money and security."

"That doesn't make her much different from most people, yourself included."

"Perhaps, but my methods to obtain such ends are far less clumsy. I am far more careful with my activities than Sharon."

"I'm growing impatient."

"Take caution in your tone, Mr. Sharpe. I'd like to remind you that you're not growing in stature." Rushing flexed his pectoral muscles and stepped closer. His teeth were showing, sweat was forming on his forehead. "My patience with your self-righteous attitude is wearing thin. I'm attempting to be cooperative. Perhaps it's time I taught you some manners."

"Let's put a pin in that." Carpenter appeared from behind the Cadillac with a .38 revolver aimed at Rushing's chest. He stepped in front of Rushing, making sure not to stand so close that he could make a quick move and take the gun. Rushing had the strength, but Carpenter was taller by six inches. The six inches, plus the gun, plus knowing how to use it made Carpenter an even fifty-six feet tall in this exchange. Eli breathed easy.

"Talk," Carpenter said. "You mentioned something about an accommodation."

Rushing backed away from Eli, his hands aloft. Where Stuckey was a woman used to failure, Rushing was a man used to victory. A crafty expression appeared on his face. He produced a red silk handkerchief from his pocket and wiped the sweat from his brow.

"*Mea culpa.* Mr. Sharpe, you'll pardon my methods. Intimidation works ninety-nine percent of the time. I can see it will not work against you and your mustachioed partner."

"Neither will flattery," Eli said.

"Quiet." Carpenter spotted Stuckey coming toward them, and he put his revolver behind his back.

The pills he'd given her had taken affect. Her head wobbled. Her shoulders sagged. The cigarette in her hand weighed too much for her, and she dropped it on the gravel. "What's up, D? This guy know where Go Go is, or what?"

"We're working on it, Sharon. Go back inside."

She wobbled back into the kitchen, leaving the door open behind her.

"There is no need for the weapon," Rushing said. "We're working toward the same end, Mister…?"

"Fuse," said Carpenter. "Mr. Short Fuse. Talk."

"As I'm sure you know, Almario has been involved with Sharon for some time."

"Since Almario tore up his knee more than a year ago," Eli said. "I heard he met both of you here, at the Earl."

"He met Sharon here, and then she brought him over to my place."

"Where you plied him with blow and booze," Carpenter said, his hand steady on the revolver.

"That is categorically false. Almario was in physical and psychological pain. He was performing poorly on the field. He was worried about losing his job, his apartment, and everything else he'd worked so hard for. He couldn't talk to anyone else. He felt trapped. I gave him half of a pain killer. Medicine that was legally prescribed to me by a licensed physician. I also made him a watered-down Piña Colada. That was all."

"You're a true humanitarian," Carpenter said. He put his gun away, placed it in his shoulder harness, keeping his eyes on Rushing the whole time. "I'll be sure to vote for you as Drug Dealer of the Year."

"Your partner is awfully hostile for an octogenarian."

"He is, but you digress. Get to the point."

"I have several points to make, but my first is this: Almario, aside from being missing, is in danger."

"From who?"

"Sharon Stuckey, of course."

"Do you have any proof?"

"Not on me, no."

"But you have something somewhere that proves Almario is in danger and Stuckey is the threat?"

"Yes, I do." Rushing paused for dramatic effect, and Carpenter was poised to get out his gun. "The proof is an insurance policy."

"Proves nothing," Eli said. "A lot of ballplayers take out policies. Injury is a way of life for those guys, and they don't want to be unprotected. Do you know any of the policy's details?"

"Some, yes. All told, the policy is worth half a million. Sharon's ex-husband works for Mountain Ridge Insurance. He drafted the policy."

Eli looked at Carpenter, who lit a cigar and walked to his

Cadillac and slammed the door behind him.

"What's his problem?"

"He's seen this movie before. We both have." Worse, Eli knew the ending. And it wasn't rosy. The air was humid and heavy, the stars obscured by clouds. "Please tell me the beneficiary is Maria Gato."

"I read the policy twice. The beneficiary listed was Sharon Stuckey."

Rushing explained how he came across the policy in Stuckey's apartment one night. She and Almario had snorted an eightball and drank vodka and Red Bull. While the two of them were passed out, Rushing did some snooping around and found the policy in a pouch in the freezer.

"Naturally, I made copies, one for me and one for my attorney. Be prepared, is my motto."

"That is the Boy Scouts' motto, not yours." Eli glanced back at the Cadillac. Dense clouds of gray smoke floated out of the driver's side window. "So you want to give me a copy of Almario's insurance policy in exchange for keeping my mouth shut about your drug operation?"

"I do not know to what drug operation you're referring. However, I would appreciate you forgetting my name in any talks you might have with law enforcement."

Eli studied Rushing's face for any hint of deception. Nothing. But his head swarmed with suspicions. "Let me get this straight. When I got here, you didn't seem surprised to see me. What's more, you answered all my questions. Something doesn't add up here. I meant what I said: I don't care about your 'activities.' You give me a copy of the policy tomorrow, and I won't call the cops. But I need more. The insurance policy tomorrow doesn't help me find Almario today."

"Ahh, but it does help explain why he is missing. Which leads me to the second point I wanted to make: Almario isn't missing, he's hiding."

Eli made a T of his hands. What Rushing had told him up to

that point painted an ugly yet quasi-plausible picture explaining Almario's disappearance. Maybe Sharon Stuckey marked Almario from the first night he came into the Burly Earl. Her plan: be a sympathetic ear for his struggles on the diamond, and then seduce him with sex and drugs. Once she had him wrapped around her nicotine-stained finger, she probably floated the idea of marriage and the insurance policy and God knows what else. Then maybe Rushing stepped in, filled Almario's head with ideas, and the kid, hooked on the white powder, got a little paranoid and decided to hide out for a while, rethink his impending nuptials. Hmm.

It was a theory, all right. A wild one. With plenty of holes.

"Doesn't pass the sniff test," Eli said, "what you're insinuating. If Almario dies, there would be two investigations—one by the police and one by the insurance company. Stuckey wouldn't collect a cent if she had something to do with his death. Not to speak ill of your partner, but I doubt she has the wherewithal to follow through on a scheme like that."

Rushing flashed his pulpit smile again. "I assure you, you do not know Sharon Stuckey the way I do. She is capable of being devious and clever. You see a helpless, drug-addicted anorexic. That is a façade, one I helped create. Despite what you may think of me and my chosen profession, do you believe I would have an incompetent involved in my activities? Especially when my liberty is on the line?"

"Is it on the line? Are the cops on to you?"

"Not at the moment, but Sharon has become a liability. Despite my distaste for law enforcement, police are not stupid. It's only a matter of time. From a moral standpoint, I do not approve of what she's doing with Almario, and professionally, well, I will not have any blowback."

"When was the last time you saw Almario?" Eli asked.

"Yesterday."

"Did he need drugs or money or both?"

"He was in danger. I told him about Sharon's plans, such as

they are, and then I helped him find a place to hide. Some place safe. Late yesterday afternoon, I brought him some food: a grilled cheese with brie and caramelized apples. I made it myself."

Eli thought for a minute. Like all the others in Almario's life, Rushing was enchanted by the beautiful young Cuban. It was obvious. Perhaps Rushing was playing an angle. Perhaps Stuckey was playing an angle. Perhaps they were playing an angle together. He needed to keep him talking a bit longer.

"So you were attracted to Almario. You were jealous of his relationship with Stuckey, and now you want her out of the picture. Is that why you're suggesting she intends to harm him?"

"I won't deny I was or am attracted to Almario, but my interest goes beyond that. I admire him, what he did to get to this country, how he takes care of his sister. For those reasons, I ceased our professional relationship."

"Bullshit," Eli said. "Dealers deal."

Rushing rubbed his eyes, the first real sign of his frustration, the first chink in his armor. "Believe me or don't, it is of no consequence to me. After that first night when Sharon brought Almario to my apartment, I was in awe of him, his beauty, his youth and vitality. He is a Cuban Dorian Gray."

"Except this isn't a novel. If you give a kid drugs, it will kill him, sooner or later."

"I am aware. I can also tell by the tone of your voice that you care for Almario, just as I do. Which is precisely why I halted our professional interactions. To the best of my knowledge, his bride to be is his supplier now. Be advised, Mr. Sharpe, she is toxic, and I thought Almario should get away before he sank any lower."

"Says the admitted drug dealer."

"I admit nothing, except that I'm not greedy, and I like to keep off police radar. I like things quiet, Mr. Sharpe."

Best Eli could tell, Rushing was telling the truth. "One more question: you ever talk to Maria Gato or Christine Lovatt?"

"I know no Lovatt. Maria is Almario's sister, and yes, we've conversed."

"And?"

"And she threatened me. I informed her I was not professionally involved with Almario, but she became irrational. She even offered me money, which of course I refused."

"I've heard enough," said Eli. "Get in the Cadillac. In the backseat. You're going to take me to him."

"He may not be there now. He's got a serious habit and is totally paranoid. When you told me you saw him at Sharon's place, I was genuinely shocked."

"Get in the car," Eli said, "I need to talk to your partner. Alone."

"I'm telling you the truth."

"Get in the car. Or my next call is to the Asheville PD."

Inside the bar, Eli found Stuckey sitting in a booth with a fat-faced man in a rumpled suit. Wearing his striped tie like a scarf, she had her arm draped around his neck. Her serving tray was on the floor, and it was filled with empty beer bottles and highball glasses, shrunken lime wedges floating in amber liquid. Eli joined the party.

"Who invited you?" asked the fat-faced man.

"I'm a detective, sir. Your new companion is a drug dealer. Are you looking to score?"

The fat-faced man drained his highball in a gulp and untangled himself from Stuckey's thin, tentacle-like arms. When the man left the booth, she lit a cigarette, blew smoke in Eli's face. Her eyes were alert now; she was no longer stoned and helpless. Eli figured she must have snorted a little pick-me-up, maybe a line or two to get her back in fighting shape. She tossed the striped tie on the table.

"I'm going to marry Go Go," she said. "It's love. The real deal."

"I'm afraid I have objections. Many, in fact."

"I've known guys like you. Think you're so superior. Look your nose down at everybody."

"Your friend D told me an interesting story about Almario. One that painted you in an unflattering light. Care to tell your version?"

"I'm working." But she didn't move, just kept smoking, bobbing her head to a Zeppelin tune on the jukebox: "Communication Breakdown."

"D said you talked Almario into a half-a-million-dollar life insurance policy. Had him name you as the primary beneficiary."

"It's only right, we're getting married. He wants to take care of me."

"D tells me Almario isn't missing, he's hiding."

"Hiding from me?"

"Something about you wanting the half a million sooner rather than later. You follow? No? Yes? Maybe?" Eli fanned smoke away from his face. "All right, I'll make it clearer. Maybe you were or are planning on hurting Almario. Maybe you and Brad Newman had a plan to take him out, make it look like an accident of some sort and collect the insurance money."

"Fantasy land."

"Your ex gambles. You abuse cocaine amongst other vices. Put simply, you both have problems, but half a million could solve most of them. What do you have to say?"

"For a guy who spends all that time in the gym, D is a coward. He's jealous, too. Of my relationship with Almario. And as for my ex, he's a stuttering moron."

Her mouth formed a sly, all-knowing grin. She assumed a more feminine posture—back straight, head held at an angle. She smoked her cigarette daintily, as if the Burly Earl was the Asheville Country Club and her name was Veronica Kathryn Kensington III, not Sheri Stuckey. For the first time, Eli saw something of what Almario must have been attracted to. Her audacity. Perhaps Rushing was right about Sharon's "carefully-crafted persona." Perhaps she wasn't so helpless after all. Eli sat back, studied her and she let him; she didn't look away, just mouthed the words to "Communication Breakdown." That was the problem with drug people. Too erratic. Ten minutes ago she was a frightened, nervous wreck. Now: calm. Calm and in control.

Eli said, "All right, you love him. I'll go get him tonight and if he wants, I'll bring him to you. The two of you can talk. Just tell me where he is."

"You're the smart guy, not me."

"D said he knows where and is going to take me. D says he stopped supplying Almario with blow. He says you're Almario's supplier now."

She held up her left hand. "This diamond has the three Cs: carat, clarity, and color. Almario bought it for me. That red Prius in the parking lot. Almario? Best daycare in town for my little girl, five hundred a week. Almario. Why would I want to hurt him?"

Eli asked if she'd ever met or spoken to Maria Gato, and she said no. Christine Lovatt? Homer Hodge? No and no.

Eli snatched the cigarette from her hand, stubbed it out in the ashtray. The billiard balls cracked behind him. The jukebox switched from Zeppelin to the Allman Brothers, "Ain't Wasting Time No More."

"D said he stashed Almario someplace safe and quiet. He's taking us there now. Care to join us?"

"Can't," she said. "I'm working." A single tear fell down her cheek.

Eli went to the bar, gave Summer his cellphone number, told her to keep an eye on Stuckey.

"Last chance," Eli said, but Stuckey picked up her drink tray and wandered over to a couple of Bikers playing nine ball.

The last thing Eli heard when he left the bar: Stuckey's flirty, over-the-top laughter.

CHAPTER 11

When Eli joined Rushing in the backseat of Carpenter's Cadillac, Eli smelled sickly sweet cigar smoke, saw Carpenter glaring at Rushing in the rearview mirror, giving him the thousand-yard stare the old Army vet had learned in Vietnam forty-some years prior. Eli fanned smoke, his eyes burning.

"Stuckey stonewalled me," Eli said. "But our friend here has agreed to take us to Almario's hiding spot."

Carpenter grunted, kept his eyes on the bulky drug dealer in the rearview mirror. "That's all well and good, but our friend back there needs to understand something: I expect this trip to pan out. You hear me, Mr. Rushing? Whatever deal you made with my partner is null and void if this goes sideways."

Rushing turned his nose up and sniffed. Either he was offended by Carpenter's insinuation or the cigar smoke disagreed with him. "Yes, well, as I informed your partner, I care for Almario."

"I think I believe you," said Eli. "And we're wasting time."

Carpenter tossed his cigar. The fine leather seats made a noise as he turned to face Rushing, who had his hands on his knee caps and a nervous expression on his face. "Mr. Rushing, I was a homicide detective with the Asheville PD for more than two decades."

"Was that a fact or a veiled threat?" Rushing asked.

"Both," Eli said.

"Let me explain my expectations, so there's no miscommunication. First," Carpenter said, holding up his right thumb, "I expect this ride, wherever it takes us, to get us closer to finding Almario. And second," he held up his right pointer finger, "I expect all of us, even you, to come back safely. We understand each other?"

Something passing for a chuckle escaped Rushing's mouth. Buckled into the backseat, he didn't seem nearly as imposing a physical specimen. "Mr. Carpenter, have you ever been a thespian?"

"Kid, our new friend isn't hearing me. Make him comprehend."

"What my partner is trying to say is, we want Almario, and we expect you to help lead us to him, safely. No bullshit. No tricks. Do that and I promise to make good on our arrangement. Don't and we'll make some phone calls and you'll be out of business before the week is out."

"Not to mention wearing an orange jumpsuit," Carpenter added.

"Message received and understood. Turn left out of the parking lot."

With that, Carpenter headed south on Tunnel Road, through the traffic lights and past the Asheville Mall and the movie theaters and the big box retail. The lights of the McMansions on the surrounding hills twinkled. The Cadillac hummed, rode smoothly over the pavement. Out of the corner of his eye, Eli saw Rushing's barrel chest rising and falling rapidly.

Six minutes later, Rushing led Carpenter onto I-70, away from the city lights and out into the more rural part of Buncombe County. Trees and foothills and winding stretches of darkened two-lane highway. Eli checked his Seiko: 11:43 p.m. Carpenter drove the speed limit, every half mile the Caddy's arced headlights catching a glimpse of a deer by the side of the road. Rushing began reiterating his admiration for Almario, and Eli's mind shifted into overdrive. The two of them—Rushing and Stuckey—

were up to something. Both of them had offered up a wealth of information, but Eli wondered how much of it was on the level. Could Almario really be hiding from his fiancée? Or was he coked out and paranoid, running away from his professional failures, just as Eli had once done?

Eli asked how much farther.

"Just another mile, mile and a half," said Rushing. "The road has no name. No sign. No marker. Just slow down and keep your eyes open."

Carpenter crested a hill, the highway bent to the left, and he eased into it, gently pumping the brakes.

Eli told Rushing to roll his window down, and he obeyed. Eli craned his neck, focused on the shifting shadows and the perfect arc of the headlights. A bag of trash. A dead dog. Other debris strewn along the highway. Humid summer air rushed through the window. Carpenter slowed to thirty miles per hour, flicked on the brights, and Eli spotted an opening in the woods.

"There," Eli said. "That gravel turn-off. Pull over."

Once safely on the shoulder, Carpenter flicked on the hazard lights, killed the engine, and adjusted the rearview mirror, making sure he could see both Eli and Rushing. Carpenter unholstered the .38, clicked the safety on, commanded Rushing to face the back window.

"I assure you I'm not violent." Rushing threw up his hands. "I've never held a gun."

"We're cautious people," said Carpenter.

"And trust must be earned," Eli added. "Remember our expectations."

Rushing faced the back window, laid his hands flat against the glass.

Carpenter passed the revolver, and Eli gripped it, the metal warm and purposeful in his hands. As part of Eli's apprenticeship, Carpenter had taught him gun safety and maintenance, had taken him to the gun range to practice four days a week for nearly six months. When Eli passed the test and received his license to carry a firearm, Carpenter even purchased Eli a brand new Smith & Wesson revolver, which was still sitting in the original box in Eli's desk drawer. When his heart rate slowed, Eli clicked the safety off, told Rushing to turn around, sit on the opposite end of the bench seat.

"Farther. All the way against the window."

"You have trust issues."

"I had a turbulent childhood," Eli said. "And I like a wide berth."

Rushing leaned against the window.

Carpenter cranked the engine, drove down the gravel drive and into the woods.

The path started out clear and wide enough for one and a half cars to pass through comfortably, but after three hundred yards or so the path narrowed and the gravel ended. The gravel was replaced by bumpy red clay, lots of dips and divots and holes. As Carpenter drove, the Cadillac bounced and shook and tree branches and brush scraped against the hood.

"There goes my paint job," Carpenter said and let loose a string of curse words.

Rushing leaned out of the opened window. The sound of briars ruining the paint job helped Eli focus, helped him stay alert for whatever was at the end of the trail. The farther they went, the thicker the woods got. The thicker the woods got, the more his senses heightened, the more natural the .38 felt in his hand, the more he recalled those trips to the shooting range with Carpenter. He remembered the smell of cordite and his own sweat as he breathed and squeezed the trigger and his ear drums suffered. Eli checked his Seiko: 11:50 p.m. He asked how much farther.

Rushing said, "Not long. Just up ahead."

After half a mile of scraping and bumping, the path opened up onto broken pavement. At the end of the broken pavement sat a dilapidated four-story brick building. The building was square with four even rows of barred windows on each floor.

Overgrown grass and bush surrounded the crumbling structure, and there were thick woods on either side.

"Kill the headlights," Eli said. "Park on the pavement."

Carpenter dimmed the high beams, and the building disappeared.

Rushing said, "This used to be a rehabilitation facility. For the mentally-disturbed."

"Our boy is in there, right?" Carpenter asked, his voice calm and authoritative.

Eli heard Rushing nodding vigorously in the dark. "Almario is in the common area. At least he was yesterday when I brought him food and toiletries."

"The common area?" Eli asked.

"On the first floor, next to the kitchen. My older sister spent a year here before it closed. That must have been ten years ago, maybe more." Rushing sighed. "Bipolar disorder. She killed herself with Seconal."

Eli waited a respectable length of time and then asked Carpenter for an assessment of the situation.

Carpenter opened the glove compartment, pulled out a Taser C2, checked the lithium-powered magazine.

"Let's go get Almario," Carpenter said. "Got a heavy duty flashlight in the trunk."

Rushing asked for permission to open the car door and Eli followed, keeping his distance, gun at the ready. With the interior car lights still on, Eli quarterbacked the game plan.

"Dantonio, you'll take point. We'll be behind with the light."

"And the weaponry," Carpenter added.

Rushing laughed anxiously. "Look around you, we're miles from civilization."

"Which is kind of my partner's point," Eli said. "Now let's go."

Rushing walked toward the building with his hands by his ears, refusing to lower them.

Carpenter shined the light on a concrete pathway with weeds

sprouting out of the cracks. Crickets and other insects of the night spoke. The air was saturated. Eli kept his eyes focused on a ring of sweat on the back of Rushing's pink, button-down shirt. To avoid tripping on the broken asphalt, Eli counted his steps. Carpenter hummed. Rushing's breathing was labored.

"That's the problem with you drug dealers," Carpenter said, "not enough cardio."

"I can bench press almost twice my body weight."

"Which will serve you well when you're doing a nickel for distributing narcotics."

"Gentlemen," Eli said, "if you please." The building came into flashlight range, and Carpenter aimed the light at the front entrance. Graffiti on a rusted-out metal door. A big rat with a long tail and red eyes scurried away as Carpenter shoved Rushing forward. Rushing produced a silk handkerchief, used it to turn the broken door knob, moved forward, sucked in air. Carpenter and Eli followed.

"He should be over here to the left," Rushing said. "Should I call him?"

"Was anybody else staying here with him?"

"There wasn't anybody here yesterday. Squatters stay here, but the police run them off every couple of days."

Carpenter shined the light on the common area: a large, open room with a brick fireplace on the wall. Mildewed furniture scattered about the room. Broken wine bottles and cigarette butts littered the floor. The air was close and stifling. Damp. Moldy. Eli struggled to breathe normally.

"Over there," Rushing said and moved toward the far right corner of the room. "Almario? Are you here?"

Silence.

Carpenter shined the light, and Eli followed its yellow path to the corner of the room. A black blanket neatly folded in half. Eli touched the fleece material. Wet. He bent and sniffed. Rain water? Mildew? There was something hard hidden beneath the fold, something made of metal, and he unfolded the blanket, carefully. Almario's sledgehammer. Same aqua-blue handle. Beside the sledgehammer were two books bound together by a rubber band. Removing the rubber band, he placed the books side by side. *The Bible* written in Spanish. *Self-Actualization: How to Achieve Greatness in Your Chosen Profession.* He turned the self-help book upside down, fanned the pages out. Nothing. Ditto *The Bible.* Nothing.

Carpenter asked about the sledgehammer, and Rushing said, "It was his father's."

"He's right," said Eli. "Maria told me Almario brought it with him from Cuba."

Eli took a corner of the blanket in his hand, rubbed the damp material between thumb and forefinger, dropped it to the ground.

"Keep looking," Eli said, trading the .38 for Carpenter's heavy duty flashlight.

He moved down the hallway over broken glass, entered the kitchen, shined the light around. Rats scurried. Cobwebs everywhere. A dimmed EXIT sign above a large metal door.

Outside, he shook the cobwebs from his hair, got his bearings, shined the light slowly from side to side. Woods to the left and right. Straight ahead: a concrete footpath leading into the trees.

He followed the path, weeds brushing up against his pant leg, blood coursing through his veins. He counted his steps along the path, and every fifth one he called Almario's name, shined the light on some suspicious shadow. But there was nothing around. Just gnats and highway noise in the distance.

Wiping sweat from his eyes, he quickened his pace, moved to the end of the concrete path, stopped, turned off the flashlight, waited for his breathing to steady.

He listened. Water. Moving water. He turned on the flashlight. Where the concrete path ended, a dirt path began, and he moved down it, deeper into the woods. The rush of water grew louder with every step, and the louder it got, the faster he moved.

He speed-walked, jogged, ran. As he ran, he kept the light aimed forward, kept his feet pumping until he saw a body lying face up on the muddy banks of a creek.

The body was shaped like an X: arms and legs spread out as if interrupted by death while making a snow angel. His boots were muddy, clothes, too: black pants and black T-shirt. Eli shined the light on his face. Only this wasn't the same handsome countenance Eli had seen four hours prior. This face was grotesque. Large black spots on both cheeks and forehead. Rotten flesh? An infection? His nostrils were caked with dried blood, his lips encrusted with vomit, his eyes wide open.

Eli backpedaled away from the body, dropped the flashlight, and swung on an oak tree, his pointer finger snapping like a matchstick on impact.

It was a long, painful walk back to the Cadillac.

CHAPTER 12

Borrowing Eli's cellphone, Carpenter called APD first, asked for the Criminal Investigations Division and gave them precise directions to their location. Then he called nine-one-one. Using the clipped language of a veteran police detective, he told the operator what had happened.

"Body in the woods. Male. Eighteen. Identity unconfirmed."

"It's Go Go," Eli whispered as he tried to flex his broken finger.

The EMTs were first on the scene. An ambulance bumped to a stop beside Carpenter's Cadillac. Two large women in dark blue uniforms and matching hats got out, and Rushing climbed into the backseat of the Cadillac, crying softly. Carpenter brought the EMTs up to speed while Eli studied their faces to take his mind off things. The younger EMT with a cherubic face looked young and restless. She asked what the plan was, and the older and heavier EMT scrunched up her face.

Carpenter said, "We wait for the CID Unit and Forensics."

"And," Eli said, "we make sure to steer clear of the area where Almario was found. No contamination."

The younger EMT asked who Almario was, and the older EMT pointed to their rig, told her to make sure they were ready for when company arrived. The younger EMT pouted but obeyed.

While they waited, Carpenter reached through the driver's

side window, turned on the highbeams, and the one-time rehabilitation facility appeared out of the darkness.

"Creepy place," said the EMT. "Are we even within city limits?"

"We're pretty far south," Carpenter said. "But this must be Baker."

"You sure it's not the Charlie District?" Eli asked. "We must be four, five miles down I-70."

"Charlie only covers south central Asheville. Unless they redrew the district lines since I collected my gold watch, we're in Baker, and Baker means Detective Meachum."

"What's this Meachum like?" Eli asked.

"He needs a haircut." Carpenter grunted. "Capable detective though."

Eli checked his Seiko: 1:05 a.m. He couldn't wait any longer. He called Veronica Craven. She answered on the first ring.

"Tell me you found him," she said.

Eli steeled his insides and spoke. Halfway through the report, she started crying. Then cursing. Eli absorbed her insults without retaliating. When she ran out of steam, he told her to sit tight, that the detectives would want to talk to her and Maria soon. Veronica stopped crying, took a deep breath. Then another.

"I'll tell her," she said. "I'll go there now and tell her."

Silence.

Then, "Full refund," Eli said and instantly regretted saying it. He prepared himself for a fresh onslaught of insults. None came.

"Keep the money," she said flatly.

"I can't. I failed."

"Oh, I'm going to make you earn it. Starting now: I need you to talk to Waring and his two sycophants. They're staying in my hotel."

A moment to think. By failing to save Almario Gato, Eli had failed Maria Gato. The one person—the one woman—who needed his help the most. Whiskey. His mouth watered at the thought of a drink, of drawing the shades and diving to the bottom of a fifth of George Dickel. But his conscience gnawed at him. His brotherly feeling for Maria wouldn't allow him to self-destruct. As tough as she was, Maria still needed someone. And Eli, stuck between a boulder of failure and a hard place of self-destruction, needed her to need *him.*

"Have they been bothering you?" Eli asked. "Waring and his flunkies?"

"Incessantly," she said, regaining some of her professional poise. "Waring has been calling every half hour demanding updates on your progress. Complaining that he gets your voicemail every time he calls."

"I must have turned the phone off. I'll deal with Waring."

"Yes, you will."

More silence.

Eli said, "Meet me tomorrow at Two Guys Hoagies on Charlotte Street at noon."

"For a meal? Or absolution?"

A fair question.

"Veronica?"

"What is it?"

"Nothing," Eli said. "Tomorrow at noon."

Sirens wailed and as the blue and red lights drew nearer, Eli called Frank Waring, and Gifford, the cauliflower ear, answered.

"The boss is pissed."

"So am I," Eli said, "but for different reasons, I'm sure."

"The boss has a reason to be pissed. Why haven't you answered any of his calls?"

"Put Waring on the phone."

"He's in the john. He told me to deal with you."

"Get Waring. He'll want to hear what I have to say."

"You got a smart mouth, Sharpe. Our paths cross again I just might slap it for you."

Staring down at the purple bruise forming on his hand, Eli counted one Mississippi, two Mississippi, three Mississippi.

"I'm hanging up now, Gifford. When your boss gets out of the bathroom, have him call me." Gifford started to make another wisecrack, but Eli hung up before the punch line.

Thirty seconds later his phone rang.

"Frank Waring here. You got an update."

Eli explained what happened. It was no easier to tell on the second go round.

Waring muttered a few sympathetic phrases, and then began asking questions.

"I can't tell you any more than I've told you already," said Eli, angry at how worthless and true the words sounded. "The city police are on their way to investigate."

Waring cursed, began talking like a calculated businessman again. "You call me and tell me one of my most valued assets is dead, and that's all the information you can muster up? That's unacceptable."

"Almario is not an asset."

"This whole thing was bungled from start to finish."

"If you want to meet tomorrow I can give you a report on my investigation. As a professional courtesy. Because I know you cared so much for Almario Gato as a human being. Short of that, Mr. Waring, fuck off."

Forensics arrived in a black, unmarked SUV, red siren still flashing on the dashboard as a team of three—two women and one man—exited the car. Dressed in dark slacks and a polo shirt, the man strode toward the Cadillac with an oversized bag slung across his shoulder. The two women wore blue windbreakers with FORENSICS written in yellow across the front and back. The man looked at Eli and then Carpenter and then the two women behind him.

"Mitchell. Forensics. Where's he hiding?"

"Behind the building," Eli said. "Where the path ends. Beside the creek."

"You touch the body?"

"I don't think so."

"Either you did or you didn't."

"I might have checked for a pulse."

"Might have?"

"I can't say for sure. I was angry."

"Angry over what?"

"Angry a man was dead. A man I was hired to find."

Mitchell shook his head. "What about the rest of the scene? You didn't handle any evidence, did you?"

Carpenter stepped between Mitchell and Eli. "How about we leave the questions to the CID boys."

"I have questions now," Mitchell said, looking up at Carpenter, who had him by half a foot, easy.

One of the women on the forensics team took the oversized bag from Mitchell, smiled at Carpenter. "Our boss is only trying to determine the integrity of the scene."

"So we can do our jobs more efficiently," the other woman added cheerfully.

"Fair enough," said Eli. "No, I didn't handle any evidence."

Moments later, several cars rolled to a stop on the grass—two squad cars and a Crown Victoria. Three uniformed police officers got out of each of the squad cars, all of them holding rolls of yellow tape and heavy duty flashlights like the one Eli had carried.

Bill Meachum, a homicide detective, exited the unmarked car and stood in the headlights of the Crown Victoria, looking like no cop Eli had ever seen. Standing well over six-four, Meachum had jet-black hair pulled back into a ponytail, deep-set eyes, and the kind of deep tan you get from working out in the sun for long stretches at a time. A hemp necklace hung from around his hairy neck. He wore an Indian-red leather motorcycle jacket with a purple Phish T-shirt underneath. Packing his left cheek with Skoal, he spat brown juice and shook Eli's hand, nodded at Carpenter. He produced a leather-bound notebook from his jacket, slapped the back of his thigh with it.

"So," Meachum said, "who found the body?"

"I did," Eli said.

"He inside?"

"Behind the building. Follow the path—"

"Show, don't tell." Meachum whistled, and the police officers, forensics, and EMTs gathered around. He cleared his throat. "Ladies and gents, it's too hot and way too late, so pay attention. Here's the play. To my left is Eli. He's gonna show us where to. The unit are gonna tape off the scene and secure the area while forensics collects evidence and I try to determine if we've gotta crime scene on our hands or an accidental. When we're done, the EMTs are gonna give the dearly departed a ride to St. Joe's, and I'll take official statements. Questions?" No one said anything. "Fantastic. Everybody keep your eyes open. You see something interesting, yell out, 'Evidence.' Forensics'll take it from there. Eli, lead the way."

Meachum and the others started off.

Carpenter tugged on Eli's shirt, waited until the rest were out of earshot.

"That man loves the sound of his own voice. I'll babysit Rushing. See if he has anything illuminating to say."

Meachum, forensics and the uniformed officers stood several yards off, checking flashlights and bitching about the ungodly hour. Meachum whistled, shined his flashlight in Eli's face.

"On the hop, Eli. Time's wasting. And tell your ancient partner to sit tight. Tell the bulky one to compose himself. He blubbered like a baby when the EMTs confirmed the kid was dead. I'm gonna need statements from them."

Carpenter muttered something under his breath.

Eli led the group to the end of the footpath, stopped, and pointed straight ahead. Half a dozen flashlights shone on Almario, a lifeless X sprawled out in the mud. Everyone was silent. Except for the creek rushing by. One of the uniformed officers broke the silence with a comment about Almario's face.

Meachum said, "Keep your thoughts to yourself, officer. Let's go to work."

As he drew closer to the body, Eli was startled again by the state of Almario Gato. Under the harsh glare of the flashlights, Almario's face looked gruesome, like something out of a B-horror movie. The black, rotted flesh. The shocked look in his eyes. The dried up blood. And yet Eli couldn't avert his gaze. The knot of failure in his stomach tightened.

This wasn't the first time he'd been hired to track down a missing person, and the person ended up dead. It was the second time. The first one, a reckless alcoholic who drove his Harley into an oak tree, wasn't easy, far from it. But that first one wasn't eighteen years old. That first one didn't have a twin sister to look after. That first one hadn't come all the way to America on a boat with a change of clothes and his father's sledgehammer. That first one hadn't been alive and well and mere steps away from Eli before he slammed into that oak tree. Almario had.

A hand gripped Eli's shoulder.

"I need your statement." Meachum held an iPhone in front of him. "No worries, son. Just tell it like it happened. No adverbs. No embellishments."

Eli obeyed. It was not easier telling what happened for a third time.

Meachum put away his cellphone, said Eli did fine. Meachum wrote down Eli's cellphone, office phone, address.

"That's all I need for now. We'll talk tomorrow."

"What about Dantonio Rushing?"

"Don't worry, son. The EMTs'll take care of him."

Eli shook his head. "I'm talking about the bulky one in the back of the Cadillac. He led us here. He may have vital information."

"I'll get his statement, too." Meachum opened his can of Skoal and offered it to Eli. Eli shook his head. Meachum put in a fresh plug and spat.

"Before I go, maybe I should fill you in on the people in

Almario's life."

"No need. We're gonna work the scene first, see what kind of evidence we got before we go labeling. At a glance, I expect the ME will find plenty to chew on. I'll keep on him, but it'll still take a day, maybe two for a preliminary workup. A full tox screen and blood analysis'll take six weeks, minimum." He spat, nearly hitting Eli's shoe. "Meantime, tell your ancient partner and the bulky one to come down here. I need statements."

Meachum walked over, crouched beside Almario's body, spoke softly into his iPhone. Eli surveyed the scene. Yellow tape everywhere. Officers tiptoeing around the woods, watching their step, shining light into dark places. Forensics had the kit out and was collecting evidence. Eli followed the path out of the woods, the knot in his stomach tighter than before. To Meachum, Almario was just another dead body. But to Eli Sharpe, Almario was a symbol—of wasted youth and talent, of hope and promise. Had a butterfly flapped its wings in Thailand twelve years ago, Eli could have easily wound up like Almario, dead beside a muddy creek. But he wasn't dead. He was alive. And while Detective Meachum was running the show on the official investigation, Eli wasn't about to sit on his hands and wait.

CHAPTER 13

Carpenter whipped the Cadillac into the Burly Earl parking lot and killed the engine. Glaring into the rearview mirror, he ordered Rushing out of the car.

"How can you be cross with me?" Rushing asked, squirming in the backseat. "I told Detective Meachum everything I know. I've already professed my admiration for Almario, and you're still suspicious of me?"

"Imagine us being suspicious of a drug dealer."

Eli reached over Rushing, opened the door. "Time to go."

"You're angry with me, too? I'm the one who tried to get him away from Sharon, remember? I refused to sell to him."

"So now you admit you're a drug dealer," said Eli. "It's no longer your 'activities.'"

"What right do you have to be hostile?"

"Call it a moral imperative," Carpenter said.

"I'm befuddled. Truly. I tried to help Almario."

"My partner is suggesting this whole thing stinks. He is suggesting you held something back."

"That's your game," Carpenter said. "You come across as well-spoken and accommodating. You play the good drug dealer, as if there were such a thing. Meanwhile, you had something to do with Almario's death."

"I'm flabbergasted."

"Save the flabber and the gas." Carpenter gritted his teeth; Eli could see his mentor's capped incisors in the rearview mirror.

"Talk or get out," Eli said, and Rushing exited the car. Eli yanked the door shut, rolled the window down. "By the way, I dropped your name and Sheri Stuckey's to Meachum. Might have even hinted at a drug connection. So if the investigation turns up anything fishy, I'll know which direction to point."

"And we still want a copy of Almario's insurance policy," said Carpenter.

"Tomorrow. Here. Three o'clock. Bring the policy."

Rushing's pink button-down shirt was un-tucked. Rings of sweat had formed under his armpits. Under the streetlight, he didn't look nearly as big. Or handsome. Eli watched him walk back into the bar and then climbed into the passenger seat.

"Speak to me, kid. Tell me what's on your mind."

"I'm curious."

"Me too. You found Almario in what, twelve hours? Who does that?"

"Maybe Jim Rockford. Maybe." Eli pointed to Stuckey's red Prius in the parking lot, checked his Seiko: 1:43 a.m. "The bar closes in fifteen. She might have made the Caddy earlier. Let's use my car."

Carpenter turned right out of the bar, dropped Eli off at Walmart. Eli started his truck, picked up Carpenter, parked in the First Citizens Bank across the street from the Burly Earl. Decent view of anyone coming or going.

They didn't have to wait long. Eli's cellphone rang. It was Summer inside the Burly Earl.

"All right, skinny man, Sheri is leaving work now. Without cleaning her section. Again."

"She seem upset? Nervous?"

"Nervous? No. Half in the bag? Yes. She snuck a few rum-and-cokes during the late night rush. Right now she's checking her cellphone."

"Ask if she's acting squirrelly at all," Carpenter said.

Eli held up a finger. "Does she seem in a hurry?"

"Of course, she's allergic to work."

"Did you see her talk to Rushing?"

Clinking beer bottles. Summer barking orders at the kitchen staff. "Nope. Dantonio came in and got to work. Same as it ever was."

"And where is he now?"

"On the floor, clearing tables. He always helps me close up. Gays make the best employees. If he didn't deal blow, I might enjoy working with him."

Eli said he owed her.

"Wait. Tell me what happened with Almario. Did you find him yet?"

"Yes," Eli said. "I found him."

Stuckey inched the red Prius out of the parking lot and turned left onto Tunnel Road, stopping at a yellow light to send some texts. Eli slowed, pulled into the turn lane, waited until the light turned green and then accelerated. At the next stop-light, Stuckey turned right onto Kenilworth and made another quick right into an all-night convenience store. Eli drove down Kenilworth, past the convenience store.

"Know where she's going?" Carpenter asked.

"Ex-husband's place."

"The one who wrote the insurance policy?"

"The same."

Eli drove past Newman's decrepit bungalow, found a nicer house two doors down with a Century 21 Realty sign stuck in the newly sodded lawn. The driveway had privacy hedges. He parked, killed the engine.

"Can't see Newman's place from here," Eli said. "Ideas?"

"Which one's his?"

"Bungalow with the steep driveway and sagging front porch. Two down, on our side."

"Needs a landscaper," Carpenter said. "And a wrecking ball. Done any surveillance of late?"

"My camera's in the trunk. I'll spy, you keep lookout. Anyone shows, text me. I'll have it on vibrate."

"Get in position, kid. Our Mother of the Year could arrive any time now."

Leaving the keys in the ignition, Eli popped the trunk and retrieved his Nikon digital camera, making sure the memory stick was functional. He turned off the flash, snapped a picture of the privacy hedges using a long exposure, reviewed the picture on the screen. Still worked. Shutting the trunk, he crept up the driveway and into the backyard. He scaled a chain-link fence, ducked under a gazebo in the middle of the yard. He peered into the next yard. When the coast seemed clear, he hopped over the fence, and floodlights came on. Sticking to the shadows, he hurried toward Newman's property line, hiding behind an elm tree. He looked up at Newman's house. Lights in three windows. Music playing. The backyard had a covered patio with rusty deck chairs and a table with an umbrella. Behind the patio was a large grill for barbecue, the kind a restaurant would use. A good hiding place, Eli thought and sprinted for the grill, crouching behind it. Decent vantage point. Through the sliding glass door, he could see into the kitchen and the living room: half a dozen laptops on the coffee table, two black cats skulking around the kitchen, and Newman gawking at one of the computer screens, punching keys, his foot tapping along to the music. He finished typing, pumped his fist, turned his attention to a different screen, and pulled at his hair. This screen got the middle finger. Eli snapped several pictures as Newman snatched a remote off the couch, pressed some buttons, and the music got louder. Heavy metal. Screeching guitars. Rapid, thunderous drum beat. Eli's pocket vibrated. PRIUS, the message read.

Two minutes later Sheri Stuckey appeared in the living room, cigarette in one hand, pink wine cooler in the other. She plopped down on the couch beside Newman, and Eli snapped away. Newman slapped her knee, pointed at one of the computer screens, and pumped his fist. He put his arm around her; she pushed him away. Laughing, he pressed some buttons on the remote, and the music got louder. She yelled over the music, opened the sliding glass door, shooed away one of the black cats, and lit a cigarette. Newman came outside, petted the cat who'd circled back around.

"Do you love him?"

Stuckey drank her wine cooler, ashed on a broken patio chair. "He's good to me. Good to Crystal. I'm going to get help."

Her voice was calm, even. She didn't know Almario was dead, Eli thought. Rushing hadn't told her.

Stuckey spent the next three cigarettes explaining to Newman all the things Almario had done for her and Crystal. The car. The daycare. She went on to say how she'd made arrangements to check both herself and Almario into rehab.

She said, "I told him I wouldn't be his supplier no more, that he'd have to find it someplace else. Even told him how much Crystal loved him and wanted him to come with me to Whispered Promises. D had Almario so paranoid he ran off. Didn't even tell his coach where he was going."

"My l-l-landlords came by today," said Newman, still stroking the cat's head. "They had a d-detective with them."

"Sharpe is his name. He came by the Earl tonight. Thinks his shit don't float, but I hope he finds Go Go."

"Y-you really going to rehab?"

Stuckey nodded, flicked her cigarette into the yard. "We're both going."

Stuckey and Newman went back inside, and Eli sneaked back to the truck, tossing the camera in the backseat. Carpenter started the truck, drove down Kenilworth.

"Well?"

Eli told him what Stuckey had said about cutting Almario off from her supply of cocaine and getting them both into rehab, about all the things Almario had done for Stuckey and Crystal. By the time Carpenter pulled into the Walmart parking lot, half of Eli was convinced Almario's death was an accident.

But that still left his other half, which was suspicious. Highly so.

CHAPTER 14

At a quarter after eight the following morning, Eli rolled off the lumpy futon in his office, kicking empty Red Bull cans as he shuffled toward the window. The rusty Saab in the parking lot was still stranded, windows broken, graffiti all over the body.

"Apropos," Eli muttered, tasting his own sour breath. He moved to the bathroom, opened the mini-fridge, and drank OJ from the carton while examining his reflection in the mirror. Dark circles under the eyes. Facial tic from the previous night's caffeine intake. Hair: disheveled. Teeth: in need of a thorough cleaning. When he'd made it back home the night before, all he wanted to do was drink and forget. But his conscience wouldn't let him, so he bought a twelve-pack of Red Bull, spent the small hours poring over his case notes and trying to shake the images of Almario's black, rotted cheeks and shocked eyeballs. The OJ turned his stomach, and he slammed the refrigerator shut. Stalked to his desk. Got out the whiskey. Stared at the label. *Est'd 1970 George Dickel Sour Mash Whiskey Brand No. 8.* Unscrewing the cap, he inhaled. Oak and corn, a bit of molasses. He took a sip, a dainty one, and swallowed. He heard a knock on the door and hid the bottle.

"I'm in no mood for company," Eli said, wanting to lock the door but getting there too late.

Waring followed by Gifford. Waring was wearing pleated

slacks and a collared golf shirt with the Colorado Rockies logo on the breast. Gifford was wearing a navy blue suit, his barrel chest threatening to bust through the fabric at any moment.

Eli stood in the opened doorway, watched Gifford sidestep the Red Bull cans. Waring sat behind the desk, jerked a thumb toward the picture of Eli Sharpe in a Tampa Bay Devil Rays uniform.

"You never quite made it, did you, Eli? Oh, you had the talent, but everybody in this business has talent. You came *this* close." Waring held his thumb and forefinger a millimeter apart. Then shook his head. "But you never put it all together. And now you live here. With your memories and spy novels and posters of Tricky Dick."

"Pathetic," Gifford said.

Eli gritted his teeth. "I attempt to move from failure to failure without loss of enthusiasm. Speaking of which, where were you last night, Mr. Waring?"

Gifford uncrossed his arms.

Waring held up his hand. "Easy, Mr. Gifford, he's just letting off some steam after a trying night. But I'm glad you mentioned failure, Eli, as I've come here to express my disappointment in you."

Eli moved to the center of the room and yanked the cord, quickly remembering the ceiling fan was broken and he hadn't gotten around to moving to an apartment with central air. Not that he ever would.

"I should get this fixed. Fans are good for allergy sufferers. I read that somewhere."

"I expected more from you, Eli. You should have gotten to Almario sooner."

"He should have gone to the police, Mr. Waring."

"My client didn't want to involve the police."

"Then for Almario's sake," said Waring, "you should have persuaded her, Eli."

"You can be persuasive, can't you, Sharpe?" Gifford had a

day's worth of stubble on his chin and a nasty gleam in his eye. "You persuaded your client you were capable of finding Almario, right? More capable than the police? Than us?"

"Mr. Gifford has a point." Waring wagged his finger. "Our organization is significantly larger than DMSI."

"And we work together," Gifford added. "We're plugged into a network of private investigators and police departments across the country."

"You work by yourself is the point," said Waring. "Now that may have served you well in the past, but in this case it hurt you. Which means it hurt us. This is a PR disaster."

Eli spun the ceiling fan. Dust bunnies rained down on Gifford. "It hurt Almario, not us. As for you, I don't give a damn about your public relations disaster. Now if you don't mind—"

"Ah, but I do mind. I didn't come here to argue with you, Eli. I came here for a full report. One of my valued employees is dead. I owe it to the organization to find out precisely what happened."

"Tell us about the drugs, Sharpe. We know there was a drug connection somewhere."

"What Mr. Gifford means—"

"Stop translating English to English," said Eli. "I know exactly what he means."

"As an executive, it is my duty to protect the organization from any legal entanglements that could arise from this tragedy. Do you understand?"

Eli opened the middle desk drawer, pulled out his leather notebook. "Get out of my chair."

"I don't care for your tone, Eli."

"One more time for the hearing-impaired: I don't care if your owners have 'legal entanglements,' Frank. A kid is dead."

"Come now, Eli. Tell us about the drugs. Maria admitted Almario had a substance abuse problem. What did you find out?"

"You're only interested in covering your ass."

Gifford told Eli to back away from Mr. Waring. Eli ignored him, continued glaring at Waring's shiny bald pate. "Maybe I'll do a little digging into your past, Frank. I'm sure there's a skeleton or two in your closet somewhere. Maybe I'll dig up a juicy tidbit about you, give your bosses something to think about."

A hand gripped Eli's shoulder blade, and he spun on his heel. A hairy fist hurtled toward his face, and Eli jerked his head and right shoulder back ninety degrees, watched Gifford's punch land squarely on the picture of Eli in a Tampa Bay Devil Rays uniform. The glass frame shattered. Gifford yelped like a wounded animal. Waring fell out of the chair, stumbled toward the door, his hands up, his eyes scared.

"Steady, Eli. Don't do anything rash."

Gifford straightened to full height, examined his bloody hand with a mixture of fascination and rage. He looked at Eli and then at the shards of broken glass on the desk. When Gifford bent to pick up a piece, Eli lowered his shoulder and drove Gifford into the wall. Another yelp. Followed by a thud on the floor. Waring sprinted out the door, leaving behind a trail of threats.

"Your boss really had your back."

"Don't need his help," Gifford said and retrieved a spring-loaded sap from inside his suit jacket. With his good hand, Gifford swung the sap low and hard, aiming at Eli's kneecaps, but Eli stepped to the left, out of harm's way. Gifford swung again, harder and wilder, and Eli stepped to the right. *Whiff.*

"Gifford, I think you work for an asshole."

"Sharpe, I think you're an asshole." Gifford swung a third time, throwing himself off balance, and Eli landed a decent punch on Gifford's cauliflower ear. The sap fell, and Eli picked it up, took two steps backwards. Gifford was on his knees, doubled over in pain, one hand holding his bleeding ear, the other rubbing the small of his back. Gifford looked at the hand that had been holding the cauliflower ear. Speckled with red blood.

"Truce?" Eli tossed the sap onto the futon, offered Gifford a hand. Gifford sucker-punched him and stood up on his own.

"Truce."

They both caught their collective breath. Eli laughed. It hurt his kidney.

"I'm meeting with Veronica Craven later today. Afterward, I'll write up a full report and send it to you."

Gifford shook his head. "Waring won't like it. The report has to be addressed to Waring. Chain of command."

"Will it help you out?"

"It will. And I'll owe you."

"How can I say no to a man who tries to break my kneecaps? That hand needs stitches." Eli called urgent care, spoke to and flirted with Elizabeth, fiancée number four, and then wrapped Gifford's hand with a bath towel and walked him outside. No Waring. Surprise, surprise. Eli gave Gifford a ride to urgent care on Lexington Avenue.

"Just ask for Libby. Chestnut hair. Pretty as a prayer book."

"Obliged." Gifford opened the door with his good hand, leaned through the opened window. "Almario Gato. What happened?"

Eli weighed the serious look in Gifford's eye against the pain in his own kidney. He slid the gear into neutral, told the tale a fourth time. Gifford listened hard, took a while before responding.

"This coke dealer, Rushing. He took you right to the body?"

"More or less."

"And the fiancée, Stuckey, she stood to gain financially from Almario's death?"

"An insurance policy, yes. Half a million, I'm told, but don't know for sure."

Gifford nodded as blood trickled down his neck from his ear. "In your gut, you believe it was an overdose?"

"My gut tells me there's more to it."

"You going to investigate?"

Eli spread his hands.

"I have a son a year younger than Almario." Gifford laid a bloodied business card on the dashboard. "Call my cell if you find anything."

"I might take you up on that."

"About Waring badmouthing you. Word is he's on his way out. I hear whispers around the water cooler."

"A pity."

"The man's a prick."

"Make sure you tell the receptionist to bill Frank Waring."

At noon, Eli entered Two Guys Olde Style Hoagies, ordered a Submaniac and a Killian's, and carried his lunch into the dining area, the smell of freshly baked sourdough bread temporarily lightening his mood. He found Veronica Craven in the corner by the window, hiding behind oversized Gucci sunglasses. On the table before her sat a small garden salad, untouched.

Eli sat down. An uncomfortable silence followed. His empty stomach growled.

"Sorry. Only had Red Bulls for the past ten hours."

More silence.

"I haven't eaten since before it happened," said Craven.

Her cellphone buzzed. She typed a text, removed her sunglasses, gave Eli the Boardroom Glare. But her heart wasn't in it. She looked good enough to shoot a Crest commercial. Hair styled. Makeup flawless. Clothes fresh from the dry cleaners: tailored black trousers and a red Calvin Klein top that showed off part of her freckled shoulders and all of her long, moisturizer-scented neck. But this wasn't the same take-no-prisoners businesswoman he'd met only the day before. This woman was sad. Her eyes. They were a darker shade of green. They no longer sparkled like emeralds.

"Stop staring and eat."

Eli unwrapped his sandwich. Vinegar and olive oil leaked onto the table. He cursed, wiped his greasy fingertips on his jeans, looked out the window. An elderly black couple in matching sweats limped down Charlotte Street. They were both smiling, both holding two-pound weights in each hand. Eli touched the breast pocket of his seersucker jacket, felt the bulging envelope of cash. One part of him wanted to give Veronica Craven back her money, wanted to walk away and spend the next three days swimming in George Dickel and self-pity and regret. A second part of him couldn't bring himself to admit failure to a client, especially one as beautiful and as accomplished as she was. Still, a third part of him believed the case wasn't over, that Almario's death wasn't an accidental overdose.

"The emotions you're feeling, they're called hybrid emotions. Or so my shrink informs me."

Eli pushed the envelope across the table. "The advance is all there, minus a bit for taxis and gas. The VISA card is in there, too. All in, I worked about fourteen hours on the case."

"You could have prorated your fee."

"I failed."

"You work, you should be compensated."

"Not for this."

"What about expenses?"

"I'll live." Eli cringed. "Poor choice of words. My apologies."

"We're past apologies. In any case, you have nothing to apologize for."

Eli took a bite of his sandwich, had trouble swallowing. He plopped the sandwich down in a pool of oil. "How's Maria?"

"Hysterical at first. I gave her a Valium, but she's not up for making funeral arrangements. Or talking to the police. I had to identify the body. She couldn't do it." Eli stood up, made a move toward her, but she waved him off. He sat. She covered her mouth with her hand. She recovered quickly, cut her eyes left and right to make sure no one else saw.

"I can't leave her here alone. She has no one, now. No one."

Veronica put on her sunglasses.

Eli gulped at his beer, thought about the words *alone* and *no one.*

"If I thought it would help Maria, now is when I'd tell her about the first thirteen years of my life. How I spent most of that time in public libraries, alone."

"Where were your parents?" Veronica asked, her voice still shaky.

"Breaking into cars and houses. Trying to hustle up enough money for Dead tickets and magic mushrooms."

"Didn't you go to school?"

"My old man drove us from one corner of the country to the other, and then back again. Every new town, he'd pull up to the public library and hand me a dollar. I taught myself to read and write. With the help of some very nice librarians."

"My God, I thought *I* hated my father. You must really hate yours."

Eli peeled the label off of his beer. "Not anymore. Best education I ever got, really. I learned how to take care of myself, how to talk to women—I have a big soft spot for librarians. I even learned how to tell a good lie when the situation warranted one. Like when Social Services wanted to separate me from my parents."

"Your parents are criminals."

"Were. Past tense. But it all worked out in the end. When I was thirteen, my old man found a job at the VA hospital here in Asheville, and I made damn sure he kept it. We rented a nice house, and I went to school and hit a growth spurt and discovered baseball. So it goes." Eli finished his beer, ashamed, as usual, at how cathartic it felt to tell a woman—an attractive, whip-smart woman—his story. He pulled out his leather-bound notebook, leafed through the pages, stalling for time. Although he'd been rehearsing what he'd say to Veronica Craven, he still wasn't sure which details to include and which to leave out. One thing he knew for sure: full disclosure was not an option. Confessing his own failure to confront Almario—face to face—when he'd had the chance would assuage his own guilt, but it would do Veronica Craven no good. And it would devastate Maria Gato.

"Things moved quickly," Eli said. "I had to act on information as soon as I received it."

"I meant what I said. I don't hold you responsible for what happened."

"Did Maria tell you about Almario's drug problem?"

Veronica shook her head. "Some bubble-headed blonde on the morning news mentioned something about a possible overdose. Maria said nothing."

"What did Maria tell you?"

"Just that Almario was mixed up with a single mother, that he was trying to help her and her daughter."

"That's true. Sharon Stuckey, the single mother, is or was involved in distributing cocaine. She and Dantonio Rushing, her partner, work at and deal out of a dive bar on Tunnel Road called the Burly Earl. A few sources confirmed Almario frequented this bar. That's where he met Stuckey and Rushing."

"So how long had Almario been associating with drug dealers?"

"Going on a year, maybe more. Right around the time he injured his knee."

Veronica picked up a plastic fork, pushed a cucumber around her plate. She pushed the salad away from her, looked Eli dead in the eyes. "In hindsight, I should have been more supportive. A good agent—no—a decent human being would have understood the situation. What kind of person does not see a teenager being crushed under colossal expectations? I was too concerned about my own career. Always have been." Her eyes welled with tears, but she didn't look away. "This Stuckey person. What is she like?"

"Crafty, is how I would describe her. Almario was planning on marrying her."

"You cannot be serious."

"I called the county recorder. Both Almario and Stuckey filed for marriage licenses on the same day. Almario took out an insurance policy and made Stuckey the primary beneficiary. Half a million. But I haven't confirmed that yet. Stuckey was planning on checking herself and Almario into a rehab facility called Whispered Promises."

"So she wasn't just after Almario's money?"

"I didn't say that. What I can say is, Almario Gato and Sheri Stuckey had rooms reserved at Whispered Promises beginning next Monday. I already called and confirmed that. According to Stuckey, she told Almario about her plans, and he split. Wasn't up for detox. Rushing had a different version of events."

"Tell me what he said," Veronica demanded.

"That Almario ran off because he was scared of Stuckey, worried she might contrive some clever accident and collect the insurance money."

"Are you suggesting Almario was murdered?"

Eli spread his hands.

Veronica fussed with her silver antique watch. "It seems impossible Almario would have taken out another insurance policy without consulting Maria. And Maria would have asked for my input. I am, or was, Almario's agent and lawyer."

"Like I said, Rushing and Stuckey could be lying. I can't say for sure, until I meet Rushing later this afternoon. He said he had a copy of the policy. He also claimed Stuckey's ex-husband was the one who had it drawn up."

Veronica excused herself, walked to the counter, and came back with two mini-bottles of Cabernet. She opened one and drank half of it.

"This whole thing is fucked." She finished the first bottle and opened the second. "Tell me what else you know."

"I know both Stuckey and Rushing claimed to have stopped selling Almario coke. Stuckey told me she wanted both her and Almario to check into rehab, and that's when Almario disappeared."

"He refused to go?"

"She refused to give Almario drugs, allegedly. Said if they were to be married, they were going to rehab. It spooked him, and he went into hiding."

"Hiding? So this whole thing was over Almario not wanting to go to rehab?"

"Maybe, maybe not. There's another wrinkle: I think Rushing had a crush on Almario. Rushing claimed Stuckey was using Almario and that Almario was in danger. Almario was probably already paranoid from drug use, and Rushing filled his head with all sorts of scenarios. Rushing told him it would be best if he disappeared for a while. He led us to the abandoned mental health facility where we found Almario last night. If nothing else, this whole thing deserves a closer look. I suggested as much to Meachum last night."

She finished the second mini-bottle. "It sounds to me like both of them had motives and opportunities to do Almario harm. Rushing was jealous of Stuckey's relationship with Almario. That is his motive. Stuckey wanted Almario's money. That is hers."

"You could be onto something."

"Do not patronize me. Tell me what else you know."

"Last night, after we found Almario, I followed Stuckey to her ex-husband's house. Snapped a few pictures. Did some eavesdropping. I don't think she knew Almario was dead. She didn't know where he was hiding, either. My sense is, Almario was good to her and her daughter, and she appreciated it."

"You really believe she stopped selling Almario cocaine?"

"No way to know for sure, but yeah, I do. Which leads us back to Rushing. Who, in my professional opinion, is too smart."

"Agreed. Nobody with any thought of self-preservation would lead detectives to a dead body if he had anything to do with the death. So where does that leave us?"

"In the hands of Bill Meachum. He's in charge of the death investigation."

"I saw him on TV this morning. I've never seen a policeman

with a ponytail. Or a leather jacket."

"Carpenter tells me Meachum's plenty capable," Eli said. "Maybe he can answer some of the questions we can't. Either way, I'll call him later today."

"You will not call. You will go to his office and speak with him." She slid the envelope of cash back across the table. "I want you to assist in the investigation. I need to know what really happened to Almario."

"You don't need me," Eli said, pushing the envelope back where it came from.

"Yes, I do. Police must adhere to policies and procedures. They're bound by laws. They have chains of command to follow. You don't." She picked up Eli's hand, placed it gently atop the envelope. Her face softened. "Please."

Eli walked Veronica outside to her rental car, watched as she drove down Charlotte Street, heat trails rising up off the asphalt. Sweating from the midday heat, he jammed his hands in his pockets, the scent of her perfume mingling with the cooking pavement. His cellphone rang.

"Mr. Sharpe?"

"Speaking."

"Donna Rogall here. We met yesterday evening."

"Mr. Newman's landlord, I remember."

"You asked me to call if Mr. Newman's ex-wife showed."

"She's there now?"

"She was five minutes ago. Her daughter was with her. Police took them both away."

Eli thought a moment as he watched a pink-haired teenage girl with gold-rimmed glasses ride a skateboard down the sidewalk, her nose stuck in a thick book. "Was one of them really tall? Long hair? Might have been chewing tobacco?"

"Lord, yes, he was a giant. And I didn't think policemen could have long hair."

"He's a criminal investigator, Mrs. Rogall. Different rules."

"Criminal investigator? What's this about? Hank fixed the

bathroom and got the place cleaned up, not that Mr. Newman said one word of thanks."

"How did Newman's ex react when the police arrived?"

"Hank saw the squad car pull into the driveway and called me over to the window. From what I saw, she was an emotional wreck. She was crying and looked like she was about to fall over."

Meachum must have told Stuckey about Almario, hence, her reaction. Either that or she was a hell of an actress.

Eli thanked her, checked his Seiko: 12:49 p.m. Looking both ways twice, Eli jogged across Charlotte Street to the Ingles grocery store, bought a copy of the *Asheville Citizen Times.* Back in his truck with the air conditioning on full tilt, he scanned the front page. Above the fold was news of yet another suicide bombing in Afghanistan with grainy but unsettling pictures. Below the fold, two stories. One about a house fire in Biltmore Forest, the other about an escaped convict wanted for bombing an abortion clinic in Buncombe County. Authorities had been looking for the bomber for years, figured he was living somewhere in the Blue Ridge Mountains and surviving off the land. Eli unfolded the paper and looked inside. Page three. The story of Almario Gato took up about four inches of space. Meachum was quoted by the reporter, "I'm not gonna espouse theories, although there was some evidence of drug use. I can tell you we've collected evidence from the scene. The ME is gonna examine the body. Post mortem tests will be a top priority. From the tests we'll make a determination of death, but it'll take time, weeks probably."

Eli finished reading the article, and then read it a second time. And then a third. And a fourth. After the fifth reading, he began thinking about the people in Almario's life and looking for motives, methods, and opportunities. "Find the MMO," Carpenter has said all those years ago.

As Eli drove to DMSI Investigations, the knot in his stomach began to loosen.

CHAPTER 15

Carpenter was in his office, glued to the ancient color TV perched on the end of his cluttered desk, his mustache dusted with white donut powder.

Eli moved a pile of folders and sat on the edge of the desk so he could see the TV. Bill Meachum being interviewed by the local TV news.

Carpenter said, "He needs to cut that hair. He's not the cool high school quarterback anymore."

"You got a history with Meachum?"

"A long one. Goes all the way back to senior prom."

"I'd like to hear it."

Eli moved to a chair. Carpenter pulled a cigar from out of the breast pocket of his purple and gold Hawaiian shirt, sniffed it, put it back in his pocket.

"Just don't like him. Cops are like dogs that way."

"Territorial?"

"It's deeper than that. It's visceral. I never liked him. But he's smart. Well, smart enough. I just don't like his act." Carpenter switched off the TV and leaned back in his chair, put his hands behind his large bald head.

"I didn't sleep for shit last night."

"You know why, don't you?"

"Sure, I know. A kid is dead. A drug addict, maybe, but a

kid just the same. 'A real detective won't sleep until he puts the shit back in the donkey.'" They both tried to laugh, but it didn't work. Eli took a hard look at the pictures on the wall. Carpenter in his Army fatigues, M16 at the ready. Carpenter in his suit and tie, his Saint Bernard face studying the cordoned-off crime scene. Carpenter and his daughter before prom. She was wearing a candy-apple colored red dress and silver tiara, blonde curls cascading over her shoulders. Carpenter stood behind her, had both arms wrapped around her, shielding her from an unforeseen future.

"You know something seems off," said Carpenter. "Too many questions about this one. Speak to me. Tell me what you're thinking."

"I think Stuckey and Rushing are telling the truth."

"You said Almario bought her a ring, paid for the daughter to go to day care. Sounds like she had motive to keep him around, not get rid of him."

"But there's also the insurance policy. Half a million is a lot of money. I can't shake this feeling."

"That feeling is guilt," Carpenter said, his voice rising. He aimed a finger at Eli. "And you can't let it go. So control it. Use it."

"Gladly. Just tell me how."

"No, I won't. I'm the snappy dresser. You're the smart one. You tell me how."

Eli looked at Carpenter and then at the pictures of Carpenter behind framed glass. Good father. Honorable soldier. Decorated cop. Mentor. Father figure. Eli had no firsthand experience with parenting techniques, but every time Ernest Carpenter paid Eli a compliment, it meant something to him.

Eli looked back at Carpenter.

"I saw him. Yesterday afternoon. Alive and well. He couldn't have been more than forty feet away. I saw him and he saw me, and I let him go, let him run right into the woods." Eli studied the backs of his hands, clenched and unclenched his fists. "His sister's got nobody now."

Carpenter pounded his fist on the desk. "Congratulations, you're a human being. I froze in Vietnam, five, six times. I froze while walking a beat. I froze just before my wedding ceremony. The goddamned priest had to drag me out of a supply closet. Look at me, son. I said, look at me. Did you have anything to do with Almario's death?"

"No, I didn't."

"Then you've got nothing to be ashamed of. That guilt you feel." He patted his gut. "Hold on to it. Use it. Don't wait around for Meachum or anybody else to tell you what happened to Almario. Figure it out yourself. I'll help. Just as soon as you stop feeling sorry for yourself."

Eli scrolled through the pictures he'd uploaded to his phone. Newman sitting in his living room staring at six laptops. Newman and Stuckey standing on the patio, Stuckey smoking a cigarette and drinking a pink wine cooler. Eli thought out loud.

"Stuckey's ex-husband wrote the insurance policy, right?"

"Newman's his name. But we don't have confirmation on that."

"And we don't want to wait to hear from Rushing. So."

"So you got an idea?"

"Let's go talk to the man with the stutter."

Newman's house on Kenilworth. Eli bounded up the steps and onto the sagging front porch, pounded on the door. No answer. Carpenter blew the truck horn, signaled for Eli to look in the windows. Eli did. A black cat with neon green eyes stared back at him from Newman's couch, showed its teeth. Eli checked under the welcome mat for a spare key. Termites. He looked under a potted plant, which had died long ago. Spiders. He pounded on the door again, called Newman's house phone, heard it ring itself out. He called Newman's cellphone. Voicemail.

Carpenter blew the horn again. "Neighbors," he yelled

through the window and pointed to the Rogall's much nicer bungalow, two doors down.

On the second knock Hank Rogall appeared in the doorway, still clothed in head-to-toe denim, his face splattered with burnt orange paint. He looked at Eli, and then at the paint roller in his hand, and then back at Eli.

"Mr. Sharpe, my wife is at spin class. Do you know what a spin class is?"

"Stationary bike. Good cardiovascular exercise, or so I'm told. Probably why your wife looks like she's still in her thirties."

"I'll tell her you said so, she'll be so tickled. Hey, I slept better last night knowing our house wasn't going to float away because of a leaky toilet. Thanks a million for getting us inside."

"Maybe you want to help me sleep better tonight?"

"How could I do that?"

"Tell me where Mr. Newman works."

"You still huntin' the ballplayer?"

"You didn't read the paper this morning?"

"Just the funnies."

"You're a wise man. Yes, I found the missing ballplayer. Now I'm trying to find out why he ended up where he ended up. I think your tenant might have some information. Important information."

"Say no more," Hank said holding up his free hand. "He works at Mountain Ridge Insurance. Across town on Haywood Street. He writes policies. Wears a suit and tie to work. I see him most mornings."

Hank Rogall smeared orange paint on Eli's hand when he shook it.

From Kenilworth, Eli took Tunnel Road to I-240 West, and then I-70 to Haywood Road. The neighborhood: brick starter homes on quarter acre lots. Gravel driveways with carports. Silver-haired ladies in track suits walking the cracked sidewalks. Clean-cut black kids tossing Nerf footballs. A nice, affordable place to live. The Allstate office was the largest and best-kept house on the street, complete with an inviting front porch and a newly paved, eight-space parking lot. Eli picked a spot and killed the engine.

"I'm in there with you?" Carpenter asked.

"In the chair next to me," Eli said. "Just follow my lead."

"Lead on, protégé."

Eli told a pack of harmless lies to the receptionist, and within five minutes of arriving, Eli and Carpenter were sitting in cushioned swiveling armchairs inside an office with drab carpeting, one window and zero charm. Behind the desk sat Brad Newman. Early forties. Full head of wavy, salt and pepper hair. Ruddy complexion. Puppy dog eyes. Feminine mouth. He wore a tan, off-the-rack suit and a bright green necktie. Beside his laptop sat a steaming mug of tea, the bag still in it. It smelled like Earl Grey.

"Gentlemen, w-what type of policy are you looking for?"

"The one you wrote for Almario Gato," Eli said. "We'd appreciate the details."

Newman's salesman smile vanished. He reached for the phone.

Eli said, "Mr. Newman, we know your ex-wife sells blow, yet she still has partial custody of your daughter."

Newman put the phone down, sucked air as if he was out of breath. "W-w-w-woman judge. Biased."

Carpenter said, "Sounds like you need to grow up. Women run the world, Newman, and thank the good Lord they do."

"Amen," said Eli. "Look, Mr. Newman, I just need the details of Almario Gato's insurance policy."

Newman shaped his lips into a cryptic smile. He opened the window a crack, made sure the Venetian blinds were closed, and then reached into a desk drawer, came up with a silver cigarette case. He lit a hand-rolled joint, blew the smoke toward the window. Earthy smell. Undertones of citrus. Newman took another long drag, exhaled a contrail of smoke.

"Is that dope?" Carpenter asked.

Newman held up a finger and took another hit, exhaled. His puppy-dog eyes glazed over. He sat down, held the joint away from his suit.

"S-speech therapy didn't work. Ss-Psychotherapy. C-cannabis is the only thing that w-works."

After Newman finished smoking, he doused himself with Canoe cologne and sprayed Lysol everywhere. By the time he was finished clearing the room of pot smoke, Eli was dizzy. Newman put Visine in his eyes, looked at Eli, muttered a string of nonsense phrases. No stutter.

"So you want to know about the dead man's policies, correct? Don't look so shocked. I read the newspaper, too. Sharon phoned twenty minutes before you arrived. The cops came to question her. She'd been staying at my house for a day or two. She was quite frightened."

"You don't sound too concerned," Carpenter said.

"Crystal is all that matters to me."

"Then why aren't you at the police station right now?" Eli asked.

"Because I have appointments. I have rent to pay."

"And online poker to play," Carpenter said.

"You were in my house," said Newman. "You went through my internet history. Those are crimes."

Eli grinned. "He wasn't, but I was. Don't look so shocked. The Rogalls invited me in. Very nice couple. Hank was worried about the shape his house was in. Did you know the toilet was leaking?"

"How did you find out where I live?" Newman asked, his pupils widening.

"I was hired to find Almario. I tracked you from cellphone records, but I'll come back to that in a minute. For now, tell me when you met Almario and wrote the policy."

Newman crossed his arms. "I can tell you that just as soon as you get authorization to force me to disclose confidential information. I'm not risking my job for you or anybody else, so tell your mustachioed bodyguard to glare elsewhere. If you wanted to find out about his insurance policies, you should have found him sooner and asked him yourself."

Carpenter white-knuckled his armrests.

Eli moved toward Newman, who put his hand on the telephone. "Touch me and I call the police."

Eli reached inside the desk and snatched the silver cigarette case. He looked at Carpenter. "I count five joints. Could be an eighth, no?"

"More like a quarter ounce," Carpenter said. "Possession. No muss, no fuss."

"A possession charge? No jail time, but it's more than enough to get you fired."

"Might get him to watch his tongue, too. How 'bout it?"

Hand shaking, Newman put the phone back on the receiver. "If I lose my job—"

"You lose Crystal, you lose your home. You're getting the idea."

"Maybe that's not such a bad thing," said Carpenter. "The guy smokes dope on the job."

"And he doesn't care that the mother of his kid snorts and sells blow. Doesn't bat an eye when the mother of his kid gets hauled away by the cops."

"No, no, maybe he's trying to do right," Carpenter said. "That's medicinal, a way to cope. Talking to people is part of his profession. And the gambling, well, hell, he's going to get that under control, too, right?"

Newman kept quiet.

"But in the meantime," Eli said, "he's going to tell us what we need to know, right, partner?"

"For his own sake, I hope so. I hope he bends the rules and gives us what we need."

"I hope so, too. After all, an eighteen-year-old-kid is dead behind this mess. Or do you not have a conscience, Mr. Newman?"

Newman's puppy dog eyes were scared now. Yanking his tie loose, he tossed it on the desk, took a few deep breaths.

"I can't divulge confidential information. But I can tell you a story."

Eli got out his leather notebook, clicked his pen.

Newman took another deep breath. "Suppose a highly paid athlete wants to get married. Having already been seriously injured on the job once before, he wants a life insurance policy to make sure both he and his bride are protected. Normally, obtaining a policy on an eighteen-year-old wouldn't be a problem. No medical examination would even be necessary for a policy worth up to, say, fifty to one hundred thousand, depending on income.

"But, given the young man is in a volatile profession and injury prone, if he wants a policy worth more than that, he would have to submit to a physical. And a drug test, you understand?"

"Let me guess: you know a doctor."

"I know m-many doctors."

Eli wrote in his notebook. "So, hypothetically speaking, this highly paid athlete would go to a doctor who would give him a clean bill of health and clean urine?"

"More or less, hypothetically speaking. So he would pass his physical and drug test, and the insurance agent would ask a few questions and then apply various formulas to determine how much the policy would be worth."

"Talk about the formulas and questions," Carpenter said.

"For example, what is the goal of the policy? Does he want the beneficiary to be able to stop working after his demise? Does he want all debts to be paid, both his and the beneficiary's? Et cetera."

Eli said, "And our injury prone athlete, how would he answer those questions?"

"Prudently, remarkably so, given his age and experience. He would want enough for the beneficiary to pay down all debts and have an annual income of forty thousand dollars for the next ten years. He would want a significant portion—let's guestimate seventy-five thousand dollars—for any offspring the couple could produce. Personally, as a family man myself, I think the seventy-five-K is a very wise thing to do."

"Are you saying Almario wanted policy money set aside for Crystal?"

"I'm n-not saying that at all. This is purely a hypothetical." Carpenter grunted, asked how much the policy was worth, all in. "Half a million," Newman said.

"The policy," Eli said, "when was it written?"

"It could have been written any time, seeing as how this is a fictional scenario. However, I would say about two, three months ago would have been an ideal time."

Eli flipped pages in his notebook, checked to see when Gato and Stuckey filed for marriage licenses. Two months ago.

"The last step would be to name a primary and secondary beneficiary and then divide up the money. He would want to name his wife-to-be and a second person, a parent or sibling, perhaps."

Eli held up a finger, and Newman stopped talking. Why hadn't Almario gotten a bigger policy? Half a million was chump change compared to what he could have secured for his bride-to-be. Newman's voice interrupted Eli's train of thought.

"Look, I want to help you g-gentlemen get at the truth. Since we're discussing this fictional young athlete so openly, I should inform you that it is possible, likely even, that he would have a second policy. A m-much bigger one."

Eli bargained with Newman to get more information: a second joint for the details of Almario's second policy.

"Yes, please. The stuttering gets w-worse when I'm under stress."

Eli slid the silver cigarette case across the desk, and Newman opened it with trembling hands, lit another of the hand-rolled joints. He inhaled, exhaled. Smoke escaped through the opened window. Newman's hands stopped shaking.

Carpenter said, "All right, Cheech. You've had your fix. Now talk."

Newman stubbed the joint out on the window sill. "Have you gentlemen ever heard of the four percent withdrawal rule?" They both shook their heads, and Newman continued, "I know nothing about Almario's first or second policy. I remind you, this is all hypothetical."

Carpenter said, "Next time you use the word 'hypothetical,' I'm gonna smash the fancy frames those Better Business Bureau accommodations are in. Understood?"

Newman sprayed more Lysol and sat back down. "The four percent withdrawal rule is how one determines how much money one will need to retire. We also apply it when writing life insurance policies. In the case of our hypo—I mean fictional—young athlete, he would have used the six percent withdrawal rule when the second policy was written."

"Slow down," said Eli. "Explain the six percent withdrawal rule."

"First, let me correct myself. This would not be his second policy; it would be his first. It would have been written almost a year in advance of the ah, the aforementioned policy."

Eli saw Carpenter's fists tighten, but he let the annoying word pass. He thought for a minute. So Almario's first policy was written at another insurance agency almost a year before the one Newman wrote. And this first policy was worth much more money.

Eli said, "You never explained the six percent withdrawal rule. What is it? How does it work?"

"It is quite simple. Step one, you add up all the policy holder's debts. Step two, you calculate the desired annual income for the beneficiary and multiply by six percent. That is how you would arrive at how much the policy is worth."

"I flunked math," Carpenter lied, for Eli knew his mentor was a college man. GI Bill. Phi Beta Kappa. "Just tell us how much."

"I'll get to all that. Let's say the fictional athlete had no debts, but he would want to estimate at least ten thousand dollars for accidentals. That's standard in most policies. As for the annual desired salary, he would want the beneficiary to never have to work again, so an annual desired salary of four hundred thousand dollars over twenty years is the figure I would suggest. The rest is a question of math."

Eli scribbled the numbers on his notebook: eight-point-two million dollars. He asked who the beneficiary was.

"In cases such as these, it's usually the spouse, a parent, or a sibling."

"You don't know who the beneficiary is?" Carpenter asked.

"No, I don't. After all, this is only a—"

"Hypothetical," Eli said. "We get it." Eli thought. Maria was Almario's only living relative. She took care of him. She loved him, tried to help him. Maria Gato made the most sense. Eli asked where the policy was written.

"All I can tell you is it wasn't written by me or by anyone in this office."

Eli slid the silver cigarette case across the desk. Carpenter removed one of the Better Business Bureau citations on the wall, placed it on the ground, and carefully stepped on it. Then he thanked Newman for his time.

In the truck, Eli cranked the AC. "Were you playing good cop, bad cop?"

"I'm not a cop anymore. And I don't play games. The little weasel just pissed me off. What's next?"

"We talk to another weasel," Eli said. "A much bigger one."

CHAPTER 16

Dantonio Rushing pulled into the Burly Earl parking lot in a hunter green Chevrolet Cavalier, backed carefully into the space next to Eli's truck, and got out. He was dressed for the gym—mesh cap, blue tank top, baggy black shorts and black cross trainers. Every oversized muscle and bulging vein was on display, and Eli wondered aloud how many hours a day it took to become a body builder. But Carpenter noticed something else.

"No tinted windows or flashy rims for our boy. No boom-boom music, either."

"A smart drug dealer," Eli said. "Chevrolets don't attract police attention."

Carpenter grunted. "Smart drug dealer, huh? My least favorite kind."

Eli soaked up five more seconds of AC, and then stepped into the mid-afternoon sun.

"Tell me you brought Almario's insurance policy," he said.

Rushing stopped dead in his tracks, crossed his very large arms over his very large chest.

"Is that it? No 'I'm sorry a close friend of yours died alone in the middle of the woods'? No 'I'm sorry you spent the night being interrogated by police officers and crying your eyes out'?"

Rushing's eyes were red rimmed and swollen. After stringing together another half dozen rhetorical questions, he burst into a fit of sobbing, which ended with him kicking a sizable dent in a nearby dumpster.

Then he produced a red folder from the backseat of his car.

"What you wanted," Rushing said and stuffed the folder in Eli's breadbasket, knocking the wind from his chest. "Almario's insurance policy. Despite my chosen profession, I am a man of my word."

Shielding his eyes from the sun, Eli scanned the pages. The details of the policy were just as Newman claimed. Sharon Stuckey was the primary beneficiary and stood to collect half a million dollars should anything unforeseen befall Almario Gato. The policy's date: April 4—roughly two and a half months prior. Almario's signature and initials were at the bottom of every page. The policy was notarized and official.

But did it mean Rushing was right about Stuckey's intentions? Could Almario's death been the result of foul play?

Eli had a hunch. A couple, in fact.

But hunches weren't proof.

Eli removed his sunglasses, looked Rushing in the eyes. "My apologies for being so mistrustful of you and your intentions. I appreciate you bringing the insurance policy. And for attempting to help Almario." Even though one of Eli's hunches told him this dealer of narcotics was a better friend to Almario than most, Eli played the manipulator, hoping to get more information.

"Bottom line," Eli said, "I feel guilty about Almario. I think you feel guilty, too."

"There is a major distinction between feeling guilty and being guilty."

"Fair enough. But I think you feel something else, something more than guilt."

"Please don't psychoanalyze me. I fled my parents' house at sixteen because they sent me to a shrink."

"We're not trying to get into your head," Carpenter said, his voice gentler than usual, grandfatherly and casual. "We're trying to help your friend."

"My partner is right, but I'll go a step further. Dantonio, I feel responsible for what happened to Almario. I think you do, too."

"Don't patronize me," Rushing said unconvincingly. "You didn't lose a friend. I did."

"All right, let me put it another way: you are responsible for your friend's death. At least in part. Maybe not for his actual death, but you're responsible for his decline."

"I'm telling you I had nothing to do with it. I tried to help him." Rushing's voice rose and fell in waves.

Carpenter said, "Enough of this bullshit. You're a drug dealer."

"I'm not going to have a moral debate. With either of you."

"But you are going to help me," Eli said, his voice more insistent, more accusatory now. "You are going to help me figure out what really happened."

"What else do you want me to do? I didn't know Sharon wanted to take Almario to rehab. She doesn't tell me every little half-formed thought or idea that enters her drug-addled brain, okay? I thought I was protecting him."

Eli was half-convinced Stuckey's intentions were good. Whatever happened to Almario that night, Eli didn't think she was involved. Ditto Rushing. But there was no evidence to prove these hunches. No hard evidence, anyway. Hunter S. Thompson once said, "Never turn your back on a drug." And these were drug people. With oblique agendas and plenty to lose. Best to keep pressing, keep his guard up.

"Maybe you are helping us," Eli said, "and maybe you're not. Maybe you and Stuckey weren't supplying Almario his dope."

"But somebody was supplying him," Carpenter said. "We want to know who."

"I want to be able to go to Maria Gato and say I did all I could."

"If I knew who his supplier was, I would gladly tell you.

Honestly."

"Honestly," said Eli, "I want the name of a supplier. A competitor. Anyone Almario might have come in contact with connected to drugs."

Rushing reached into his car, found a pack of cigarettes in the glove compartment and lit one. He puffed twice. Stubbed it out. Exhaled. Lit another one.

"Ah, fuck it. I don't use the asshole anymore." He recited the phone number from memory.

Eli wrote the number down in his notebook. "What else can you tell me about the person on the other end of this phone number?"

"Not much, regrettably. I've only spoken to him on the phone. I can tell you he has a booming voice, projects every word and every syllable like a Shakespearean stage actor. That's all I know."

"A name," Carpenter barked. "We need a name."

"I don't know his name. I know his voice, which I've already described."

Eli said, "So this number, he's your supplier."

"Former supplier. I've taken my activities elsewhere."

"Tell me how you arranged things with him."

"I called. He set up a dead drop for the pickup. Just like in a spy novel. Very clandestine, although there is no need for such measures in a peaceful, low-crime city like Asheville. Anyway, there's a big house with spires and a flowerbed out front. Behind the last row of tulips is a box that holds gardening tools like shovels and hoes. Packages were left inside a ten-pound bag of fertilizer." Rushing tossed his latest cigarette. "Now, I've told you more than enough."

Rushing's cellphone rang. He turned on the engine and drove away, inconspicuous in his American car.

Eli cranked the AC, drummed on the steering wheel.

"You want me to help you check out Rushing's lead?" Carpenter asked.

"I'll do it myself. You've done enough."

After dropping Carpenter off at DMSI, Eli drove to 23 Battery Park and parked illegally across the street. Looking up at the fifth floor of Maria's apartment building, Eli dug out his cellphone. Veronica Craven answered on the fourth ring.

"This isn't a convenient time."

"Are you with Maria?"

"Yes. She's cooking a seven-course meal. Therapeutic, I suppose."

A city cop on a bicycle stopped beside Eli's truck, tapped on the window. Eli held up a finger. "Think I might have a minute to talk to her? I would like to express my condolences. Face to face."

"She would appreciate the gesture, I'm sure, but now is not convenient. I only just succeeded in coaxing her out of her bedroom. I had to make the funeral arrangements myself. St. Ann's, the day after tomorrow."

"I'll be there." The cop tapped louder on the window, pointed to the LOADING ONLY sign. Eli cranked the car, gave him the thumbs up. The cop pedaled away. Eli killed the engine. He told Veronica about his meetings with Newman and Rushing, told her about the insurance policies.

"So what will you do now?"

"I have new information to work off of while we wait for news from Meachum or the medical examiner. In the meantime I've got some questions maybe you can answer. Did you know Almario had two life insurance policies?"

Silence. Then breathing. Then, "I know of only one, the policy I personally reviewed last spring."

"It was drawn up here, in town?"

"Correct," she said her voice on edge. "At Grand Life downtown. Big glass building on Biltmore. I flew in to oversee the purchase of the apartment and the signing of the insurance policy. Part of my job was to protect Almario."

"What can you tell me about the policy?"

"Almario had only one concern: making sure Maria was protected in the event he suffered a career-ending injury, or worse. With no other living relatives, Maria would be all alone, and he didn't want her to be burdened financially."

"So Maria is the primary beneficiary?"

"Of course."

"He didn't name a secondary beneficiary?"

"As I said, Maria is his only living relative, and, as far as I knew, the most important person in his life."

"How much is the policy worth?"

"Seven, eight million, I think. Pretty standard. Memory serves, we calculated a mid-six-figure annual income and multiplied by twenty years to arrive at the final figure. Almario wanted to ensure that Maria was well-provided for." She breathed into the phone, her tone sharpened. "But I can assure you, she has no need for money."

"How so?"

"Maria made wise decisions, especially with Almario's signing bonus money. I helped her find a trustworthy accountant, and she saved enough money for her and Almario to live on for the next ten to twelve years, at least."

"A girl after my own heart," Eli said.

"Agreed. I should put her in charge of my finances." She said something in Spanish, and Maria responded. Veronica lowered her voice. "Truth be told, Maria was worried Almario's career could end abruptly. She is superstitious."

He stared out his dirtied windshield. Across the street a European-style sidewalk café was filling up with hipster artists, too hip to remove their vintage wool cardigans despite the mid-eighty degree heat.

"I'll call you later after I talk with Meachum."

"No call. Let's meet for a drink. I need a break from all of this grief."

"A drink sounds good."

Very good, Eli thought.

***

Asheville Police Headquarters sat at 100 Court Plaza, on the corner of Spruce and Majorie. A series of brick buildings of varying heights, headquarters took up about a half a block and always reminded Eli of a public library in downtown Birmingham he'd spent the night in when he was nine years old. Seeking a warmer climate to ride out January, his parents hitchhiked into town, dropped Eli off at a massive library in a sketchy part of downtown, and then promptly got arrested. Vagrancy and marijuana possession. When they finally came for him—thirty hours later—his hatred for his old man had grown stronger, but his fear of the dark, once crippling, had all but vanished. A fitful night's rest in the cave-black periodical section had cured him.

Eli parked his truck on Spruce, in front of a Gothic-looking church with spires reaching up into the clear blue sky. As he walked down the block, he felt grateful for the shade the buildings provided. Entering the lobby of the smallest of the headquarters' buildings, he emptied his pockets and passed through a metal detector while a uniformed black woman stared at his skeleton on a computer screen. He collected his wallet and cellphone on the other side.

"Could you tell me where Bill Meachum's office is?"

"CID is not in this building. Go out the way you came. Turn left. Follow the stairs to the tall beige building. Sixth floor."

Eli followed her directions.

The elevator in the tall beige building was out of order, so Eli took the stairs. By the time he found Meachum's cubicle, Eli was drenched with sweat.

Meachum had his feet propped up on the desk, his right cheek packed tight with Skoal. He was wearing a Widespread Panic T-shirt beneath a leather jacket. His desk was littered with dirty Styrofoam cups, none more befouled than the one in his hand.

Eli pulled a rolling chair from a neighboring cubicle and sat down.

"I'd advise against thieving Howard's chair. It's ergonomic. Had it made special."

"I won't be here long. I just wanted an update."

"I give my boss updates. I give victims updates."

"How about witnesses? I found Almario."

Meachum passed Eli an official-looking document. "I have your statement all typed up and ready for your John Hancock."

Eli read it twice and signed. "I have new information."

"It's too early for theories. Especially from private detectives who never walked a beat."

Stalling, Eli looked around. Through the window, a nice view of downtown. On the cubicle walls, APD's mission statement. Eli tapped the poster with the mission statement written on it. "Integrity. Fairness. Respect. Professionalism. You wrote that?"

"Not a word." Meachum spat in his cup, chuckled like Jolly Ol' Saint Nicholas. In the daylight, his legs sprawled over the desk, he appeared taller—taller and, with the thick beard and long hair, even more formidable.

"I asked Carpenter about you. He said you're capable. A real detective."

"High praise, indeed."

"I owe it to Almario's sister to find out what happened."

"Funny, I thought that was my job."

"I'm not trying to jam you up."

"All evidence to the contrary."

"The sooner you tell me what you have, the sooner I move on."

"How old are you, son?"

"Old enough to recognize the Wise Elder routine when I see it. And take offense."

Meachum pointed a finger in Eli's direction. "Take caution in your tone. I've already been dealing with the press, my bosses, and Frank Waring. The vic's lawyer called me first thing this morning, demanding I put a rush on the autopsy and tox screen."

"Maria Gato has every right to know what happened to her brother."

"Look at the bags under my eyes. Like I told the mayor, I'm on top of it."

"You on top of this, too?" Eli laid the insurance policy Rushing had given him on the desk. "Almario Gato's. It's worth half a million. Primary beneficiary is the woman you picked up this morning."

Meachum shooed the papers off his desk and back into Eli's hands. "Sharon Stuckey. I had her in the box for more than two hours. Went all over her history with Almario. She talked about how he cared for her and her little girl, but cared a bit more about snorting."

"So you've heard the rehab story?" Meachum nodded and spat. Brown saliva dribbled down his chin, stuck in his beard. "I think there's more to their relationship. More to Almario's story."

"You're talking foul play. Between you, me, and the wall, the medical examiner says early signs point to overdose. Time of death was around 11 p.m. Stuckey had an alibi, as did Rushing. I had him in here for a chat this morning, too. Big son of a bitch. Well-spoken though. He took me through his relationship with Almario and Sharon. Gave me a play by play of how you and the old fart found Almario in the woods. By the way, do you have a license to carry a firearm?"

Eli ignored the question. "You say the two of them had alibis. Fine. They also had motives. Money and jealousy, for instance. Maybe they're innocent, maybe not, but this needs to be investigated."

"No, it don't. Not yet."

"If they wanted Almario out of the way, they would cover their tracks. First thing they'd do is establish alibis. There are too many unanswered questions about those two. I suspect Stuckey sent an email to Maria pretending to be Almario. In it she asked Maria not to try and find Almario. Why would she do that? And Rushing admitted he had feelings for Almario. He was jealous of Almario's relationship with Sharon. Isn't it convenient that he led Carpenter and me directly to Almario's body? That he was the only one who knew where he was?"

"All that's speculation. I work on hard evidence." He handed Eli a document with charts and numbers on it. Eli asked what it was. "I had our expert give Stuckey and Rushing polygraphs. Asked them questions about Almario's death, their role in it, et cetera. They both passed. Hell, they didn't flinch when I suggested they hook up to the box. Didn't flinch once."

Eli handed the document back to Meachum. "What did the ME have to say about the rotten flesh on Almario's face?"

Meachum clicked the mouse and a laser jet printer sprang to life. Meachum collected the pages, squinted at them a moment, and then handed them to Eli. An article from the *Los Angeles Times.* Headline read COCAINE...LACED WITH DEWORMING MEDICATION. There was a picture of a young white woman, her face riddled with dozens of black spots similar to the ones on Almario's face. Eli skimmed the opening paragraph. According to the AP reporter, batches of cocaine around the country were being cut with levamisole, a cancer medication that was also used to de-worm livestock. And make cocaine even more potent. Levamisole increased the narcotic effects of the cocaine, but also caused skin infections, sores, abscesses, thrush, pneumonia, and other serious medical problems. Half a dozen deaths had been reported in the last month, most of them in Los Angeles.

"So the ME thinks he died from levamisole poisoning?"

"Didn't say that. Doc thought he recognized the black spots and shot me an email. Professional courtesy."

"Did they test Almario's blood for drugs?"

Meachum snorted, rubbed his eyes. "You're starting to irritate me, and bad. A full tox screen workup'll take weeks."

"But does he have a hunch?"

"His initial opinion, the kid died of cardiac arrest."

"How can he tell?"

"'Cause he's been on the job since before you popped your first pimple."

Eli asked more questions. Did they find anything unusual at the crime scene? What about on Almario's person? Did they talk to Almario's friends or his sister? No. No. And yes.

"I notified Maria Gato personally. She was distraught. As for the rest, we're interviewing all the people that were at the Burly Earl last night and everyone in Almario's circle of friends."

"Christine Lovatt? Homer Hodge? Brad Newman?"

Meachum held up his hand. "This is a sad business, but not uncommon. Kid got mixed up with drugs. Wasted talent." Meachum spat, leaned back in his chair, achieving total immobility. On the cubicle wall behind him, beside the APD mission statement, was a plaque from the mayor of Asheville. BILL MEACHUM, it read, IN HONOR OF 15 YEARS OF DEDICATED SERVICE.

"Look son, I know how you feel. You see something godawful happen, and you want to set it right. I've been there more times than I care to count. I know what it feels like." The phone rang. Meachum picked it up, but didn't answer. "I'll call you if the doc learns anything new. Now, if you'll kindly shove off, I got work to do."

Back home, Eli changed clothes, poured a shot of George Dickel, drank and spat it in the bathroom sink, and then looked over his case notes. He typed up the official report to present to Veronica Craven, proofread it four times, and placed it in a manila folder.

Then he took out the picture of Almario in his dark suit. His clear complexion, his light eyes, his dark curly hair: they all brought to mind words like youth and vitality, beauty and potential.

Potential.

Christ, what a lethal word.

Eli couldn't accept Almario's mistakes because Eli had made the very same ones. Alcohol. Drugs. Wasted talent. Just ten short years ago Eli had been in Almario's position. Playing a child's game for ridiculous sums of money. The pressure had gotten to Eli, but he came out the other side. Almario hadn't been so lucky. Like the lone survivor from a plane crash, Eli had limped away from his misspent youth, but Almario Gato had crashed into the side of the mountain. Only question was: did he have help?

Eli licked his lips, stared daggers at the half-empty fifth of George Dickel on his desk. Ever since the day he rammed that Greyhound into the Bull, Eli had received untold tidbits of life wisdom, all of it worthless save one. "You have an overactive mind," Carpenter once said, "so stay busy." Eli calmly took the bottle of whiskey in hand, poured its contents into the toilet, flushed, and resumed his seat. He glanced out the window, trying to control his overactive mind. In the parking lot an orange cat was sleeping atop the rusty Saab, the sun cooking down on her orange and gray fur. Eli thought about what he would say to Maria at the funeral and instantly regretted flushing the liquor. What could he say to Maria Gato? *You're alone in this world. Your twin brother, the one you followed to America, the one you loved and cared for, is gone. And what's worse, I didn't do enough to stop it.*

Turning back to his desk, Eli ripped Almario's picture into halves, quarters, eighths, sixteenths. He dropped the confetti into the wastebasket, waited to feel closure. But never did.

So he drove up the Blue Ridge Parkway, hiked up Cold Mountain, swam naked in the frigid Pisgah River until he couldn't feel his arms and couldn't see Almario's rotted out face in his mind's eye.

Afterward, sitting on the hood of his truck drip-drying, he looked west beyond the sun-dappled mountains and drifting clouds toward the Tennessee border. Beautiful. Scenic. But his third eye refused to open, and his thoughts drifted to something Aubrey Meekins, his first fiancée, once told him. "You're a mechanism," she'd said when Eli, just seventeen, refused to give his newborn daughter back to her mother to be fed. "Just wind you up and set you in motion."

Thinking of his daughter, who was thirty-six days young when she died of SIDS, Eli checked his Seiko: 3:45 p.m. The watch—silver quartz LCD with a black leather band, waterproof—was a gift from Aubrey on Eli's seventeenth birthday. Even though he hadn't spoken to Aubrey Meekins since the day of their daughter's funeral, he'd worn the watch every day for the last eighteen years. He'd told every fiancée the watch kept good time, but he knew the real reason.

A family of overweight travelers spilled out of a minivan, complaining loudly about the heat and the curvy drive up the mountain.

Eli got in his truck, cranked up the AC, and called the telephone number Rushing had given him. The outgoing message was generated by a computerized voice. No names. Eli left his cellphone number and drove down the parkway and back into town to Montford Park, a historic neighborhood filled with old Victorians. He spent an hour walking along the streets, using his cellphone to take pictures of every house with spires and a flowerbed out front. There were dozens. He couldn't be sure he was even in the right neighborhood.

When he climbed back inside the truck, his cellphone rang.

"I need carbohydrates," Veronica Craven said. "Do you like Italian?"

CHAPTER 17

At Modesto Trattoria, a dimly-lit Italian restaurant on the hip and happening end of College Avenue downtown, Veronica Craven ordered a double-Absolut martini, a plate of squid ravioli for herself, and a whole Mediterranean sea bass on wood-fired ratatouille for Eli.

"And a Coke," Eli said. The waitress smirked, and Veronica said something in Italian. The waitress nodded, scurried away. Veronica raised her martini glass, and Eli clinked it with his own. She was wearing an ivory button-up blouse and gray pin-stripe trousers, her emerald eyes sparkling in the candlelight.

"I feel overmatched," Eli said tugging at the lapels of his best and only blazer. "In more ways than one."

"I apologize for ordering for you."

"In Italian, no less."

"I'm so sorry. Truly." A spot of color formed on her freckled cheek. She gulped the remainder of her drink, chewed and swallowed the olive stuffed with gorgonzola. "I speak it so rarely. As a child, I spent my summers in Tuscany. Father had a villa with land. Olive trees. A vineyard."

"Sounds idyllic."

"Father was never around, always off on business, but the fields were our babysitter." She held her martini glass aloft, tapped on the side until the waitress acknowledged her. "Just listen to me. Tuscany. Vineyards. I must sound spoiled. And callous. I should not have left Maria at home."

"Is she doing any better?"

Veronica put the martini to her lips, quickly realized it was empty, and blushed. She scratched her thumb with her pointer finger, and a spot of blood rose to the surface. "It was the oddest thing," she said when she noticed the blood and stopped scratching. "Maria made this dinner reservation. Even helped me pick out this outfit."

"Then she's to be commended," Eli said.

"You're not totally unpresentable yourself."

"May I ask what you're going to do now? About work, I mean."

She scratched her thumb twice, winced. Laid her hands flat on the table. "I do have other clients, but I must confess none of them pay the bills nearly as well as Almario. Nonetheless, I need to figure it out soon. L.A. is expensive. Perhaps I'll go back to the law."

"Plenty of clients in Beverly Hills."

The waitress carefully set a replacement martini on the table and hurried off. Veronica sipped. Her shoulders relaxed. "I could open my own firm, concentrate on divorce. Although I sincerely doubt clients would be too impressed with my seven-hundred-square-foot studio apartment on the Wilshire Corridor. I can't afford a separate office."

"Money isn't everything."

"Said the boy-man with no debts."

"I have plenty of debts," Eli said. "Just not those kind."

A nervous laugh. Another sip of martini. "I envy you. I think I even *like* you."

"Veronica, we need to talk about Almario."

She clenched her jaw. "Your timing is impeccable. Here I was feeling vulnerable and you listened with your kind eyes and pretended not to understand the menu, so I could show off, and then you had to ruin my good time by calling attention to the elephant in the room. You just had to bring me back down to Earth."

Eli waited.

Veronica fumed for a bit, silently sipping her drink. "I'm not a cold-hearted bitch. I just wanted a break."

Eli waited some more, wished his Coke contained a heavy dose of Tennessee bourbon instead of industrial quantities of corn syrup and sugar.

"Remember I told you Almario had black spots on his face? Meachum received an email from the medical examiner. Turns out the cocaine Almario bought might have been laced with something called levamisole."

"That rings a bell somewhere. Why?"

"Internet says it's used to de-worm livestock. And drug suppliers use it to increase the buzz."

Veronica snapped her fingers. "Oh yes, I remember. My stepmother, the second one, the one I liked, died of colon cancer. She took levamisole. So what does this mean? Almario was deliberately poisoned?"

"Not sure. A toxicology report will take up to six weeks. But almost half of the cocaine in circulation is laced with levamisole. Meachum polygraphed the two most likely suspects, Stuckey and Rushing. Both passed."

"Those tests are inconclusive."

"My sentiments exactly. That said, my gut tells me Rushing cared for Almario. Stuckey, too."

"So Almario killed himself?"

Eli finished his soda. "I have my official report back at the office."

Her eyes tearing up, Veronica excused herself and Eli listened to her high heels on the black and white tile floor. When she returned, her eyes were clear, her makeup restored to its previous glory. She set her shiny black clutch on the table.

The food arrived, and they ate in silence.

Eli checked his Seiko: 9:13 p.m.

"I'll take you back to Maria," Eli finally said.

"No, I can't go back there right now." Clutch in hand, she stood up, grabbed Eli's wrist, and squeezed. "Let's go somewhere else. Anywhere. Just not there."

Eli's pulse quickened. Her perfume. Her vodka-laced breath. The vulnerability in her impossibly green eyes.

"What about the bill?" he asked.

"It's taken care of." She let go his wrist, tilted her head toward the door, and walked, leaving perfume in her wake. Light Blue by Dolce & Gabbana. Eli followed, a million and one thoughts racing through his brain.

Half an hour later, Eli stared up the cracked ceiling in his apartment. In the semi-darkness he could make out the Tigris and Euphrates Rivers snaking over the popcorn ceiling. The scent of Veronica Craven filled his nostrils. He tasted her on his lips and tongue, felt her naked and warm beside him.

"I'm out of shape. I need oxygen."

"What you need is a proper bed. A grown man should not sleep on a futon." Veronica straddled him again. She leaned down to kiss his forehead, her hair tickling his face. He wrapped his arms around her waist, pulled her in close enough to feel her heart beating against his bare chest.

"I cannot believe I just made love in a studio apartment. On a futon. To a private detective."

"Private investigator, Miss Craven."

"'Private investigator, Miss Craven.'" She buried her cheek in his chest, giggled and then was silent.

"I hope that's not post-coital regret you're feeling."

"Not at all. It's just, I get it now."

"Get what?"

"Your history with women. All the fiancées. Why so many have fallen for you."

"Reciprocity is the key."

She pulled his chest hair. "I'm not talking about sex, asshole.

But since you broached the subject, you're merely proficient in that arena. I was referring to the way you deal with people, how you talk to them. Like Maria. You told her that story about your father and Cuban coffee to make her more comfortable talking to you. You were open and honest, and you're so at ease with yourself, you encourage others to do likewise. It is, well, unnerving."

"I know you said romance was out of the question, but just in case this turns into something more, I have a confession: that story I told Maria wasn't completely true." She sat up, brushed her hair behind her ears as he added, "But it wasn't a lie, either. It was a half-truth. My father did drag us to Florida, but I've never had Cuban coffee before."

She rolled over to her side of the futon. Sighed. Stared at the ceiling a beat. "Have you told any other lies?"

"Half-truths."

"What about you?"

Eli thought of Almario's sledgehammer, how Almario had sprinted right by Eli and into the woods, but before he could confess his failure, Veronica took his erection in her hand.

"You said you had new information. Tell me about it."

The next morning Veronica Craven was gone, but her perfume lingered. Half awake, Eli buried his face in the sheets. Smiling, he rolled off the futon, removed his T-shirt and boxers on the way to the bathroom. He checked his reflection in the mirror. Disheveled hair. Sleepy eyes. Scratches on his stomach and shoulders. He stepped into the shower, whistling. With a beautiful, intelligent woman lying naked beside him, he'd slept soundly. No nightmares. No bouts with his conscience. He was in such a good mood he didn't mind that Veronica hadn't said goodbye or left a flirty note.

But when the cold water hit his face, it all came back to him. The guilt. The image of Almario's rotted face, his youth ruined.

The nagging suspicions about his death. Eli shampooed his hair as more images swarmed in his head. Maria in a black dress, standing over the casket with a red rose in her hand. Eli scrubbed and scrubbed his scalp, his chest, his arms, his legs, but he still felt dirty.

Dressed in khakis, a white T-shirt, and a seersucker jacket, Eli opened the front door and retrieved the morning newspaper. Sitting behind his desk, he skimmed the front page. Stock market up and down. Terrorist attacks in Iraq. Global warming. All in all: status quo on planet Earth. He found Almario on page four. The medical examiner, according to the reporter, had put a rush on the post mortem tests, but early signs pointed to accidental death by drugs. Meachum was quoted again. "This is an unfortunate case. By all accounts, Almario Gato was a good kid, a ballplayer with a bright future." Frank Waring was quoted too, but it was the usual platitudes. Invaluable to our organization. A human tragedy. Vague talk of starting a foundation in Almario's name. *Asshole*, Eli thought and continued reading. The article provided a brief bio of Almario Gato and went on to describe how he ended up in America. The story took up seven inches. The life of Almario "Go Go" Gato took up a paltry seven inches.

Eli tossed the newspaper into the recycling, the knot in his stomach steadily tightening with every moment he wasn't out seeking the truth about Almario's death.

Eli opened his leather notebook, found the information Rushing had given him on his drug source. An 828 telephone number. A booming voice. A dead drop at a big house with spires and a flowerbed out front. On his cellphone Eli scrolled through the pictures he'd taken of the houses on Montford. They all looked annoyingly similar, but after consulting Google Images, he realized only five of the houses had actual "spires." And only two of those houses had a flowerbed out front that contained tulips. Getting closer. Eli studied both houses with spires carefully, paying close attention to the architectural details and the rows of tulips and the lawns and anything else that might indicate the presence of drug activities. But he couldn't find anything. He put his cellphone away, checked the 828 number Rushing had given him against Maria and Almario's Verizon records. No match with Almario: he'd neither called nor received a call from Rushing's supplier.

But Maria had. Over the past two months, she'd made and received several phone calls from the number in question.

And the number in question belonged to Homer Hodge. Cranky psych professor. Former civil rights activist.

And mentor to Maria Gato.

After a quick call to Rubio to confirm Hodge's address, Eli gathered supplies. An Igloo cooler filled with bologna sandwiches and Cherry Cokes. Binoculars and a camera and the lock-picking kit his mother bequeathed to him years ago.

Eli checked his Seiko: 9:01 a.m.

Sixteen minutes later, Eli parked on Monteford Avenue, a street lined with Dogwoods and Maple trees. Fit women ran down the sidewalks wearing workout clothes and headbands and pushing baby strollers. The lawns were a surrealistic green and freshly mowed, the houses all old, mostly Victorians and Tudors, some extravagantly restored, others elegantly decayed. The one Eli had his eye on—221 Monteford Avenue—was a square-shaped Victorian with three sharpened spires sticking out of the roof. A rectangular tulip garden sat to the left of a cobblestone walkway, just waiting to be photographed for *Better Homes & Gardens*. Three cars were parked in the drive, none of them as expensive as the cars parked in the other driveways on the street. When a shapely woman ran by, Eli nodded politely, hoping she'd notice the magnetic sign he'd slapped on the side of the truck, EARNEST APPRAISALS, LLC, which was a real company started by his second fiancée in the winter of '07. Now, Eli kept the sign when he needed to blend in while doing surveillance. When the shapely woman disappeared around the corner, he aimed his binoculars at his target. Four different mail slots by the front door. 221A, 221B, 221C, and 221D. Another runner appeared, and Eli lowered the binoculars, pretended to check his phone for messages.

About an hour into his wait, three college-age girls came out of the house, none of them, Eli assumed, possessing booming voices.

But shortly thereafter, a short, heavyset black man with close-cropped silver hair emerged from the house, fumbling with his car keys. A moment later a black woman appeared beside him, wearing a knit cap and a terrycloth bathrobe. She was hunched over. In obvious pain, she clutched the man's forearm for support as she turned away from the hot summer sun. Eli peered through his binoculars, zoomed in nice and tight. The black man had mottled skin and a large head. He wore white sweatpants and a red polo shirt. The pieces assembled themselves slowly in Eli's head. A man with a booming voice. A sick wife. This was Homer Hodge, Rushing's mysterious drug connection, the man Maria had called more than a dozen times in the last two months.

Eli lowered the binoculars, his mind racing. A dead drop at your own house? How would that work? A possibility occurred to him: maybe Rushing pretended to be the gardener. He watered the tulips, planted a bulb or two, and then carried off a package of blow disguised as fertilizer. Genius. Who would ever expect a senior citizen with an ailing wife to distribute cocaine right out of his flowerbed?

With great care, Hodge helped his wife into the passenger seat of an ancient Volvo that was once green. He kissed her forehead, shut the door and got behind the wheel. Eli started his truck, ducking as Hodge drove by.

Hodge turned onto Biltmore Avenue and headed south, Eli staying two cars back, his eyes focused on the NPR sticker on the Volvo's rusty bumper. The Volvo eased through a yellow light, and Eli stopped, drummed on the steering wheel, turned on the radio, turned it off. Questions flooded his brain, mostly about the connection between Hodge and Almario, Hodge and Maria.

The light turned green, and Eli accelerated, caught up just as the once-green Volvo turned into St. Joseph's Hospital. Hodge stopped in front of the EMERGENCY drop off while Eli veered off into the long-term parking lot. After finding a space, he got out his binoculars. Hodge, with the aid of two nurses, placed his wife in a wheelchair, kissed her forehead once more, and then waved as the nurses wheeled her through the automatic doors. After staring inside the hospital for a full minute, Hodge got into the Volvo, pulled away from the hospital and stopped. Eli cranked the car, waited, watched. Hodge made fists of his hands and slammed them down on the steering wheel. He shouted. He cursed. Then he slowly pulled out of the parking lot and headed back the way he'd come.

Eli put down the binoculars and followed him north along Biltmore and then west on Hilliard Avenue to Aston Park, a multi-purpose complex with a playground, picnic tables, basketball courts and tennis courts. Hodge parked on Hilliard in front of the ten or so tennis courts, while Eli continued farther down the street and parked in front of a fire hydrant. Making sure he wasn't seen, Eli got out of the car, waited for Hodge to emerge with a Wilson tennis bag slung over his shoulder.

Aston Park comprised two different worlds. At the bottom of a hill sat well-maintained tennis courts and a pro shop that sold energy bars and overpriced bottle water. Lawyers, professors, and investment bankers hung out there, sometimes sneaking away from their corner offices for a quick set or two before the afternoon deposition or meeting. At the top of the hill, in the shadow of the only non-luxury apartment high rise in Asheville, sat basketball courts, a playground, and picnic tables. There were plenty of trees and green grass, but one had to be careful not to step on any hypodermic needles or syringes.

As Hodge walked to the pro shop, he sidestepped a homeless man. Eli followed, his camera slung over his shoulder, pretending to be interested in the summer sunlight reflecting through the trees. Eli hurried to a stone bench situated between the tennis courts and sat down. Good vantage point. He aimed the camera up, snapped some random pictures of birds and deciduous trees, all the while keeping an eye on Hodge.

Hodge bought a Gatorade at the pro shop and then wandered onto Court 7, where a middle-aged white man in an orange and white Prince shirt was stretching. They shook hands, and Hodge got out his racquet and walked to the other side of the court, stopping only to set his tennis bag and Gatorade bottle beside the other man's tennis bag. Eli noticed that they both had the same bag: red with the word WILSON in white lettering. The man trotted back to the baseline, racquet in hand. Hodge hit a serve, and they began to play. They were pretty good. Most of their shots landed in the court, none with much power or precision, but they could maintain a decent rally.

Eli walked to the pro shop. A teenage boy sat on a stool watching a TV mounted to the gray concrete wall. Eli cleared his throat. The boy blinked at Eli from beneath a thicket of unruly strawberry blonde hair. A fan whirred nearby, blowing hot air around.

Eli held up his wallet. "The man on Court 7, I think he dropped this."

"The white dude or the black dude?"

"White. What's his name? I want to make sure this is his before I give it back."

"You mean Mr. Hanson?"

"Do you know his first name?"

"I'd have to check the club registry."

"I'll wait."

The boy sighed as if he were being asked to scale Mount Everest without oxygen canisters. He opened up a thick three-ring bound book, flipped to the middle. His fingers scanned the pages. He looked up. Something interesting happened on the TV, and the boy turned away.

Eli said he was in kind of a hurry, and the boy scowled, read the name off the three-ring binder.

"The white dude's name is Stan Hanson." The boy made a face. "I think I had him for Chemistry. MBS."

MBS. Major Boring Shit. Eli left the boy to his TV watching.

At 1:09 p.m., Hodge put his Wilson tennis bag in the trunk of his Volvo, and Eli followed him to the campus of AB Tech. With early afternoon classes yet to begin, the parking lot in front of the Humanities Building was only a quarter full, and Eli parked beside a souped-up Honda Accord. Hodge parked in the faculty lot, in a nice shady area beneath a line of mature elm trees, and speed-walked inside, head down, eyes focused on his cellphone. Donning a book bag filled with evidence, Eli followed Hodge inside, taking the stairs when Hodge selected the elevator.

On the third floor, Hodge, still sweating profusely from his tennis match, unlocked his office and shut the door.

Eli checked Hodge's schedule posted on the door. Office hours from 1:30 p.m. to 5 p.m. It was 1:22 p.m. Plenty of time to gather evidence.

Back in the parking lot, Eli waited for a group of loitering students to clear out before approaching the dented Subaru parked beside Hodge's off-green Volvo. The Subaru had no faculty parking decal, and the rear bumper was covered in dust and Widespread Panic stickers. Textbooks with uncracked spines sat in the backseat, the covers fading from the constant exposure to the sun. Eli patted his pockets, pretending to look for his car keys. He sat his book bag on the trunk of the Subaru, unzipped the smallest pocket, came up with a leather pouch containing the fourteen-piece stainless steel lock-picking kit his mother gave him on her death bed.

Old sensations came back to him. Tingling fingertips. Galloping heart. Calm mind. Making sure he was alone, he opened the leather pouch, selected the handy key extractor and a tension wrench and went to work.

In one minute forty-eight seconds he was inside Hodge's trunk, inventorying the items. Tire iron. Fix a flat. He opened the Wilson tennis bag. Three identical Wilson racquets with yellow strings. A can of Dunlap tennis balls. A water bottle with the AB Tech logo. A damp towel, redolent of sweat and aftershave. He looked under the towel. An unwrapped box of cigars. He opened the box, found a freezer bag half-filled with white powder. *Shit*, he thought, glancing around the parking lot. He thrashed his hand inside his book bag. Using his digital camera, he snapped pictures of the cigar box, the powder, the Wilson bag and its other contents. He took pictures of the name tag hanging from the tennis bag's straps. Homer Hodge, 221B Monteford Avenue. He took pictures of Hodge's license plate, put the camera back in his book bag, used Hodge's sweaty towel to remove all traces of the break-in and shut the trunk. He uploaded the pictures to his cellphone, sent an email to Carpenter with the photographs attached, and walked back into the Humanities Building.

Eli entered Hodge's office without knocking.

Hodge removed his glasses and stood up, his dark eyes glaring with a mixture of curiosity and hatred.

Book bag slung over his shoulder, Eli stood in the opened doorway, cellphone in hand.

"Leave before I telephone security."

"Call security? That's a good idea. I could show them what one of their longest tenured and most trusted instructors keeps in the trunk of his faded green Volvo sedan. In a red Wilson tennis bag. Underneath three oversized Wilson racquets with cat gut strings. Inside a cigar box." Eli enlarged the picture of the baggie of white powder on the phone's display screen, turned it so Hodge could see the picture. "Don't tell me this is part of a new course on entrepreneurship, Mr. Hodge."

"Shut the door."

"Your voice," Eli said, trying to hold back his anger, "it's no longer booming."

"Shut the door and come in."

"You come out into the hall. I need answers."

"And if I refuse, you'll do what exactly? Inform administration? Get me terminated?"

"For starters."

"Go ahead," he said bitterly. "My career at this so-called institution of higher learning has been a farce, a sham from beginning to end. You would be relieving me of a painful burden."

"When you're fired, I'm certain the school will want to contact the police, press charges against the professor—excuse me, I mean, the instructor—who soiled the school's reputation. The headline will read SELF-PITYING PSYCHOLOGY INSTRUCTOR DISGRACED."

A snort of derision, a smirk of misplaced pride. He crossed his arms, unapologetic for his crimes, unafraid of his punishment. "Do what you feel is right, Mr. Sharpe. Call the president of the school. Call the police. You'd be doing me a personal favor."

Eli examined the pictures of the famous African-Americans on Hodge's wall. Above his desk were half a dozen pictures of Hodge and his wife, pre-cancer. It was difficult to tell who was happier in the pictures.

Eli said, "You told me you've seen the inside of a police interrogation room before, but I'm betting you've never been formally charged."

Hodge's smirk widened; his dark eyes flashed amusement. "Detained, never formally arrested. I was a political protester. What's your point?"

"My point is, this drug charge would be your first official crime. Hell, a guy like you? Never been arrested, led a decent and productive life? A guy like that might not even serve time. You'd receive a suspended sentence, most likely. Sure, you'd get fired, but the school might not want to taint its own reputation. Maybe they downplay it in the newspapers. Sweep the whole thing under the rug. Have you take early retirement." Eli raised his voice. "But what about your wife?"

"My wife has nothing to do with this."

"How will she feel when she finds out her doting husband, who drives her to the hospital for appointments and makes sure she gets her medication and helps her bathe and dress and go to the bathroom and cope with the prospect of dying a very painful death, is selling cocaine to students? Do you think that will help hasten her recovery? Do you think she'll be proud?"

Hodge stepped out into the hall, his hands clasped behind his back. He glared up at Eli.

"Repeat that," Hodge said. "Repeat what you just said."

"Happy to, Professor. Just tell me which part." Eli straightened Hodge's shirt collar. Hodge slapped Eli's hands away, aimed a punch at Eli's nose. Eli bent his neck to the left, and the punch landed on the wall. Hodge cursed, doubled-over, clutched his bruised right hand.

"What do you want?" Hodge asked. "You want to know how I obtain the cocaine?"

"Later. Tell me what happened to Almario Gato. Tell me everything and I'll give you a chance to explain yourself to your wife before I turn you over to the police."

Hodge straightened up, caught his breath. "What's stopping you from hearing my version of the truth, and then reneging on our deal?"

"Nothing but my conscience."

"That's amusing, you claiming to have a moral compass."

"It's a nuisance, I admit, but I prefer to sleep at night."

"Sleep," he said as if it were some vague notion from his distant past, now long forgotten. "Mr. Sharpe, I'm almost sixty-five. You might grasp the concept of growing old, but you cannot know the *experience.* You cannot know what it is like to watch the decay of your own body, to witness your own slow and steady descent. Worse, you cannot know what it is like to look on as your wife withers and rots before your very own eyes." His theatrical voice had returned. He was playing a role now, and Eli let him. "As I've gotten older, the truth has become more relative. Oddly enough, the more lies I tell and the more secrets I keep, the more I value honesty in others. Mr. Sharpe, I appreciate your candor."

"And I demand yours. Either way, you're going down for possession and distribution. I emailed the pictures to a friend of mine, had him run a check on Mr. Hanson, too."

"Mr. Hanson has nothing to do with this. He is merely a tennis partner, nothing more."

"Then who supplies you with the cocaine?"

Another smirk. "Some investigator you are. I was a double major in college. *Magna cum laude.* Psychology *and* Chemistry. For purposes of research. I am my own supplier." His facial muscles relaxed. The hatred drained from his eyes. Something inside him, something he'd been holding on to for a very long time was let go. He looked at Eli, and then at the students at the other end of the hall.

"The things I did, I did out of love."

"Love? Love for who?"

"Maria," he said, his eyes already wet with tears. "Maria Gato."

After speeding through three red lights and weaving in and out of downtown traffic, Eli parked in front of DMSI and jogged up to Carpenter's office. He opened the office door and found Carpenter signing expense reports and muttering to himself. Carpenter finished the last signature with a flourish.

"Got the pictures, kid. Do I want to know the particulars?"

Eli told the quick version.

"Disturbing," Carpenter said and tweaked his mustache a time or two.

"When I confronted Hodge, he didn't bother to deny it. He almost seemed proud."

"Scumbag."

"My sentiments exactly. I figured he'd offer up some sort of pseudo-political or psychological explanation for selling drugs to his students—an intellectual justification for his crime—but he didn't. He didn't bat an eye when I threatened to turn over my evidence to the school and the police."

"Major scumbag," Carpenter said, his voice sounding more tired than angry.

"But as soon as I mentioned telling his wife, his whole demeanor changed. He got emotional. He took a swing at me."

"Slow down and sit down. Tell me how all this connects with Almario."

Eli sat. After the Hodge confrontation, Eli had walked back to his truck, dazed, soaked in sweat. With the air conditioner fully cranked, he'd read over his case notes while the recycled air cooled the sweat on his forehead. He didn't want to believe Hodge's story, couldn't believe it.

Eli said, "Hodge was having an affair with Maria Gato."

"Goddamned scumbag. Explain the connection. Start from the beginning."

Eli obliged. He told him how Hodge had been Maria's instructor and mentor for almost a year now—hence, his number popping up on Maria's cellphone records. He told him how Hodge had been helping Maria with her research—something about twins and their parents—and had become involved with her.

"Romantically?"

Eli nodded. "He made it clear he had deep feelings for Maria, and she for him. He went on and on about her intelligence and 'Rubenesque' physique and youth and innocence. He made several references to her family history, her 'harrowing personal narrative' was what he called it. He said his wife was dying, and he felt helpless and angry and vulnerable."

"And Maria needed a father figure. How long has Hodge been dealing blow?"

"A little less than a year. Right around the time his wife was diagnosed with stomach cancer. He said it killed two birds with one stone: it earned him money to pay the extra medical expenses—"

"Surely that asshole has health insurance."

"He claimed the school's coverage was a joke, which was the second bird his dealing killed."

"He must have really wanted to stick it to his employer."

"On our first encounter, Hodge made half a dozen remarks about the school's shortcomings. Lack of faculty diversity. Low pay. Not enough recognition for exemplary work. He seemed bitter. Distributing drugs to students who then sold them, right under the school's nose, is the perfect little FU to the employer who undervalued him."

"All right, that explains how he got involved with Maria. Not the first or the last time a teacher took advantage of a naïve student." Carpenter bit the end off a cigar and spat it into the waste basket, lit the cigar. Plumes of dense gray smoke filled the room. A pleasant smell.

"Try this," Eli said, fanning smoke away from his face. "The May-December tryst ended sour. Maria wanted to move on, she wanted to concentrate on her studies, et cetera, and Hodge got to thinking about what his life was like before this eighteen-year-old girl entered it. A dying wife. Medical bills. Unfulfilling job. Seems to me, this whole thing could be about revenge. In his own way, Hodge has been practicing psychology for more than twenty years. He knew Maria cared deeply for Almario, would be all alone in the world if he were gone. He knew hurting him would destroy her. Ruin her life the way that his was ruined."

"Which is exactly what a jilted lover wants. There's your motive. How about method?"

"The method is drugs. I have picture proof Hodge is dealing. He admitted to it, admitted to having a degree in chemistry as well. With basic knowledge of science, he could cook his own cocaine. The kicker? When I asked Hodge where he was on the night we found Almario, he clammed up. 'I can't say,' was his response."

"Can't or won't?"

"Can't."

"With no confirmed alibi—"

"He had an opportunity. The rotted flesh. Almario had black spots all over his face. The ME told Meachum he'd seen it before in drug cases. Possible levamisole poisoning, but no confirmation until tox screen comes in official. I did some research, though. Veterinarians use it to de-worm livestock. Oncologists use it to treat cancer, and his wife—Gladys Hodge—has cancer. Anyway, put levamisole in coke and it enhances the narcotic effect. The articles I read said the same thing: a majority of the cocaine in this country, something like sixty percent, is already laced with the stuff. All Hodge had to do was spike up a high-powered batch and make sure Almario got it. Simple."

Carpenter rubbed his chin.

Eli stopped talking. Then, "What am I missing?"

"A possibility you haven't considered." Carpenter looked away, out the window.

"Maria," Eli said after a moment of reflection. "You don't know her."

"I know she had a motive. Big insurance policy. Big money."

"She dotes on Almario."

"Doted."

"She didn't do this," Eli said. "She couldn't kill anyone. Besides, she has an alibi."

"I believe you, kid, and I like Hodge for this, too. The evidence is pointing in his direction. But you know my motto.

"Always check your blind spot." Eli made a mental note to recheck Maria's alibi. "Look, Maria must have told Hodge about Almario's drug problems. Maybe she even mentioned talking to Stuckey, begging her to leave her brother alone, to find another man to sponge off of, to find someone else to deal blow to. Hodge could have slipped the hot dose to Almario and watched the cops go straight to Stuckey."

Carpenter put his cigar in an empty coffee mug.

Eli went into Carpenter's filing cabinet, got out a bottle of Maker's Mark, filled two Dixie cups and passed one to his mentor.

"Indigestion," Carpenter said and Eli downed both shots, the liquor blazing a path down his throat.

Carpenter took the bottle away, but Eli was too keyed up to care.

It fit. Everything fit. Motive. Method. Opportunity. Hodge, a desperate and angry old man, manipulated a naïve and trusting young girl. He exploited her emotionally and sexually, and when she came to her senses and ended it, he took his revenge. With a dying wife and a job he loathed, what else did he have in the world?

Another theory. With holes.

A lump of bile rose in Eli's throat.

"He cried," Eli said. "The son of bitch said he loved Maria Gato. He refused to give me his alibi."

"That doesn't make him guilty."

"I'm not going to blow the whistle yet. He knows I got him on distribution. He knows I'll tell his wife. He's not going anywhere. And if he was involved in Almario's death, I need more evidence before I go to Meachum."

Eli stared out the window. Downtown Asheville looked peaceful—the buildings, the sidewalks, the people. The anger returned. The knot in his stomach tightened.

He checked his Seiko: 3:13 p.m. He called Meachum. Voicemail. He left a message to call him back once any news on Almario's case came in. He called a second time, left another message. And a third. Just in case. He checked his Seiko: 3:17.

Against Carpenter's fatherly advice, Eli consumed three more drinks, and then lay down on Carpenter's couch and slept without dreaming. When he awoke, the office was dark. The moonlight shone through the window. There was a note on Carpenter's computer screen:

Eli,
Stepped out on another case. Call me when you hear from Meachum.
P.S. I hid all my liquor.

At 9:10 p.m., Eli found Christine Lovatt slumped against the front door of his apartment.

Holding a Visa card and a bottle of Popov vodka, she was wearing a strapless black dress and leopard high heels, the right heel a full inch shorter than the left. She waved the Visa card in Eli's face and then slipped it into the padding of her bra.

"Totally doesn't work," she said with a drunken giggle, "using credit cards to break in. Guess I'm not cut out to burgleling. For burgled. For burgling. I'm not cut out for burgling."

Eli helped her to her feet, and she put a hand on his shoulder to steady herself. Kicking off her heels, she offered up the vodka, which had a shade of gloss on the lip that matched the color of her BMW convertible.

"No clear liquids for me, thanks."

"All I can afford is bottom shelf. Father cut me off. The man I love is dead. My life is a fucking country song."

"Come inside. I'll make coffee."

"I'd rather fuck."

She drank, winced as the medicine went down.

"You shouldn't talk like that," Eli said.

"In case you missed it, I'm offering you my body."

"I'm flattered."

"But not tempted."

"Very. I'm flattered and tempted. I'm also old enough to be—"

"Don't fucking say it. Seriously, I'll puke."

"I was going to say, I'm old enough to be your much, much older brother." Eli opened the door, and in one continuous motion he gently shoved Christine inside and snatched the bottle from her hand. She plopped down on the futon. He made two cups of strong coffee, happy to have some mindless task to take his mind off of Homer Hodge.

After forcing Christine to drink her coffee, Eli gobbled four Advil for his own aching head and sat down beside her. "I'm truly sorry about Almario. I feel terrible."

When she'd cried herself out, she talked about the time she and Almario went camping in the Blue Ridge Parkway. "We set up camp on a batch of peat moss three feet away from the mountain's edge.

"Sounds nice."

"He was sixteen," she said, her voice all dreamy and sad. "I made him eat magic mushrooms, and he flipped out and ran away. He broke his ankle and I had to drag him back to the car and take him to the hospital. I remember we waited for hours in the emergency room for his X-ray. He was so depressed about having to miss games because of his stupid ankle. I gave him a blow job. Just pulled the curtain shut and swallowed his cum."

She started to cry again, and Eli lifted the coffee mug to her lips. She stopped crying and drank.

"Christine, why didn't you tell me Maria was sleeping with her teacher?"

"We're not friends like that. Maria and me. I mean, I knew she was with someone, an old guy. Not like you old, but really old. Ancient. Maria's way smart. But very weird."

"Weird how?"

"Weird like I wasn't surprised she was dating a senior citizen. That kind of weird. Look, I didn't come here to play twenty questions."

"Nor did you come here to sleep with me."

"You're not my type. No offense."

"None taken, but you did come here for a reason: to break into my office. The question is why. What aren't you telling me?"

"I can see why you've never been married, why you live in this shitty apartment, alone." She over-enunciated the word *alone.* "I came here to read your stupid notebook, all right. I want to know what all you found out about Almario. I thought if I could see your notes or whatever I could find out what happened. I loved him. I want the truth."

No tears this time. Just a determined gleam in her eyes.

"I'll make you a deal. Tell me everything you know about Maria Gato, and I'll let you look at my notes."

"Deal." She picked up her coffee, sipped, complained about the temperature and the use of Sweet'n Low instead of real sugar and then sat her coffee down on the floor, making a new ring in the hardwood.

At first, Christine spoke of Maria's shyness, her cooking, her work ethic.

Eli asked if Maria ever talked about her family.

"Sometimes. Mainly about Almario. He was her favorite subject. She was always telling me stories about what Almario was like when he was little, how the neighborhood kids followed him everywhere, how their parents fawned all over him, especially her father. He was some kind of teacher, the father. Taught language or something, I can't remember. I don't think she liked him."

"Why not?"

"The usual bullshit. Nagged her about her weight and keeping her grades perfect and making sure Almario made good life decisions. I don't think she liked her mother, either."

"And what about Homer Hodge?"

"She never told me his name, just that he was old. I swear, I didn't know he was black."

"Did you know he sold drugs?"

"No. I seriously doubt Maria knew either. She was always worried about Almario drinking. I tried to get her stoned once, and she didn't speak to me for three days. Every once in a while she would mention a teacher who was helping her do research, but she never said a name. The way she talked about this guy, I never would have guessed she was banging him. I had her pegged as a virgin from the first time I meet her."

"Have you ever seen Homer Hodge?"

She shook her head. "I'm not into old dudes or doing blow."

"You told me you scored for Almario. From Stuckey and Rushing. Maybe you scored for him more than once."

"That was one time, okay? And Almario was really hurting. Shaking and sweating. I thought he was going to have a seizure. I had to do it." She called Eli some names, cried a bit more, and then apologized. Eli handed her his leather notebook.

She took her time reading, and when she'd finished, she asked a bunch of questions all at once, most of them involving Sheri Stuckey. Was Almario really going to marry that skank? Did Almario really take out a half-a-million-dollar life insurance policy for that skank? Did Almario really want to play house with that skank's daughter? She ended the questions with a decree.

"This is all your fault." Pacing the room, she directed her anger at Eli, cursed him for having stupid Nixon posters on the wall, cursed him for sleeping on a futon in lieu of a real bed, cursed him for not being able to find Almario in time. Out of expletives, she threw her high heels against the wall, smashing a framed poster of Nixon watering his L.A. house during a fire. Barefoot, she swung open the front door and stood in the threshold as moonlight spilled inside.

"If someone killed Almario, I'll give you my BMW to find out who."

Eli called her a taxi and put her in it, gave the driver a twenty.

"I won't be at the funeral," she said through the window. "Does that make me a bitch?"

"It makes you human. One thing, though. Where were you when I found Almario?"

"At the dorm with Courtney Mullins and Whitney Carver."

"Be at the funeral."

"You're a prick."

"You'll regret not going."

Christine shouted at the driver, and the taxi sped away.

CHAPTER 18

Bill Meachum called at precisely 9 a.m. the following morning. Eli was still in bed, staring at the Tigris and Euphrates in the ceiling.

"Accident by drugs," Meachum said. "But that's unofficial."

"Anything else you can tell me? Unofficially?"

"That sarcasm I hear?"

"No, just trying to wake up."

Meachum grunted down the line. "ME and his boys in the lab found traces of cocaine in Almario's nasal passages and on his lips. They were able to analyze a sample of the drug. There were trace amounts of levamisole."

"How much cocaine? How much levamisole?"

"Can't know until the tox screen comes back next month. Point is, drugs killed him." Meachum breathed down the line. "Have anything to share with me, Sharpe?"

"That depends."

"On what?"

"On what else is in the ME's preliminary report."

"I told you what I know. Don't push it."

Eli got out of bed, moved around, got the blood flowing. "I did some reading. According to my research, seven hundred milligrams per liter of blood of levamisole is toxic. The least amount of cocaine that has ever proven lethal is around ten milligrams per liter of blood. If there was a non-lethal amount of cocaine in Almario's system and a toxic amount of levamisole—"

"That would suggest intent. But the ME can't say precise amounts. Not until the tox screen comes back official."

Eli looked out the window. The boys were out by the Saab again, playing whiffle ball and taunting one another. "Does the ME have any preliminary findings?"

"Just that cocaine, even in small dosages, can be lethal. Said a majority of blow in this country is laced with levamisole, and odds are someone who didn't know what he was doing mixed up Almario's batch. Probably wanted to make the package last longer by adding more filler and less coke."

"What if someone who did know what he was doing and had a motive and opportunity to harm Almario mixed up a hot dose?"

Meachum grunted. "Don't like hypothetical scenarios. I polygraphed Stuckey and Rushing; they're clean. I talked to Brad Newman; his alibi is solid. I talked to Maria Gato and Veronica Craven. Whatever it is you know, or think you know, you need to tell me. And now."

Eli's head pulsed like a blinking neon sign. His encounter with Christine Lovatt the night before coupled with the prospect of attending Almario's funeral sober and conscience-laden had led him right back to George Dickel. But hangover or no, he didn't want to tell Meachum about the Homer Hodge connection, if for no other reason than he refused to have Maria Gato's name dragged through the mud. He did, however, have a selfish motive for withholding vital information. Atonement. He'd failed to find Almario in time; he'd failed to recognize Homer Hodge as a predator during their first encounter. He'd fucked up and he wanted—no, he needed—to fix it. Himself. No one else.

"I was just speculating," Eli said. "Thinking out loud."

"Withholding information from the police is frowned upon. Especially in a death investigation. Mind you, there are consequences for such actions. Serious ones, you follow?"

"I follow."

Meachum spat, and Eli pictured brown tobacco juice clinging to the cop's thick beard.

"You sure you don't have anything on your mind? Something pressing?"

But Meachum didn't wait for an answer, leaving Eli staring at his cellphone screen, weighing his options.

Option number one: Get Hodge to confess. Although the cradle-robbing instructor had refused to supply Eli with an alibi, Hodge also vehemently denied having anything to do with Almario's death. All he would cop to was selling large quantities of cocaine to his students. And having an extra-marital affair with one. While his own wife lay ill with terminal cancer.

Eli chucked the cellphone across the room, and it landed safely on the futon. The morning sun was rising slowly above the mountains, and he leaned against the window, watched the wispy clouds float by the mountain peaks.

Option number two: Talk to Maria Gato. Surely, a smart girl like her had an inkling of Hodge's predilection for drug dealing. Maybe she'd seen something or heard something, anything that could be used against Hodge in a court of law, anything that would put more pressure on the psychology instructor. At the moment all Eli had were pictures of drugs in the man's Volvo. Pictures he'd obtained illegally. Pictures that could, technically, get him arrested.

Eli ran a hand through his hair, which was greasy. He needed a shower. And evidence. Once the evidence was in place, Eli could turn everything over to Meachum. Meachum was already prepared to call this one an accidental death, and without knowledge of Hodge's connection to Maria Gato, he would—technically—be correct. The police department would be thrilled to keep their murder numbers low—Asheville got very few a year. The medical examiner would be covered too: Almario, a known drug abuser, just took it too far. Cocaine was a highly volatile drug, and levamisole was present in a majority of cocaine in the United States. It was up to Eli to find the truth. And assuage his own guilt.

Basking in a hot shower, Eli thought of more options. Emailing the pictures of Hodge's stash to a friend at the *Asheville Citizen Times.* Phoning in an anonymous tip to the police, implicating the lot of them: Hodge, Stuckey, and Rushing. Paying Gladys Hodge a visit, letting her know what kind of man she'd been sharing a bed with for the last few decades.

But none of them sat right, and as Eli exited the shower and defogged the bathroom mirror, cooler heads prevailed.

"Option number one," Eli said to his reflection, "with a twist."

Eli dressed in a tan linen suit bought off-the-rack at Men's Warehouse, a white button-down shirt with a black tie, and Italian leather shoes he'd stolen from his old man, who'd stolen them from a flea market in Jacksonville, Florida, fifteen years prior. While combing his hair, he steeled his insides to face Maria Gato at the funeral.

Local news reporters were camped outside St. Anne's Catholic Church, microphones in hand, cameramen trailing behind them. The parking lot teemed with news vans and regular cars. Eli parked a block away on Charlotte Street, entered the church through a side entrance. The monsignor, a stout man in a long purple robe, greeted Eli with a limp handshake and bad breath, and Eli hurried inside, trying to block out memories of being stood up at the altar by his first fiancée.

Despite all the cars in the parking lot, only the first two rows of the sanctuary were filled. Eli recognized two faces: Herbie McClure and Coach Burns. Without uniforms on or sunflower seed shells dangling from their lips, they looked out of place, as if they were waiting for the saints in the stained glass windows to come alive and escort them outside. Eli walked to the end of the front row and took a seat next to Herbie. They nodded at each other. Herbie's big blue eyes were watery and sad. Eli gripped the old man's forearm and squeezed. Herbie wiped his eyes.

Eli spotted Dantonio Rushing, Sheri Stuckey, and Brad Newman sitting together in the second row. Rushing and Newman wore shirts and ties, but no suits. Stuckey's face was thin and frail, her eyes wounded. Her black dress was too short and too wrinkled. Stuckey's daughter, a little blonde girl with a red bow in her hair, sat on Newman's lap, blowing spit bubbles and giggling at her own thoughts. In the row behind them sat four of Almario's teammates, some of them stealthily checking their cellphones while the rest pondered the Virgin Veronica on the ceiling. None of them looked at the casket in the vestibule.

But Eli did.

The undertaker had done an admirable job on Almario's face. No black spots on his cheeks. No busted blood vessels on his nose. His luxurious black hair covered the satin pillow beneath his head. His face was young and handsome, his suit pressed and clean for all eternity. Eli checked his Seiko: 9:55 a.m. Still no Maria. Or Veronica.

At the side entrance the monsignor turned away a reporter, a pushy young brunette in a beige pantsuit. Eli scanned the sanctuary once more. No Christine Lovatt. No Homer Hodge. The monsignor coughed, and in walked Frank Waring, Caulder, and Gifford, all dressed in dark suits. Waring led the other two to the front row nearest the side exit.

At precisely 10 a.m., Veronica Craven entered the sanctuary wearing a form-fitting black dress, a string of pearls, and heels that made her six and a half feet tall. As she moved across the sanctuary, Almario's teammates craned their necks. When Stuckey's daughter pointed and said, "Pretty lady," Veronica blew the little girl a kiss and sat down beside Eli. Veronica's perfume triggered memories.

Eli said, "You couldn't fix yourself up a little."

"Your tie is misshapen."

"Where's Maria?"

"In the car. Talking to a picture of Almario."

"There's a lot of press out there."

"I parked a half a mile away. They won't find her."

"She'll regret not being here."

Veronica removed her Lady Stella Hat, rearranged her hair, greeted the others in the pew.

Eli went and spoke to the monsignor, asked him to delay the ceremony for ten minutes.

"I'll give you five," the monsignor said.

Eli jogged down Charlotte Street and turned onto Lee, where Veronica's rental car was parked in front of a bed and breakfast with an elaborate porch swing. Pouring sweat, Eli knocked on the passenger side window, but Maria ignored him, continued staring down at a photograph of Almario in her lap. Maria was wearing the same black designer dress as Veronica Craven, only two sizes larger. Her hair was a dark, tangled mess, and her makeup did little to hide a cluster of angry red pimples on her right cheek. Eli tried the door. Locked. Maria kissed the photograph, leaving behind red lipstick. Same shade Veronica Craven was wearing.

"Maria, we need to talk. Let me into the car." Eli walked to the driver's side door. Locked. A man carrying a bag of groceries passed by, flashed Eli a disapproving look.

"Maria, I know about you and Homer Hodge. We need to talk."

Sweat dripped into his eyes, burned. His cellphone buzzed. A text from Veronica. UPDATE? Eli texted back: SCARED.

Kissing Almario's photograph a second time, Maria placed it on the dashboard and then studied her reflection in the rearview mirror. She brushed sweaty bangs from her forehead, wiped away a clump of mascara from under her eye, forced a smile. Lipstick on her teeth. Sighing, she opened the door and made eye contact with Eli, which quickened his pulse and chilled his blood. It was Maria's eyes. The hurt there was different than what he'd seen in Christine Lovatt the night before. Beneath the overt sex talk and drunkenness, Christine had been shocked and outraged and confused that someone she loved—someone *she* loved—could be snatched away. But not Maria. There was something infinitely more profound behind her dark Spanish Princess eyes: resignation. Here was a girl totally alone. And Eli had failed her.

"I'm truly sorry about Almario."

"I know." Maria straightened the knot in Eli's tie. "My father's tie was always crooked, too."

"Tell me about Hodge."

Maria stared out the window, a dreamy expression on her face. "He's a good man," she said. "I learned much from him."

"He took advantage of you. He sold drugs to his students."

She sighed. She muttered something in Spanish that sounded like cursing. "I didn't know about that, but it doesn't surprise me. I just know he was good to me."

"But he was bad to everyone else. He—"

"No one takes advantage of me, Mr. Sharpe. From the first day I saw Homer in class and heard him speak, the way he commanded the room with his voice—the way he looked me dead in the eye when he spoke to me—I knew I wanted to be with him. I didn't care about his age. I didn't care about his black skin. I didn't care about his wife. Homer had what I'd always wanted."

"Which was?"

"Confidence. But in my family..." Her voice trailed off. "Homer was emotional. He spoke of children, making a life together. Why are men so soft? I never lied to him, Mr. Sharpe. I spoke to him *cara a cara*. 'You're a phase,' I said, and he wept. He told me he loved his wife and she would be dead soon, and I ended it. It had to be done."

"How did he take it?"

"He stopped coming to class. He begged me to take him back, said he wouldn't smother me. He said he didn't care if I really loved him, he just didn't want to be alone. When I refused, he got angry. He threatened me."

Maria reached into a leather satchel she had at her feet. She removed an envelope and handed it Eli. The letter was written in cursive.

"Read it," Maria said.

Eli obeyed.

> Dearest Maria,
>
> If your love for me is dead, then I am truly bereft of hope, and a man without hope is a nasty thing. I offered you guidance. You offered me a shot at redemption. We both sinned, we are both guilty. Youth absolves you of your transgression while age condemns me of mine. This is as it should be. Your conscience is clear. In retrospect, our May-December affair was ill-fated, doomed from the start, but a man in love is nearsighted, and I do so love to hold you near.
>
> But now that you've made your decision, I glimpse what must be done.
>
> I do not apologize for it, nor shall I make excuses.
>
> Together we mined the depths of our hearts and souls. We attempted to make sense of the nonsensical. We failed, but in failing we became more human. For this I thank you. But never forget: I know you better than you know yourself. I know who you are and where you come from and where you are going. I know what you fear. I know what hurts you the most. I know what you love most in this world. I know what you cannot live without.
>
> Reconsider me.
>
> Shamefully yours,
> H.H.

It certainly sounded like Hodge's style. Rhetorical. Theatrical. Pretentious. Eli read it a second time and got angry.

As if reading his thoughts, Maria said, "I was ashamed of my affair. I told no one."

"When did you receive this letter?"

"The night Almario died."

"But if you knew Hodge was threatening you, and you knew your brother was—"

"I was selfish." Looking away, she muttered something else in Spanish. "I didn't think Homer would do anything. I've known him for a year now, and he talks about things. He talks and talks and talks, but he is not a man of action." Maria crossed herself and cried, softly. Calmly.

Eli considered Maria's plight. Eighteen-year-old orphan girl involved with a sixty-four-year-old married man. Who might have killed her twin brother. Eli put his hand on her shoulder, explained the tox screen results and what he thought might have happened to Almario. Through the tears she listened well, but didn't get hysterical. Her grief was controlled, her sadness calm and intractable.

"Where was Hodge the night Almario was killed?"

Maria clutched Almario's picture to her chest. "You dropped me off that night at seven-forty-five. Homer called me while I was riding the elevator up to the apartment. He told me he had something to give me. He asked me to meet him at a park near his house. He sounded calm, so I agreed."

"Do you remember the time?"

"Eight. It was already getting dark."

Eli remembered the ME put Almario's time of death between 11 p.m. and 12 a.m. "What did he want to show you, Maria?"

"An X-ray of his wife's chest. It was full of white specks. Homer said he loved his wife dearly, but she would be dead soon, in a few weeks, maybe. He said he could bear it if we were together after she was gone. I told him I didn't want to be with him anymore. That's when he gave me the letter and demanded that I read it in front of him. I told him to leave me alone. No one takes advantage of me. No one."

"What time did he leave?"

"Eight-thirty."

"Are you sure?"

"The park had tennis courts with lights. The sign said the lights automatically come on at 8:30 p.m. on weekdays. As I was leaving, the lights came on."

Eli slowed down his train of thought, focused on the time line. If Hodge left by 8:30 p.m., that would give him plenty of time to meet up with Almario and give him the tainted drugs. Now all Eli needed to do was prove Hodge deliberately spiked the drugs and delivered them to Almario. With no witnesses: a tall order.

As Eli wondered how he might go about filling that tall order, another question bubbled to the surface: could someone have given Almario the tainted drugs earlier in the day? Could he have waited to consume them? Eli chewed on that bone a moment, and then came to a logical conclusion: Almario was a heavy drug user in need of rehab. No way would he have waited to do the drugs. No, Hodge was the culprit. Eli could feel it in his bones.

A woman walking a pug waved at Eli as she moved down the sidewalk. Eli waved back. He looked at Maria. The rims of her almond-shaped eyes were red, inflamed, her lips dry.

"I'm to blame," Maria said. "I spoke to God, and he forgave me, but I cannot forgive myself. Not until the truth comes out. Mr. Sharpe, I need your help." She reached into her satchel and pulled out a silver key on a red key chain. "Take this. Go to Homer's house on Monteford Avenue. Two twenty-one B. I know his schedule. He takes his wife to the hospital every day for treatments. That's when I would go to him. You now know things about me that I'm ashamed of, things I'm glad my parents aren't around to see. Please don't think me a bad person."

Maria exited the car and walked barefoot toward the church.

Along the way she played a quick round of hopscotch with the little black girl, and then wiped the tears from her face.

Maria Gato delivered the eulogy in Spanish and then kissed Almario's cheek and closed the casket. Catholic prayers followed, and then the pallbearers—Coach Burns, Veronica Craven, and four of Almario's teammates—carried Almario to the hearse parked behind the church. While the mourners trickled out of the church and into the hot summer sun, the press kept their distance, waiting for the right moment to pounce. The pallbearers loaded the hearse, and Eli watched it roll slowly down the street and disappear into traffic.

Then the press pounced.

At 12:13 p.m., Eli parked outside 221 Monteford Avenue, slapped the EARNEST APPRAISALS, LLC sign on the driver's side door and donned a ball cap, also bearing the company name.

At 12:28 p.m., Hodge emerged from the house with the spires, carrying his wife in his arms. He gently placed her upright in the back seat of his faded green Volvo, wrapped her shawl a little tighter around her slumped shoulders, and then drove away.

When the Volvo disappeared, Eli strolled toward the house, clipboard and digital camera in hand. To sell the act to any nosy neighbors who might have been watching, he snapped pictures of the house from various angles, scribbled some notes, and then stepped onto the front porch.

Making sure the coast was clear, Eli put on a pair of latex gloves and used Maria's key to enter the house, taking the stairs two at a time to the top floor unit, 221B.

Hodge's apartment was spacious, with nice architectural details. Parquet floors and high ceilings. French doors and plenty of windows. On the living room walls were African tribal masks, reprints of Winslow Homer, pictures of Hodge and his wife in various tropical locations. A velveteen painting of Gandhi hung above the fireplace, the famous pacifist's eyes tranquil behind Coke-bottle thick glasses. All the furniture was covered in plastic, the bookshelves in dust. Everything smelled of mothballs and cough drops, and there wasn't a TV in sight.

Eli passed through French doors into what looked like a spare bedroom. A large, four-poster bed. A nightstand littered with romance paperbacks and pill bottles. Eli checked the bottles. Some were vitamins. Fish oils, omega 3-fatty acid tablets, iron, zinc. Others were serious painkillers. Oxycontin. Codeine. Sifting through the dozen or more bottles, he found what he was looking for. Levamisole. The directions read:

> 50 mg orally every 8 hours for 3 days (starting 7-30 days post-surgery). DO NOT EXCEED DOSAGE. CONSULT DOCTOR IF ALLERGIC.

Eli shook the pills in the bottle.

A threatening letter to Maria Gato.

Access to levamisole and cocaine.

Knowledge of basic chemistry.

No alibi.

A powerful motive.

The case against Homer Hodge was getting stronger.

As was Eli's anger. He slipped the bottle into his jacket pocket, went through the living room and into the second bedroom. In the corner sat a twin bed. Beside the closet was a bookshelf filled with political memoirs, college textbooks, dozens of back issues of *Psychology Today* and other magazines—some popular, others obscure. Skimming the titles, Eli pulled out a thin, yellowed publication called *Journal of African-American Literary Arts.* It was dated Winter, 1983. In the table of contents, under the poetry section, Eli found the following entry: "Of a late winter day," by Homer Bartholomew Hodge.

Eli flipped to the page indicated in the table of contents and read Hodge's poem. Sixteen lines. No punctuation of any kind. Totally devoid of imagery. Eli flipped forward several pages and found a Polaroid picture wedged deep in the spine. Maria Gato, completely naked, lying on the floor of what looked like Hodge's office at AB Tech. She had large, brown nipples and a round belly and a thatch of dark hair between her thick thighs. But it was the frank expression on her face Eli found disturbing. Her eyes were hungry, feral, like those of a tigress in heat, ready to scour the jungle for a suitable mate. Eli slipped the photograph into his pocket, ashamed of the semi-erection filling his pants.

After making sure the apartment was just as he'd found it, Eli pocketed the latex gloves and went outside. Not caring if the neighbors wanted to call the police, he dropped the clipboard and camera on the lawn and tramped through the tulip garden, flattening a row of purple and yellow blooms. Behind the last row of flowers, he found a wooden box. Inside the box were some gardening tools and a ten-pound bag of fertilizer. Using his car keys, he cut open the fertilizer and learned that Rushing had been telling the truth.

And that Hodge was as arrogant as he was guilty.

When Eli opened his apartment door, he stepped on a blue folder with a handwritten note taped to it.

> My friend,
>
> I was saddened to learn about Almario Gato. He was a gifted young ballplayer with a bright future. My wife and I prayed to the Holy Mother for him last night.
>
> As for your case, I called an associate of mine in Miami who specializes in information retrieval. In the folder

is what he came up with on the Gato defection. I skimmed it. It looks like fairly standard reporting.

I wish I could have done more.

—Rubio

Eli dropped the folder on his desk, still reeling from his visit to Hodge's apartment. The background info could wait. Right now, he needed to get out of his suit and into a stiff drink. With more comfortable clothes on, he sloshed three fingers of Dickel into a coffee mug and sat down at his desk. The sun was out, but dark clouds hovered over the mountains to the west. Eli touched the folder. He wasn't anxious to learn more about the family Gato. He was only interested in bringing Homer Hodge to justice. His cellphone rang.

"I need to see you," Veronica said.

Images from their night together flickered in his mind. His pulse quickened, he finished his drink. "My office," he said.

"Be there in ten."

Eli called Carpenter and launched into a condensed version of what he believed happened to Almario Gato. Hodge fell in love with Maria, a young, exotic student. She broke his heart. He begged for another chance. She refused. Then, under considerable emotional strain from his wife's terminal illness, he sought a way to hurt Maria. Aware of her devotion to Almario and Almario's drug use, he figured out a way to make Maria feel as horribly as he did: kill Almario. Kill the only family she had left. Take revenge.

"It's more than just conjecture." Eli put down his drink, untouched. "I have evidence."

"Anything that would hold up in court?"

"I have a handwritten letter that Hodge wrote to Maria after she ended things. No specific references to Almario, but it does say..." Eli dug the letter out of a drawer, smoothed it out on the desk, "'I know what you love most in this world. I know what you cannot live without.'"

"Too vague. Speaks to motive, sure, but it's not enough. What else you got?"

"A bottle of levamisole in Hodge's apartment. The prescription is in his wife's name, Gladys Hodge. Put that together with the pictures I took of Hodge's stash in the trunk of his car and the three ounces hidden in his tulip bed and that makes for a solid case."

Carpenter grunted. "If this were a TV show, you just hit a walk-off home run. In reality, it's just a bloop single. First, you're not a cop and didn't have a warrant to search Hodge's car, his apartment, or his tulip bed. Whatever you found in there is useless in a court of law. Second, you said the letter was handwritten. It's tough to prove ownership of a handwritten letter. You could have it checked for fingerprints, but who knows what'll turn up? Third, you said Hodge doesn't have an alibi for the night Almario died, but you still have to prove he got the tainted drugs to Almario. Remember, Almario could have gotten those drugs any time from anyone. That'll present challenges, too. The police need probable cause. Hard evidence that'll withstand the scrutiny of attorneys, judges, and juries. Your case, such as it is, won't ever make it to court."

Eli picked up his drink. Put it down. "Forget about court. Forget the police."

"As an ex-detective myself, I have a healthy disdain for the shield. But don't be rash."

"I don't want to break the law, just bend it enough to catch a murderer."

"If that's all you want, the solution is simple."

"Confession?"

"Bingo." Silence. "Murder investigations are high-stakes, kid. Bottom of the ninth and you're down to your last strike type stuff. You gotta be prepared to swing away or never step up to the plate. You ready to do that?"

Eli looked out the window. Dark clouds shifting. "Batter up," he said and downed his drink in one gulp.

CHAPTER 19

It was time to get organized.

After finishing a second drink, Eli uploaded the pictures of Hodge's cocaine stash to his computer and printed out hard copies, making sure that Hodge's license plate was visible in each photograph. Next, he made copies of Maria Gato's cell-phone records, highlighting the two dozen or so phone calls Hodge had made to Maria in the last two weeks. Then he made copies of the threatening letter Hodge sent Maria. Eli placed all the paper evidence in a manila folder and put the photograph of Maria Gato naked on top of the other evidence. Finally, he put on a pair of latex gloves and dropped the bottle of levamisole into a Ziploc bag. Removing the gloves, he typed up a concise, two-page summary of what he believed Homer Hodge did to Almario Gato, saving it in three different places. If nothing else worked, Eli would send the document to the *Asheville Citizen Times.* And any other newspaper or TV news station that would give it ink or air time.

Veronica walked in, wearing skinny jeans and a green scoop-neck blouse that showcased a constellation of freckles on her shoulders and neck.

Eli inhaled. "My third fiancée wore that scent."

"She had exquisite taste. In perfume."

"But not men."

"Are you drunk?"

"Not drunk. Motivated. Highly so." He held up the manila folder filled with evidence against Homer Hodge. "You're a lawyer. Read over my case and give me your opinion."

"What about that one?" Veronica pointed to the Rubio's blue folder.

Eli glanced at the folder, too preoccupied with Homer Hodge to get into it now. "Just some information on Almario's defection to America. Nothing relevant to the case. Read my file. I need a barrister's opinion."

Veronica sat in the director's chair and opened the folder. She looked at the pictures first, held the photograph of Hodge's cocaine stash up to the light. Eli tossed her the Ziploc bag with the bottle of levamisole inside, and she caught it.

"The medical examiner found traces of cocaine and *that* in Almario's system. I think it killed him."

"What does Meachum say?"

"Can't confirm anything until a full toxicology report has been filed. He's ready to call it an 'accident by drugs.' The ME is, too."

"Who is Gladys Hodge?"

"Homer Hodge's dying wife. Hodge was Maria's psychology teacher and a purveyor of narcotics. Among other things. Maria was having an affair with him. Look at the rest of the pictures." She found the picture of Maria naked. She put her hand over her mouth. "I found that in Hodge's apartment, tucked away in an obscure literary journal that published one of his poems. Apparently, he fell hard for Maria, and when she finally came to her senses and ended it, he cracked. He threatened her."

"Threatened her how?"

"By threatening Almario. Read the letter."

She did. Her face registered anger; her emerald eyes flashed hatred. Eli poured her a whiskey and slid it across the desk. She refused it. She read Eli's two-page case summary and then, with a poised and determined look on her face, ran a hand through her short blonde hair. She was a lawyer once again. A determined one.

Veronica said, "From a legal standpoint, you have nothing. The letter, while threatening, is vague, and you have no way of proving Hodge wrote it. The handwriting might match, but it's an inexact science. As for the drugs, possession is nine-tenths of the law. These are pictures. And murder? Well, you're a bright guy. I think you know you have an uphill climb to make that charge stick."

Eli sat on the edge of the desk, the alcohol sharpening his wits while masking his anger for Hodge. "Now that Almario is gone, you're the most important person in Maria's life. What I need to do will be ugly. Maria's name may get dragged through the mud."

She closed the evidence folder. "You saw her at the funeral. She broke down during the eulogy. She's damaged, scarred. *We* should do something."

"Is that why you asked to see me?"

"That's one reason."

"And the other?"

She pressed her body against his, kissed him long and hard. Eli encircled her waist with his arm and guided her to the futon. He carefully removed her high-heeled boots and jeans, folded them neatly and laid them on the desk. He kissed every inch of her long, firm legs, savoring the salty-sweet taste of her skin while she struggled out of her blouse and bra. He made his way up her body, kissing her bare stomach, her ribcage, her breasts... As he explored her neck with his tongue, he slid his hand between her legs, lightly touching and stroking everywhere but the most sensitive of places, teasing her until she whispered, "*Now.*"

Afterward, Eli, still prone on the futon, checked his Seiko: 2:22 p.m. Hodge's office hours began at three. Time to get a move on. He dressed quickly.

But then Veronica emerged from the bathroom in a towel, her long, lean body glistening, and a string of questions shoved all other thoughts aside for the moment. Could they be good together? Could it work if they saw each other on a regular basis?

Once she was fully dressed, Eli remembered she lived in L.A., which disappointed him and filled him with a sense of relief.

Veronica reapplied her makeup, dropped the lipstick in her purse, and opened Rubio's folder.

"I'm starting my own law firm," she said, "in L.A."

"No more sports agent?"

She shook her head. "Maria asked to come with me. Begged me, in fact."

"Could be good for her."

"But not so good for me. It would be like having a child."

"Maria can take care of herself. When will you leave?"

She closed the folder. "Soon. In the next day or two. I don't care for the mountains."

"Too much fresh air?"

"I'm a city gal," she said in a mock Southern accent. "Besides, it could take months for Almario's insurance claims to get sorted out."

"Well, I've really enjoyed meeting you and hope to see you again sometime."

Veronica laughed, rattling the framed Nixon posters. "Is that the best you got?"

"Sorry."

"Save the apologies, Sharpe. You know, I will need a good investigator."

"First things first. Don't leave town just yet."

"I can't leave town. Not until I know what happened."

"Good," Eli said, kissing her forehead. "Keep your cell on. I may need legal counsel."

Back up, too.

***

Eli entered the lobby of the Renaissance Hotel at 2:46 p.m. Plush carpeting. Heavy upholstered furniture. Watercolor paintings on the wall bespoke of a rebirth, just not the one that happened in Italy in the 1500s.

Eli asked the concierge, a plain-faced brunette in a gray pantsuit, to tell him which room Frank Waring was in, and her nose lifted a full two inches into the air.

"I cannot give out that information, sir."

Eli dropped the Ziploc bag containing the bottle of levamisole on her desk. He waited a beat. Then he laid the picture of Hodge's cocaine stash right beside the Ziploc bag. He gauged her reaction.

"Perhaps your patrons," he said loudly, "might like to know what's going on in your hotel."

The concierge pecked at a keyboard, ran her finger over a computer screen. "He checked out, sir."

"When?"

"Thirty minutes ago. The two men he checked in with are still present."

"Caulder and Gifford?"

She nodded. "They have a suite on the fourth floor. Room four twenty-four. But sir?"

"Yes?"

"Don't tell anyone I told you."

Eli knocked on 424 and elbowed past Caulder on the way inside.

Gifford was sitting on the couch reading the *Asheville Citizen Times,* his hand heavily bandaged. Eli dropped his evidence on the glass coffee table.

Gifford glanced at the Ziploc bag, and then at Eli and Caulder. Gifford picked up the Ziploc bag, and Caulder opened the manila folder and began leafing through the photographs, his eyes widening when they came to the picture of Maria Gato naked. Gifford squinted at the picture in Caulder's hand.

"Is that—"

"Yes," Eli said, "it is."

Caulder whimpered like a scared puppy.

Gifford held the Ziploc bag up to the light. "Levamisole. Veterinarians use this stuff. And who the hell's Gladys Hodge?"

Caulder finished reading Hodge's letter to Maria and whimpered again. Then he read the two-page summary Eli had written and handed it to Gifford. As Gifford read, Eli asked where Waring skipped off to.

"Owners called an emergency meeting," said Caulder. "Obviously, they caught wind of what happened down here, and they wanted a firsthand report."

"Horseshit. They've been looking to get rid of Waring for the past year. This is just the final straw."

"Mr. Sharpe, I fear my colleague is right. Frank Waring's position in the Rockies organization is in jeopardy. So are ours."

Gifford tossed the manila folder on the coffee table, scratched his cauliflower ear. "No way this holds up. But you knew that already, or you'd have gone to the police. And my squirmy friend in public relations is right: Waring goes down, we go with him."

"Maybe not," Eli said. "What if I had a way to save your jobs and get justice for Almario's killer?"

"I'd be interested," Gifford said. "Almario seemed like a good kid, got mixed up with bad drugs and worse people is all. What you got on this Hodge seems solid. Solid enough for an investigation anyway. A lot of smoke, but there's some fire."

"I don't see that we have much choice," Caulder said. "As the story stands, some of the responsibility for Almario's death has to be laid at the organization's doorstep. At best, we look incompetent. At worst, grossly negligent. The public will think we allowed an eighteen-year-old future superstar to piss his life away on drugs. Pardon my vulgar language. We *have* to help."

"What's our first move?" Gifford asked. "Confront Hodge?"

"You and me will take care of that."

"What about me?" Caulder asked.

"You're going to the hospital to visit Gladys Hodge."

Eli called Veronica Craven, told her he needed assistance.

The plan: Eli and Gifford were going to confront Hodge with the evidence and convince him to confess to delivering Almario tainted drugs. If that didn't work, Caulder and Veronica would be standing by at the hospital with copies of the evidence, ready to let Gladys Hodge know exactly whom she married.

"That's blackmail," Veronica said. "What we're doing is blackmail."

"No, what *I'm* doing is blackmail. What you're doing is accompanying an operative of mine to see a potential client named Gladys Hodge. Now here's your story: during the course of a separate investigation, I learned of criminal acts committed by her husband Homer Hodge and felt she should talk to him before the police do. You'll be there to provide her any legal assistance, should she require it. Understand?"

Veronica cleared her throat.

"Say the word and you're out. No hard feelings. Either way, I'm going after this guy."

"It's despicable, but I'll do it."

Silence.

"What's wrong?" Eli asked.

"You need him to confess," she said. "On tape. There must be a verifiable record of the confession, one that is not coerced. You understand? He needs to say exactly what he did to Almario. Otherwise, it won't do us any good."

"Leave that to me. Just be in the lobby of the hospital at 4 p.m. Look for Caulder. Medium height and build. Balding. Tan sport coat."

Arrangements made, Eli went to a heavy oak desk in the corner of the suite where a computer, printer and fax machine sat. He scanned pictures, documents, printed out copies of each. Keeping the originals in the folder, he gave the copies to Caulder, told him to go to the hospital.

Gifford tightened the bandage on his hand.

"Let's go," Eli said.

***

At precisely 4 p.m., Eli and Gifford barged into a classroom with stadium-style seating. Gifford adopted the bouncer stance: arms crossed menacingly at his chest. Interrupting Hodge's lecture, Eli whistled and waved the evidence folder in the air. Students whispered. Hodge—dressed in dark trousers, pink golf shirt, and a black sport jacket—stopped pacing the stage, put his hands behind his back. Even now, he appeared comfortable, at ease standing before an audience. His shoulders were up, his back arched. Scratching his silver hair, he looked up at the whiteboard and then back at the classroom of confused students.

"Class dismissed."

When the room cleared, Eli and Gifford joined Hodge on stage. Hodge was waiting for them, his hands clasped behind his back.

"Mr. Sharpe, if you've come for my head, it's yours for the taking. Since our last encounter I've been at loose ends."

Eli pressed RECORD on his iPhone and handed Hodge the evidence folder.

"What is this?"

"The last act," said Eli.

"Curtains for you," Gifford said.

Sighing, Hodge put on a pair of silver and black glasses and opened the folder. He saw the pictures first. No reaction. He read Eli's summary of how Almario Gato met his demise. Still no reaction. It wasn't until he read the threatening letter he'd sent to Maria that his eyes flashed amusement, pride even. He almost smiled, but stopped himself in time.

"Mr. Sharpe, on our last interview I sensed that you were upset about Almario's death."

"He was just a kid," Gifford said through clenched teeth.

"Yes, it is always a tragedy when a young man is cut down before his time. Believe me, I've seen many a young black male succumb to drugs and petty crime."

"We don't have time for sermons," Gifford said. "Admit what you did. Now."

"My partner is right," Eli said. "We have very little time. We've come to appeal to your better angels. We've come for your official confession to turn over to the police."

Hodge removed his glasses. He was calm. "I cannot do that."

Gifford looked at Eli, who put a hand on Gifford's shoulder. "I must say, for a man accused of murdering his lover's twin brother, you seem awfully tranquil."

"Quite the contrary. I'm furious, but at my age the emotion manifests itself internally rather than externally. As to your 'evidence,' I'm afraid you have been led down the primrose path."

Gifford breathed loudly through his mouth.

"Gentlemen," Hodge said coolly, "An explanation is in order, not a confession. The letter. I did not write it."

"I read the letter myself," Eli said. "It sure as hell sounds like you, Professor."

"True, the rhetorical style and syntax are mine, but write it I did not. Mr. Sharpe, you may allow your pit bull there to knock me down, if you must, but the fact remains that neither of you have looked at this unfortunate turn of events from all angles."

"I've looked at it from as many angles as I need to." Eli removed the Ziploc bag containing the levamisole bottle from his pocket and tossed it at Hodge, who dropped it and picked it up. "All signs point to you, Hodge. You were in love with Almario's twin sister and she dumped you unceremoniously. You were humiliated by an eighteen-year-old girl and wanted to hurt her as badly as she hurt you."

"That's motive," Gifford said.

"You sold cocaine to your students and other drug dealers in town, namely, Dantonio Rushing. Your wife is deathly ill and had a prescription for levamisole."

"That's method," Gifford said a little louder.

"I got a call this morning from Bill Meachum, the lead detective on the case. The medical examiner said it looks like Almario had both cocaine and levamisole in his system, and I'm betting when the toxicity report comes out it will show that levamisole killed him, not the cocaine. We know you met Maria three hours before Almario died. She had the letter you sent. You gave her one last chance to take you back, but she refused. Using your knowledge of basic chemistry, you mixed up a special dose just for Almario and made sure he got it. You don't have an alibi for the night Almario died, do you?"

"That's opportunity," said Gifford.

Hodge put his hands behind his back.

"An innocent man would get angry if falsely accused," Eli said. "Your silence is deafening."

Hodge said, "That is true. I am not innocent. I am guilty of many things. Adultery. Drug trafficking. Incredibly poor judgment. Betrayal. Et cetera." He waved the rest away as if they were beside the point. "But I'm not a murderer, and I return to my original thesis: Mr. Sharpe, you haven't examined this situation from all possible angles. In fact, you've failed to see what is right under your own nose. You, like me, have been manipulated by a most brilliant sociopath."

"What the hell is he talking about, Sharpe?"

"You say I have a motive, and so I do. I was, or am, enraged by what passed between Maria and me. I loved her the way I once loved my soon-to-be-departed wife. I also had a method by which to dispatch Maria's drug-addicted brother as well as an opportunity to kill him much in the manner that you describe. However, the fact remains that I did not kill him, would not kill him or anybody else. Occam's Razor, are you gentlemen familiar with it?"

Gifford grunted.

"A scientific theory," Eli said. "When you have two competing theories predicting the same result, the simpler of the two theories is the correct one."

"Precisely. And here is my theory: Maria Gato is a very troubled young woman. In psychological terms, she suffers from obsessive filial envy and a diabolical hatred of both parents. She feels constant guilt that her parents are dead as I'm sure she feels guilt over her brother's death. Believe it or not, she is, through manipulations both physical and psychological, responsible for the destruction of her own nuclear family."

"How is that a simpler theory than the old boyfriend did it?" Gifford asked.

"Forgive me. I'll put it more simply, in deference to you, Mr. Gifford: Maria was jealous of her brother, his talent, his money, his looks, and all the attention he received from everyone, most importantly her parents. She was so consumed with jealousy that she, not I, conspired to kill him. And now she is trying to frame me."

"Bullshit," Gifford said. "I met Maria. She wouldn't kill anyone, let alone her brother."

"She loved him," Eli said, surprised at the razor sharp edge in his voice. "She took care of him."

"What you say is partially true. Maria does, or did, love her brother, and the thought of killing him is abhorrent to her, but it is also intoxicating, dangerously so. Realize that this young girl had a lifetime of mental abuse from her parents, all of it stemming, in one way or another, from Almario." Hodge had hit his rhetorical stride and began pacing the stage, using hand gestures to emphasize his points. "Consider her plight: she has been on this planet for over eighteen years and never once has she stood in the spotlight. She has always stood in Almario's shadow. She's had eighteen years to allow this jealousy and hatred and envy to simmer and simmer and simmer inside of her until, finally, regrettably, it boiled over.

"And never forget Maria's keen intelligence. If you truly believe she is not capable of manipulating everyone around her, myself included, you have underestimated her." Hodge picked up a red Expo pen and wrote the word MARIA on the whiteboard and circled it, drew several diagonal lines stemming from MARIA. At the end of each line he wrote words like JEALOUSY and HATRED and OBSESSION and INTELLIGENCE and circled them. Finally, he wrote the word MONEY.

Insurance policy, Eli thought, *eight million dollars*. His face burned. The knot in his stomach threatened to snap completely. He snatched Hodge's pen and threw it across the room.

Eli lowered his arms to his side, listened to his heart pounding in his ears. Like a man who'd lost his way in the forest, he retraced his steps. Initially, all signs pointed to Sheri Stuckey, Almario's fiancée drug dealer, and Dantonio Rushing. Cellphone records indicated Maria had been in contact with both of them. But to what end? She claimed she begged them to stop selling drugs to Almario, but was there more to it than that? If Hodge was right, maybe Maria was using Stuckey and Rushing as patsies to deflect suspicion. Maybe Maria, not Stuckey, was the one who wrote the email to Brad Newman claiming that money—Almario's money—would be coming in soon and that would give Stuckey a motive to hurt Almario. And what about the fake email Maria received from Almario? It was riddled with grammatical errors, very similar to the email Stuckey allegedly wrote to Brad Newman. Maybe Maria wrote that one, too, to draw more suspicion on Stuckey and away from herself.

Or maybe Maria marked Hodge from the very beginning?

"Did Maria ever mention money? Almario's insurance policy?"

"Of course not," Hodge said, obviously amused by the questions and Eli's anger. "She never spoke of money, or of insurance. She spoke often of Veronica Craven, though. Her beauty, her intelligence. Maria spoke of moving to Los Angeles. 'Once things are settled,' was the way she put it, I believe.

"Now mind you, I'm not insinuating Veronica Craven had anything to do with Almario's death. I certainly have no proof, only suspicions." Hodge clasped his hands behind his back once more. "On the other hand, it makes perfect sense, from a psychological perspective. Veronica Craven, as described to me by Maria, is a statuesque blonde with exquisite taste and a superior intellect. And she is kind to Maria—unlike the disapproving mother who criticized her at every turn, who constantly compared her to Almario.

"And I hasten to add that Veronica lives in a city built on fantasy, a dazzling metropolis that might as well exist on a different planet in a different galaxy than the one in Old Havana where Maria started out. From what I gathered from Maria, Almario was Veronica's biggest client, and he was underperforming on the field. He was injury prone and a drug abuser. His future was uncertain at best, and perhaps Veronica had her own motives. This insurance policy you spoke of, Mr. Sharpe. Who did you say helped write it?"

The ground gave way under Eli's feet. Dizziness. Sweat. He breathed. He thought. Perhaps Veronica stood to gain financially from Almario's death, too. She'd said Almario was her biggest client, and that her father, a very wealthy man, had left most of his money to his wives. And now, Veronica wanted to start her own law firm. In Los Angeles. A notoriously expensive city.

Maybe Veronica and Maria had been playing him from the beginning.

Or maybe Hodge was trying to save his own ass.

Or maybe Almario accidentally overdosed.

Anything seemed possible.

Hodge said, "It doesn't feel good to play the fool, does it?"

Eli nodded at Gifford, who pinned Hodge against the whiteboard. "Call campus security," Eli said. "Have them check the faded green 1993 Volvo in the Faculty Parking Lot. Give them the evidence we have. Tell them to start interviewing Hodge's students and look for anyone willing to talk about drug deals involving the professor here."

"Instructor," Hodge said, staring levelly up at Gifford. "I never finished my dissertation. I go by Instructor Hodge."

"What about Caulder?" Gifford poked a finger in Hodge's chest. "As much as it pains me to say it, I vote we leave Mrs. Hodge out of this. She'll find out soon enough what type of sociopath she's been sleeping next to all these years."

"Whatever you choose to do, Mr. Sharpe, you cannot say you weren't warned: Maria Gato is false."

"As are you," Eli said, tamping down his anger by thinking about Hodge in handcuffs. "Gifford, tell Caulder to have that talk with Mrs. Hodge. It's high time she knew the truth about the professor."

While Gifford waited with Hodge for campus security, Eli went outside and found shade from the heat under a maple tree, watched students come and go, wondering how many of them knew Hodge was a drug dealer, how many would suspect he was a murderer. But these thoughts passed quickly, replaced by more nagging queries.

Like: was Maria Gato a killer?

And: did Veronica Craven help?

When Eli was ten or so, he finally worked up the nerve to ask why Daddy was a criminal. His mom delivered a lucid lecture on criminality.

A joint in one hand and the remote in the other, she said, "Son, there are two types of criminals. Shorts and Longs. Shorts are impatient and pick up easy money where they can. Low risk, low reward. But Longs are willing to wait as long as it takes. You need patience in spades if you're chasing big money and the stakes are high. Easy to remember: Shorts are harmless, Longs are dangerous. Real dangerous."

A car stereo thumping in the parking lot, and Eli wondered just who was the Long in the Gato case. Homer Hodge or Maria Gato?

Eli called Veronica Craven.

Straight to voicemail.

"Hodge wouldn't confess. Call me as soon as you get this."

Eli called Maria Gato next.

Straight to voicemail.

"It's over. Hodge confessed to everything. Call me as soon as you get this."

Eli called Caulder.

"Where's Veronica?"

"She never showed," Caulder said nervously. "What happened?"

"My plan didn't work. Call me if you see Veronica."

Driving away from the Humanities building, Eli passed a campus security car, its red siren flashing. He pounded his fist on the steering wheel, and the horn blew, scaring a group of joggers on the sidewalk.

Maria Gato?

A killer?

Eli needed to speak with her one more time. Face to face.

But first: Rubio's blue folder.

Which turned out to be a horrific account of Maria Gato's defection to the United States.

CHAPTER 20

At 4:21 p.m., Eli entered the Verizon Store and elbowed his way to the front of the line, ignoring the menacing looks and muttered curses directed at him.

Gripping two folders in his right hand, he said, "Get Garrett. Tell him I need to see all texts and phone calls for Almario and Maria Gato for the past two days." Eli won a staring contest with the high school kid behind the counter. Garrett, the dreadlocked manager, printed out the records and installed Eli in the same room he'd occupied days before.

"And my letter of recommendation. When can I expect that?"

"Soon. I'm a man of my word."

"I believe you said you had a lawyer, one who could recommend me. I believe that would carry more weight with my bosses. No offense."

"I'll get it done."

Garrett held his hands up in surrender and left the room.

Eli arranged his folders side by side—Rubio's blue folder and the evidence folder Eli had prepared for the press. He placed his leather notebook beside the two folders and then the new phone records beside the notebook. He hoped he wouldn't find anything damning in the phone records.

But he did.

Almario received three phone calls from Maria Gato on the

night he died. The calls were made at 8:46 p.m., 10:08 p.m., and 11:06 p.m. According to the ME, Almario died between 11 p.m. and 12 a.m. Maria had met with Hodge at the park around 8 p.m. and left the park around 8:30 p.m. Consulting his case notes, Eli established it took about twenty minutes to get from the Burly Earl to the abandoned mental health facility where Almario had been found.

Eli constructed a tentative timeline. For argument's sake. Just to see if it was possible.

Maybe the 8:46 p.m. phone call had been to arrange a meeting between Maria and Almario.

Maybe the 10:08 p.m. call was to let Almario know Maria had arrived, tainted drugs in tow.

Maybe the 11:06 p.m. call was to make sure Almario was dead.

A lot of maybes.

But factor those maybes in with the contents of Rubio's blue folder and the picture got much clearer. Uglier, too.

Eli double-checked the phone records, using a highlighter to make sure he got the correct times. When he reviewed the calls a third time, he took note of the calls' durations. The 11:06 p.m. call lasted nine seconds, the others more than a minute. This bothered him. He reevaluated the contents of Rubio's blue folder, examined the police reports and photographs. He read. He thought. He took his time coming to an unavoidable conclusion...

Maria Gato killed her parents.

And if she was capable of paying a boat smuggler a large sum of cash to make her parents' drowning look accidental, and if she was capable of lying to police and immigration officers about what really happened, and if she was capable of spending months in a mental health facility in Miami, pretending to be grief-stricken over the loss...

Then maybe she killed her twin brother, too.

* * *

The elevator door opened onto the Gato penthouse, and Eli nearly tripped over a full set of Louis Vuitton luggage. Loud Spanish music, smell of cumin. He moved into the kitchen. A boiling pot. Half-empty glass of red wine, the rim kissed by lipstick. Next to the wine: a Take Me Out travel book of Los Angeles and a first-class ticket aboard Flight 633—nonstop to L.A. out of Charlotte International Airport, leaving the following morning.

"Veronica?"

The sauce in the pot bubbled in rhythm to the music.

"Maria?"

No answer.

Eli called Veronica's cellphone. Straight to voicemail. He called Maria's cellphone. Straight to voicemail. He sat the evidence folders on the kitchen counter, turned the heat down on the sauce. The music ended in a crescendo of horns and drums and for a moment there was silence and he yelled again. Footsteps on the marble floor in the hallway. Eli followed the sound. Four doors along the corridor, two on each side, all of them shut.

"Maria, we need to talk."

The silence ended. A ballad, just an acoustic guitar and a sorrowful voice.

Eli opened the first door on the right. Bathroom with all the amenities: steam shower, heated tile floors, dual sinks, monogrammed towels. On the counter: Light Blue by Dolce & Gabbana. Same scent Veronica Craven wore. Same scent his third fiancée wore. Eli backed out of the room slowly, his eyes focused on the perfume bottle, wondering what it meant.

He checked the next door on the right. Media room complete with an endless L-shaped couch and an oversized flat screen TV. On the floor were piles of DVDs, all of them in jewel cases, all of them bearing Almario's name and different dates. Game film. Trying to figure out what went wrong with his swing. Eli had been there many times. Too many. Eli heard a door shut and hurried out into the hallway, saw the last door on the left standing slightly ajar. Almario's bedroom. He hurried inside, searched high and low. What he found: a pine-scented candle burning on the dresser beside a picture of a Catholic saint.

"Maria!"

"In the kitchen!"

Standing before the bubbling pot, Maria was wearing a canary yellow dress that was too short and too tight, especially around the midsection.

"Have you come to see me off, Mr. Sharpe?" she asked, her voice sounding chipper.

Before Eli could answer, a new song began, an up tempo number with a syncopated drumbeat, and Maria wiggled her hips, dipped the spoon into the sauce, tasted, and crinkled her nose.

"*Demasiado soso,*" she said flicking a pinch of red pepper flakes into the pot. "That means 'not spicy enough.' I'm making empanadas for Almario." She crossed herself, kissed her fingers. "I'm burning a candle to St. Louise in his bedroom."

"You dyed your hair blonde," Eli said.

"I straightened it, too. With an iron. And I bought this dress. You like?"

Eli nodded mutely. "Are you okay, Maria?"

"*Cansado.* Very tired. The night before the funeral I stayed with Almario. Funeral parlors are scary places, but we prayed together. I prayed for him. I saw the Holy Spirit take him Home, and now I have no more sadness. Today I made arrangements to have him shipped back to Cuba. My parents would have wanted it that way."

Eli remembered reading that some religions require a family member to stay with the body until it was buried, but he didn't think Catholics did that. Or did they?

"We need to talk," Eli said. "Where is Veronica?"

A smile. "I'm going with her to Los Angeles. I'm going to enroll at UCLA and major in psychology and become a counselor."

"Where is Veronica?"

"I have so many exciting things to see." Maria picked up the travel book, showed Eli pictures of all the places she intended to visit. The Hollywood sign. Rodeo Drive. TCL Chinese Theatre. Universal Studios." She reached for her wine glass, sipped. "Mr. Sharpe, I've never flown before. I've read that flying is much safer than riding in a car. Is that true? Is flying safe?"

"Where is Veronica?"

Maria's eyes glazed over, obliterating all traces of excitement. "I thought you came to see me. I'm the one in mourning. What is in those folders?"

"Hodge didn't kill Almario," Eli said and picked up both of the folders. "He'll most likely be charged with distributing cocaine, and there will be a new investigation into Almario's death. Do you understand what that means?"

Maria stirred the sauce.

"The night Almario died, you said you met Hodge, and that's when he tried to talk you into taking him back. You said he gave you this letter to threaten you." Eli opened his evidence folder and laid the letter beside her wine glass. "Maria, Hodge never wrote this letter."

"Yes, he did," she said calmly, her eyes focused on the *sofrito*. "That is *his* handwriting. You can compare it to other letters he wrote me."

Eli sat the phone records beside the letter. "Where were you between 9 p.m. and 11 p.m. the night your brother died?"

A pause in the music. An advertisement in Spanish.

"I'll answer that," Veronica said, breezing into the kitchen. She put her arm around Maria, gave Eli the Board Room Glare. "I was with Maria that night. She came to my hotel room at the Renaissance around eight forty-five. We ate dinner at Tupelo Honey on College Street. I have the receipt. Our waitress can confirm we were both there."

"Maria, I know you made three phone calls that night, all of them to Almario. Two of them would have been during your dinner at Tupelo Honey. Why did you call him?"

Veronica put her hands on her hips. Power position. Same one she no doubt used during a tough negotiation. "You don't have to answer that. The question is wildly inappropriate. Mr. Sharpe here has failed the task which was his charge, and now he's lashing out at a poor, grieving sister."

"Maria, what time did you leave Tupelo Honey?"

"Don't answer that."

"Maria, where did you go after dinner?"

"Don't answer that."

"Maria, the police will ask you these questions, and your answers—"

"Will be prepared by her attorney. Me. You will not try to implicate this poor child in Almario's death. I will not allow it. I will not—"

"Maria, what time did you leave Tupelo Honey?"

"Nine-thirty," Maria said and shrugged out of Veronica's embrace. "After we left the restaurant, Veronica was drunk, so we walked back to my apartment. It was closer than her hotel."

"And you were with Veronica the whole night? In your apartment?"

"Yes," Veronica said, "she was."

"No, that's not true. Veronica fell asleep on the couch, and I took her car for a drive to clear my head. I drove around town and I got back to the apartment around ten thirty"

Veronica crossed her arms, asked what happened with Homer Hodge, asked just what Eli thought he was doing.

"Hodge didn't kill Almario." Eli opened the blue folder Rubio had left at his office, spread out the death reports filed by the Cuban police and the last known photographs of José Gato and Manuela Gato, which were taken on the day they left Cuba. They looked happy, excited. Hopeful. Maria looked at the pictures with a vacant expression on her face. Eli picked up another document from inside the folder, and Veronica snatched it out of his hand, read it, the color slowly draining from her face.

"Maria, Veronica is holding a signed confession from the smuggler that got you and your parents out of Cuba. You paid him ten thousand dollars to 'accidentally drown' José and Manuela Gato en route to America. You paid him more money—Almario's money—to keep quiet."

Veronica read the confession aloud, her voice filled with horror.

Maria took the photograph of her parents in hand, kissed her father's face, crossed herself, placed the picture back in the folder. Then she picked up her travel book.

"St. Louise is the patron saint of orphans." Maria clutched the book to her chest as if it were the Bible. "Mr. Sharpe, I'm an orphan. People sympathize with an orphan. People love an orphan."

Veronica stepped away from Maria and toward Eli.

"Maria, you paid to have your parents' death look like an accidental drowning. But the confessor, the smuggler, is in jail in Cuba. Which means—"

"I know what it means, Mr. Sharpe. I'm not going to jail. Not here. Not in Cuba. Not anywhere."

Eli explained to Maria how she plotted to kill Almario. How she constructed a web of deceptions that cast suspicions on Sheri Stuckey and Dantonio Rushing, two drug dealers Almario knew well. He ended by explaining how she used Homer Hodge.

"At first, he was your mentor, a father figure of sorts, but he fell in love with you, and you let him think you loved him, too. But when you found out about his dealing and his dying wife, you saw an opportunity. You got him to show you how to make cocaine, a relatively easy scientific process once you get the hang of it, and then you got access to his house and his wife's drugs. Levamisole. From there, it was only a matter of time."

Maria opened her travel book, calmly skimmed the pages.

Eli continued, "Consider the timeline, Maria. You said you left the restaurant at nine-thirty and went back to your apartment, which is only two blocks away. That couldn't have taken more than fifteen minutes. Then when Veronica fell asleep, you went for a drive. So from roughly nine forty-five to ten-thirty, no one can account for your whereabouts. When the police investigate, they will look at the GPS in Veronica's rental car. It will tell them precisely where the car was between those times."

Silence.

The music started again. Another up tempo number.

"Maria? Do you understand what I just said?"

Maria closed her book. She looked down at her canary yellow dress, and then looked at Veronica, who was holding her breath. Then she looked at Eli. After a long pause, she extended her hand.

"Mr. Sharpe, I appreciate all you've done for my brother."

"I just accused you of killing Almario. Deny it. Prove me wrong. Say something. Please."

When she realized Eli wasn't going to shake her hand, she sighed like a disappointed mother.

"Say *something*," Veronica said.

"*Demuestrelo,*" she said and left the room with her travel book.

Seconds later the music stopped.

Having played with Spanish-speaking players, Eli knew a few phrases. *Demuestrelo* meant "prove it." It was a dare, a challenge. He checked his Seiko: 5:17 p.m.

"You have to do something," Veronica finally said, her voice almost a whisper.

Eli sidestepped the Louis Vuitton luggage on his way out of the penthouse.

Pint of George Dickel in hand, Eli sat in his truck, parked outside police headquarters. He drank, watched uniformed officers and men in handcuffs come and go. Stewing in his own sweat, he turned on the AC, grabbed the evidence folder off the passenger seat, read what he'd already read half a dozen times.

> At or around 2:43 a.m., the small speedboat disembarked from the Port of Havana with four people aboard: José Gato, Manuela Gato, Maria Gato, and Juan Cortez, the captain of the boat. The boat left Cuba, heading to Miami, Florida, without incident. Then at or around 3:12 a.m., the boat entered international waters, and Juan Cortez pretended to hit a coral reef.

Eli skipped down the page, past the summation of the actual event Maria Gato had orchestrated.

> ...a check made out to CASH...
> ...Maria Gato made several more payments to Cortez after the event...

Eli closed the folder of information Rubio had obtained from his Miami contact. It was true. The murder was premeditated. Maria had had a plan. Just like with Almario. The smuggler, who was wasting away in a Cuban prison on an unrelated charge, confessed the whole thing to the prison warden and a Catholic priest. But it was still the word of a convicted felon versus an orphan. With no criminal record. Who lived in a country with no extradition treaty with Cuba.

The knot in Eli's stomach tightened once more. He took a final swig, locked the pint in the glove compartment.

Five minutes later, he was sitting in Bill Meachum's cubicle in the Criminal Investigations building. Meachum had bags under his eyes. His beard needed a trim, his long hair needed a wash. But he still had his spit cup handy.

Meachum said, "Your boy Hodge is in the box, and he's talking. Didn't even ask for a lawyer."

"What is he asking for?"

"Just that his wife be looked after. Sent some uniforms out to the hospital to check on her."

Eli nodded. "Hodge say anything about Almario yet?"

"Not a thing. But he's confessed to trafficking narcotics. Said he had an affair with Maria Gato, but I told him that was beyond my purview."

"Lean on Dantonio Rushing for more information about Hodge's drug trafficking. Sharon Stuckey, too." Silence. "So he hasn't said anything about Almario Gato?"

"Why would he? We moved on the evidence your man with the cauliflower ear gave us. Brought a warrant and searched Hodge's car. Found about fourteen ounces worth of cocaine. No muss, no fuss."

Eli handed over the evidence he'd collected, both his folder and Rubio's.

Meachum spat in his cup. Took his time leafing through the documents and the photographs. Then he looked at Eli. Eli told him what happened to Almario Gato and who was responsible. This time, he didn't leave out any details.

"Circumstantial," Meachum said. "Won't hold up in court. Not unless Hodge knows something he isn't saying."

"Show him what happened to José and Manuela Gato."

"Could work."

"If it doesn't, go straight to Maria Gato. I know this is your investigation and I jammed you up."

"Save the speeches, son. I don't give a damn about appearances or playing the hero. If she did this thing, I want her behind bars. Same as you. But if she went to all this trouble, she won't confess just because I haul her downtown and put her in an interrogation room. What makes you think she'll talk?"

"She'll talk," Eli said. "She's dying to. She wants an audience. A big one."

Eli bought a Twix bar from the vending machine and ate it, thinking.

Ten minutes later, Eli went back, and Meachum demanded Maria's address.

"Twenty-three Battery Park," Eli said. "Fifth floor penthouse.

You got enough for a warrant?"

"We're picking her up now. For questioning."

"You should talk to Veronica Craven, too."

"The tall blonde? What's her play in all this?"

"I wish I knew. Did you talk to Hodge again?"

"He believed Maria was capable of 'patricide.' Claimed he never met Almario, though. Said he was at St. Joseph's from 8:45 p.m. to 5 a.m. the night Almario died. Place has cameras everywhere. We're checking the video to see if he's on the level."

"So Hodge is claiming he had nothing to do with Almario's death? He didn't help Maria in any way, influence her maybe?"

"Stick around for the interrogations and find out. I might need you as bait. There's free coffee down the hall."

Eli poured himself some coffee. Cold. Bitter. No sugar to be found. Only a partially obstructed view of downtown Asheville, out of a smudged and grimy window. In the restroom he splashed cold water on his face, held his right hand up to the fluorescent light. It shook. He gurgled with cold water and spat. But he still had a bad taste in his mouth. And it wasn't just from the coffee.

Eli sneaked down the hall past Meachum's cubicle, ducked into the stairwell.

Outside. Breathing easier, even though the early evening air was thick as soup. He walked to his truck. A black and white squad car jumped the curb, lights flashing. A uniformed cop got out and opened the backseat. Out came Maria Gato. She wasn't in handcuffs. The cop took her by the arm and led her toward the building's entrance, her marble-black eyes on Eli the whole way. The cop shoved her up the stairs and into the building. Eli swore he saw a smile before Maria Gato disappeared.

Eli pulled out of his parking space, turned onto Church Street. A black SUV sped and Eli half-waved, but Veronica Craven didn't see him. Or did she?

EPILOGUE

On a chilly night in early December, Eli sat in his apartment with Ernest Carpenter, drinking Earl Grey and watching his mentor jones for a cigar. Eli was relieved to be back in town, relieved to be in his own apartment after doing a week in blisteringly cold Detroit investigating a starting pitcher the Tigers were about to spend serious money on.

"You ever see him pitch?" Eli asked blowing on his mug of tea.

"Who?"

"Witkin. The lefty. The guy I've been talking about for the last five minutes."

"You know I'm a Red Sox fan from way back." Carpenter drummed his fingers on Eli's desk. "You sure I can't smoke in here?"

"I'm sure."

"I don't trust air I can't see."

"Like I was saying, this Witkin tips his breaking pitches every time. Nowadays, guy wins fifteen games in one season, and there's a bidding war for his services."

"The job pays. And pays well. Make hay while the sun shines."

"I don't mind the rain once in a while. Especially if I'm indoors to watch it."

Carpenter pointed to his gold watch, the one he received from the Asheville Police Department when he retired. "It's almost seven, kid."

"I'd rather watch *Jeopardy.*"

"You're not as funny as you think you are, kid. Or as smart."

Eli aimed the remote at a brand new thirty-two-inch flat screen TV mounted on the wall next to his Nixon memorabilia. An NBA game. Bucks and Celtics. "Look at the way they loaf back on defense. Shameful."

"Stop stalling," Carpenter says. "Turn it on before we miss the interview."

Eli clicked the remote. Reality TV. Something about the vapidity of rich wives. "You know I got a letter from Craven. Started her own law firm."

"How much did she clear on the policy?"

"Seven point four million, all told. Started a foundation in Almario's name. Donated some money to the drug treatment center Sheri Stuckey tried to check Almario into."

"That's something. Whose idea was it to make Veronica Craven the secondary beneficiary?"

"Wish I knew."

"You think she had any idea what Maria was up to?"

"Meachum interviewed her two dozen times and didn't think so. He interviewed the lot of them. Stuckey. Rushing. Lovatt. Newman. All clear. As for Hodge, Meachum pushed the D.A. hard. With a little help from Rushing's testimony, Hodge got the maximum sentence for distribution."

"Meachum." Carpenter grunted. "He did all right on this one. You sure I can't smoke?"

"Have a carrot instead."

"Turn the channel, smartass. It's four past seven."

Eli changed the channel, and Maria Gato appeared on the screen. Orange jumpsuit. Face gaunt and covered in makeup. Beneath the Cover Girl: zits and pockmarks. With her hands folded neatly in her lap, she broke the fourth wall and looked shyly into the camera, ignoring the sharply dressed woman preparing to ask Maria Gato all the tough questions.

"She's thin," Carpenter said.

"Prison food."

"And guilt. Guilt's the best diet I know of."

Eli nodded, but didn't agree. Quite the opposite. Maria Gato looked content, excited even. For the first time in her life, all eyes were on her, this put-upon, chubby little girl from Old Havana who turned out to be a murderer. A mastermind. All eyes were on her, and she reveled in the attention. Many a night she'd dreamt of this moment, and now it was here and the spotlight was shining on her and her alone. The final toxicology report showed Almario had nine hundred mg of levamisole and only eight mg of cocaine in his bloodstream. Conclusion: the de-worming medicine Maria spiked the coke with killed her twin brother, not the cocaine.

Maria had already confessed to her crimes and was awaiting sentencing. She'd confessed to having Almario send ten thousand dollars directly to her in Cuba and to using that money to pay the smuggler to help her drown her parents on the way to America and freedom. She'd confessed to stealing levamisole, mixing it with an eighth of an ounce of cocaine, and personally delivering it to her twin brother, who was suffering from severe withdrawal symptoms. She'd confessed to trying to frame Homer Hodge for Almario's death. She'd made her confession to the police, said she'd done it out of jealousy and rage, not for the insurance money. Said she was almost happy when she was caught. Happy.

But now was the most important moment, when she was on television before tens of millions of people. She'd already been written about in magazines and newspapers across the country, and she would, most likely, be written about in psychology textbooks for another couple of decades at least. But this was it; this was the moment. Her moment, and it was hers alone. Prime time TV.

The sharply-dressed woman said, "Tell us who Maria Gato

really is."

Maria looked away from the camera and bit her lip, feigning shyness. It was so easy to see through her act now, so easy to see what had been staring Eli in the face the whole time. Jealousy. Rage. Resentment. Contempt. But the knot in his stomach disappeared months ago. He sipped his tea, for the moment not caring it wasn't George Dickel.

"I'm no different than anybody else," Maria said. "I want to be loved."

"Indeed," Eli said and switched off the TV, silencing Maria Gato in mid-sentence.

Max Everhart is the author of the Eli Sharpe mystery series and of *Alphabet Land*, a crime thriller featuring a "problem-solver" known only as The Rook. Max's most recent work is a collection of short stories called *All the Different Ways Love Can Feel*; some of the stories in this book were nominated for or won Best of the Net, AWP Intro Journals Award, Glimmer Train's New Writer Award, and the Pushcart Prize. His stories and essays have been published in *Elysian Fields Quarterly*, *Potomac Review*, *Shotgun Honey*, *juked*, *Slow Trains Journal*, *The State*, and *Portable Magic: The Authors First Anthology*.

MaxEverhart.com

On the following pages are a few
more great titles from the
Down & Out Books publishing family.

For a complete list of books and to
sign up for our newsletter,
go to DownAndOutBooks.com.

Split to Splinters
An Eli Sharpe Mystery
Max Everhart

Down & Out Books
October 2018
978-1-948235-26-6

When a highly valuable piece of baseball memorabilia goes missing, Jim Honeycutt, a Hall of Fame pitcher, enlists the services of Eli Sharpe, a private detective specializing in professional athletes. Sharpe takes the case, but is quickly awash in a sea of suspects, all of the fairer sex: four lovely yet scheming daughters and their equally lovely mother, not to mention Honeycutt's business partner/mistress, who just so happens to be Mrs. Honeycutt's best friend. The culprit has to be someone in Jim's circle. So how difficult can it be to expose them?

Record Scratch
A Trevor Galloway Thriller
J.J. Hensley

Down & Out Books
October 2018
978-1-948235-35-8

Somewhere there exists a vinyl record with twelve songs recorded by the legendary Jimmy Spartan. Trevor Galloway has been hired to solve Spartan's murder and recover his final songs.

When his client terminates their first meeting by taking her own life, Galloway's journey takes him into the arms of an old flame, the crosshairs of familiar enemies, and past the demons in his own mind.

In Loco Parentis
Nigel Bird

All Due Respect, an imprint of
Down & Out Books
August 2018
978-1-948235-14-3

Joe Campion is the kind of teacher that any child would want for their class. He's also the kind of teacher that lots of mothers want to have. And some of them do. When he becomes aware of the neglect and abuse suffered by a pupil in his care and witnesses an explosion of rage from the music teacher in the school, he decides the systems to deal with such instances aren't fit for purpose. It's time for him to take matters into his own hands. His impulsive nature, dedication to his pupils and his love of women lead him into a chain of events that would cause even the most consummate professional to unravel.

A Healthy Fear of Man
A Paul Little Novel of Crime
Aaron Philip Clark

Shotgun Honey, an imprint of
Down & Out Books
June 2018
978-1-948235-01-3

The enigmatic loner, ex-con Paul Little, makes his home on ancestral land in North Carolina. But when he's accused of murder, the entire county comes gunning for him.

Can Paul stay alive long enough to prove his innocence and bring the real killer to justice?

Made in the USA
Columbia, SC
11 October 2021

47028548R00167